"Alice, I am having an affair with one of the girls in the mill."

Quinn Delevan could never say these words, for the Delevans would not understand. From their neat, comfortable homes on the hill, they would not see Bonny, but a crow-voiced girl with too much make-up. The other Delevans would not know that <u>they</u> were making it happen.

This is the story of a family manufacturing dynasty and of the forces that work to undercut its foundations, to buy it up as one more jewel on a giant conglomerate necklace, to wither its brains and rust its nerve ends.

It is the story of the Delevans, weak and strong, who balance greed against honor, comfort against happiness, deceit against the truth.

About the Author

JOHN D. MacDONALD, says *The New York Times,* "is a very good writer, not just a good 'mystery writer.' " His Travis McGee novels have established their hero as a modern-day Sam Spade and, along with MacDonald's more than 500 short stories and other bestselling novels—60 in all, including *Condominium* and *The Green Ripper*—have stamped their author as one of America's best all-round contemporary storytellers.

Contrary
Pleasure

JOHN D. MacDONALD

FAWCETT GOLD MEDAL • NEW YORK

CONTRARY PLEASURE

Published by Fawcett Gold Medal Books,
a unit of CBS Publications,
the Consumer Publishing Division of CBS Inc.

ISBN: 0-449-14104-7

Printed in the United States of America

19 18 17 16 15 14 13 12 11

FOR MARGIE AND DAD

"There are goods so opposed that we cannot seize both, but, by too much prudence, may pass between them at too great a distance to reach either. This is often the fate of long consideration; he does nothing who endeavours to do more than is allowed to humanity. Flatter not yourself with contrarieties of pleasure. Of the blessings set before you, make your choice and be content. No man can taste the fruits of autumn while he is delighting his scent with the flowers of the spring; no man can, at the same time, fill his cup from the source and from the mouth of the Nile."

—THE PRINCESS NAKAYAH
RASSELAS by Dr. Samuel Johnson

Contrary
Pleasure

Chapter One

This was a time of day he was most apt to like. A June evening, and a silence along the office halls after the twittering departures of the secretaries, young tamping of heels on the steel stair treads worn to silver, the last typewriter tilted back into its desk with decisive thump, the whirl and rattle and subsonic resonances of the mill itself stilled, the last cars leaving the lot.

He sat quite still at his desk, breathing the silence. He heard the sounds of the girl in the outer office, a stealthy sliding of desk drawer and the small, bright snap of purse, then her steps on the rug as she came to the doorway.

"Will there be anything else, Mr. Delevan?"

"No. You can go now, Miss Daley."

"Good night, sir."

He treated this one with controlled patience and was amused at himself because the net, to her, was perhaps an impression of kindliness. Whereas the bitterly efficient Miss Meyer, now on her annual vacation, was often target for unwarranted irritation. Meyer was his right hand, comrade in many battles, she of stone routines, of razored loyalties. The only one who seemed even less than he to have a life outside the worn and ugly walls. Together now in this place for twenty-five years. And this was the year that it was half his life. He had thought about that a great deal lately. As though the very figures had some symbolic meaning. Last year more of his life had been spent outside the Stockton Knitting Company, Incorporated, than in it. And next year the outside life would become the minor fraction. It added a haunting significance to this year, like the echo of a sound that cannot be identified. When, he thought, had he passed the midpoint of the years he would be here? A prisoner can compute his term. One who will be pensioned can estimate retirement. But a man who works to keep a thing alive cannot guess how long he will be successful.

He wondered if Meyer ever thought in this way. You could not get close to her, ever. They had come here at almost the same time. It was difficult to think of her outside the offices and more difficult to imagine her on vacation. Once, on a Saturday, he had been walking along one of the downtown streets and had seen her in a shoe store, salesman talking earnestly up at her, her lips pursed as she studied the shoe she was considering. It was strange to think of her as a person who must buy shoes, wash her face, think of the future, talk with friends. If she bought the wrong size, her feet would hurt. That was a shocking concept. And oddly heartbreaking.

This was the time of silence. It was a healing time of transition from the life inside to the life outside. On those days when his younger brother, Quinn Delevan, waited to ride home with him, the healing process was flawed. He was then too aware of Quinn down the hall, glancing at his watch, aimlessly handling papers.

Benjamin Delevan stood up and pushed his chair forward again, socketing it neatly into the kneehole of the desk. He closed his windows and closed his office door behind him. There was nothing at all on top of the secretarial desk in the outer office. Perhaps Meyer had explained, in her cool voice, "Mr. Delevan likes it that way."

He stood for a moment. The corner in its airlessness seemed faintly perfumed by the girl who had sat there these past few days. He shut the outer door of the office behind him and walked down the corridor, walked stolidly down the steps of steel and rubber to the tile of the ground floor. The watchman gave him his nightly surly nod and performed the ritual of leaning in over the switchboard and pulling the night plug from his phone.

He always yanked it free with more emphasis than necessary. Benjamin Delevan suspected that it was an evening
routine which obscurely comforted them both.

His car was in the small ell of the parking lot reserved
for the executive personnel, nosed against the brick on
which was affixed the small wooden signs of reservation.
B. DELEVAN. The car had been shaded from the late sun,
but the steering wheel was still warmer than his hands. He
drove out of the lot and down the narrowness of Hickman
Street with its sidings and warehouses on either side,
caught the green light at the end and turned out onto the
six-lane asphalt of Vaunt Boulevard, into the tapering
flow of the evening rush, up over the sleek hump of City
Bridge, and out the long glossy blue river of the boulevard
with its bright new yellow traffic-lane markings, its syn-
chronized lights, past showrooms and used-car lots, angular new shopping centers and, further out, the drive-ins,
the outdoor movies, an anachronistic and spanking new
miniature golf course. For many years he had had to fight
and inch his way through the narrow old streets of the city
of Stockton, cursing the delivery trucks, the suicidal
pedestrians, the uncoordinated lights. All the cities of the
Mohawk Valley had been like that. Strangled spasms of
evening traffic. Rome and Troy, Syracuse and Albany,
Utica and Rochester. But now Mr. Dewey's Thruway was
taking away the congestion of the cross-state traffic, and
the cities themselves were building these hushed black
rivers to drain the twisted stone swamps of the old parts of
the cities.

Though now it was much easier to commute—he could
make the trip from the plant to Clayton Village in twenty
minutes of restful driving rather than fifty minutes of
nerve fray—he often had the feeling that something had
been lost. The cars had jammed up where carriages had
once rolled. Some elms survived there, and stone quarried
long ago, and scrollwork on the Victorian cornices. There
were curbs dished by many years, and ornate iron on the
lamp standards, and the prehistoric bulge of old trolley
tracks under the skin of patched asphalt. When the main
street made an entirely unnecessary turn, you could think

of some stolid farmer of long ago who made his neighbors go the long way around his property and perhaps stood in the evening and leaned on the fence rail and gave them uncompromising stares, sound in his belief in ownership.

But now the sleek highway, through condemnation proceedings, implemented by bond issue, symbol of sterile union of slide rule and high-compression ratio, had flattened a swath through the most ancient slums, riding smoothly on rough fill that had once been buildings of old stone, bursting out into the flatlands beside the river where once there had been only marsh and discarded bedsprings and snaky adventures for small boys. It had simplified flow, enriched the farsighted, and spawned those bordering strips of plastic and glass brick, fluorescence and floodlight, where the Deal of the Day turned slowly under candy-striped canopy, where every orange was precisely the same size, and sapphire from Ceylon tipped the juke needles.

Sometimes on the drive home he would imagine a civilization where this delicately engineered river of asphalt had become too cramped, too slow, too dangerous. Then it would become secondary and the bright plastic would fade and the light tubes fail and fabrics with catchy chemical names would flap in the night wind off the marsh. It would die then, but without grace. Not the way the old city had died. The old city died in the way a forgotten doll is found up there behind trunks with rounded tops, wooden legs carved with care. And this would die like a tin toy, stamped into the ground and rusting.

When he thought that way, he could see the little indications of the decay. Streaks rusted down from the air conditioning units. Balled napkins hurrying along, enclosing mustard. A big window labeled with paint that had run. This stuff would not last bravely, with dignity. There was no stubborn persistence in it. It too quickly acknowledged defeat. There were no lost causes for it.

Ten miles from the city he turned right, a gentle diagonal right down an incline to the octagonal yellow of the stop sign, and then turned left again, through the tunnel under the highway he had just left, leaving it to hurry on westward while he turned south along the winding two-lane farm road that had led to the village square.

Off to his right as he neared the village was a new suburban development that had grown up in the past few years, was still growing. It had its own shops, primary school, playgrounds, park, social clubs. The houses had been put up in wholesale lots, with three and sometimes four variations of the basic design. This variation, plus the alterations in color, plus variations in plantings, plus subtle changes in the way the houses were placed on their lots, partially destroyed the flavor of sameness.

Once he had read in the newspaper, with a certain amount of wonderment, that each house in Amity Park contained: electric stove, refrigerator, washer, dryer, dishwasher, and disposal; attic room that could be finished off at owner's option; tile shower; breezeway; radiant-panel heat; concrete slab foundation with utility room; television corner; heatolater fireplace. And, knowing that, he would drive by, as on this June evening, by the streets with their new names—Three Brooks Lane, Dell Road, Grindstone Road, Persimmon Lane—and see the sprinklers turning and the bikes racing and the bent backs over the new plantings and the cars being washed and diapers drying—and it would suddenly look most odd and fearful. As though all these people had come from some alien place beyond the sun and through their very pronounced and exaggerated conformity sought to deceive us who were born here. The street scenes were too suburban, the young wives too consciously harassed and pretty, the young husbands too solemn and jolly, the children entirely too childlike. Where did they come from? Certainly not from the city. They had never lived anywhere else on this planet. Only here, at Amity Park, the alien eyes cold and waitful, aware of the times that were coming.

One day in the hallway at the office one of the young men in Accounting had come up to him and said, a bit too brashly because of his shyness, "Moved out your way last week, Mr. Delevan. Out to Amity Park. Ellen said it would be a lot better for the kids." Delevan said what was expected of him and then remembered that the man's

name was Fister, and it pleased him to be able to use the
man's name so easily. But he was disappointed to have the
game he played compromised in this fashion. It was better
when he had not known any of them. Then he could have
maintained some of the variations of the game. Such as all
the young men climbing into their Fords and Plymouths
and Chevvies after kissing their young wives and setting
out toward the city, but, of course, never going there,
flickering off, instead, into some obscure dimension from
which they would emerge, putting on their man-faces, at
five.

Perhaps, he thought, it is just because you cannot understand that way of life. It is in some obscure attunement
with the new boulevard, with too much electronics. Or
maybe, Benjamin, you are merely a snob.

The village square looked changed and naked and for a
few moments, as he waited for the light to change, he was
puzzled. Then he noticed the raw stumps and realized that
they had taken down more of the elms. He wondered if
they had been standing when he had driven through the
town that morning on his way to the city. Maybe they had
been gone for days. Or weeks. And he had not noticed.
Dutch elm disease was bad this year. At least there wasn't
any of it up on the hill yet. But there might be. He
decided to ask Sam about sprays. If one tree went, it cost
a fortune to get it felled and removed.

The light changed and he turned right onto Gilman
Street, accelerating for the steepness of Gilman Hill, wondering if he could get all the way up without that robot
under the hood shifting him back to a lower gear. It was a
daily contest with the robot, and it never failed to annoy
him. Yet he was unable to stop playing that particular
game. It seemed an infringement on his dignity, a continual persecution by servo-mechanism, even when he won. In
the winter he seldom won. He wished they would make
this same car with a manual shift. Every day they took
more decisions away from you.

It was nearly six thirty. A bit later than usual. The big
car moved smoothly up the hill. He decided as he neared
the crest that on this night the robot had been decisively

defeated, but at that moment a child's ball rolled into the road. He swerved away from it, lifting his foot from the gas pedal, and heard the disheartening clunk as the car went into a lower gear. He felt annoyed out of all proportion to the defeat and at the same time amused at his own childishness.

Once he was over the crest of the hill, the robot permitted a return to the higher gear. Ahead, on his left, was the land his father had purchased. Eight acres which the will had divided into four parcels of two acres each, one for each of the four children of Michael Delevan. And they had not even known he owned the land until the will was read. It had seemed a strange remote place then, a hilltop near an outlying village. But with the years, with the growth of commuting, Clayton Village had changed character. The old man had made a good guess. When the village became fashionable as a commuter community, there were the four Delevan kids with nice big lots on high ground. The four Delevan kids. Ben, the eldest. Quinn and Alice, the twins. Robbie, the kid.

It was so alarmingly easy, even at fifty, to think of yourself again as one of the Delevan kids. Half a century and yet the mind, with one deceptive twist, could wipe away the years. Fifty had a dreadful sound. The very consonants of the word itself. A withered, secretive sound. A dried bell. Half of a century. Five decades. Two and a half generations. This, you knew, was beyond midpoint. More than half of life was gone. There were some who lived to be a hundred. But it was not life. It was a trick, faintly obscene, to be treated by the working press with that familiar mixture of heavy-handed humor and bathos.

It seemed utterly unfair of the old man, Michael Delevan, to have made this one good guess on property value, thus leaving one false hint of shrewdness after having, with blind and stubborn arrogance, with both greed and carelessness, milked the Stockton Knitting Company into spavined sickness before he died. It could never come back completely. It could never be well again. It could be levered and pried and prodded along, staggering from one year into the next.

There were four parcels of land on top of the hill. The parcel nearest the village was vacant, brush-grown, wild. That was the place where Robbie, the youngest of the Delevan children, might build one day should he come back from far places.

Benjamin, the eldest, the President and Chairman of the Board of the Stockton Knitting Company, Incorporated—he who now drove this big car swiftly through the transition hour of Job to Home—lived in the middle house. He lived in that white house with his wife, Wilma, that white-haired lady who had comfortably shared so many of his years, and with his teen-age son, Brock, and with his teen-age daughter, Ellen.

Ben's was the middle house, with the twins on either side of him. In the house nearest the village lived Quinn Delevan, vice-president of the company, low-handicap golfer, mild husband of the husky Bess, stepfather of her son, David.

Quinn's twin was Alice, who shared his tallness and thinness and quietness. She was now a Furmon, having married the hearty George Furmon, having borne his three children—two of them simultaneously in accord with that hereditary gene. It was George Furmon who had built the three white houses on the hill, building his own no more honestly and solidly than the two he built for Benjamin Delevan and for Quinn Delevan—his wife's twin brother. They were rambling houses, pleasant to live in, hellish to heat, cool in the summer, designed for maximum privacy.

Ben turned in his driveway remembering again that he had forgotten to order gravel for the driveway, the coarser grade Sam had recommended so that it could not be so easily washed away by the spring rains. Sam Coward was the leathery old man who took care of the grounds around the three houses. If requested to plant something that did not appeal to him, it would be taken with some mysterious blight. Left to his own plans and programs, he made everything grow with unexpected lushness, and on this day the lawns looked remarkably well, Ben thought.

As he made the turn in the drive to park by the garages

he saw, to his instantaneous dismay, that his terrace was crowded with people. He thought for a moment that it was a party which had slipped his mind. But as he glanced quickly at individuals, he saw that it was all family. Though they lived here together, it was a rare time when everyone was together. He stopped the car and saw them there, looking toward him. Quinn and Alice with the twin stamp and the Delevan stamp on their lean faces, meaty florid George Furmon. And the two women, brought into the tribe, into the name, by marriage—breasty, vivid Bess, who was Quinn's wife. And his own wife, Wilma, sitting there with their two almost adult children, Brock and Ellen. Out in the yard, in the long shadows, the blond little girl called Sandy—Alice's youngest—turned solemn and dedicated and tireless cartwheels on the deep, soft green of the grass.

He stopped the car and reached to turn off the key, seeing them all there as people dear and well-known to him, and then suddenly seeing them all as strangers again. Very pleasant people. Sitting there in sunlight, in assurance, in their casual ease. With bright clothes and wrought-iron furniture on flagstones, and late sun prisming through the shaker and pitcher and glasses, touching the acid yellow of lemon rind. He had a sudden and vivid urge toward violence, wanting to put the big car in gear so that it would surge through the tailored hedge and bound up over the flagstone edge and into the lot of them. It was so clear an image that he could hear the screams, the sound of breaking glass, the coarse grinding of wrought iron against the bowels of the car.

He turned the key and turned the motor off and sat for a moment feeling oddly pleased with the image he had created, and somewhat shaken. The pleasure was that oblique pleasure of imagined horror. These random impulses toward violence seemed to occur too often lately. Crazy impulses. Perhaps everyone had them. But only a madman would go around responding to such impulses. Maybe with all normal people it remained in proper perspective. A game. Nothing more.

Yet when he got out of the car and walked toward the

gap in the hedge, smiling, they still looked like strangers to him, so much so that he was, in turn, sharply aware of how he must look to all of them, a rather dumpy man in a dark, rumpled suit, balding, his jowls shadowed with the day's beard, his hat in his hand, like someone approaching with faint apologetic air to beg from them, without quite knowing what he intended to ask for. Or how he would use it were it given him.

"The gang's all here," he said, almost pleased with the fatuousness of the expression.

"You're late, dear," Wilma said, and met him at the edge of the terrace for the uxorial kiss, which he implanted quickly on her soft, dry, textureless mouth. There was about her an unaccustomed air of excitement. That air, combined with the gathering of the clan, meant news. For one good moment he wondered if it meant that Brock had been accepted by a decent college, though God knew the odds were against that. He glanced at his son, but it was not a moment when he could read his son's face. Brock sat slouched, his head tilted back, eyes shut against the sun as he slowly drained a bottle of Coke.

Ben nodded and spoke to all of them, Quinn and Bess, George and Alice, Brock and Ellen.

"Shall we tell him now or wait until he sits down?" George Furman asked, his heavy voice a little loose at the edges, as it became each day of his life at five thirty. And there was a slurred bite of sarcasm which, to Ben, meant that George did not consider the news as impressive as the others did.

"I'll get a drink and then sit down," Ben said. He was aware of their faces. At least it wasn't bad news. Perhaps a local scandal of some sort that did not affect them. Yet Wilma wouldn't bring up something like that with both kids around. She avoided such topics when the children were there, even though she knew they had their own sources and would find out in any case.

Ben poured himself a martini. The glass was warm from being in the sun. The drink was acid and tepid. He sat down with it, took a sip, said, "Ready or not."

The women all tried to speak at once, but Wilma got

the floor. "What do you know, Ben? Robbie has gotten married. In Mexico City. He's flying up with her. He'll be here Saturday, three days from now."

It took him a moment to comprehend. "Good Lord," he said softly. "Is she a Mexican?"

"Oh, no, dear," Wilma said. "Her name is—was—Susan Walton, and she was a civil service person in the embassy there. I guess it was all very sudden."

Robbie Delevan, the youngest of the Delevans, only twenty-eight, had been working in Mexico City on some sort of vague project that bore a dim relationship to the State Department. They had not seen him in over two years. It was one of Wilma's self-imposed "duties" to write to him regularly, but Robbie had been neither a very interesting nor a very consistent correspondent.

"Here's the letter, dear," Wilma said. "And her picture."

Ben looked at the picture first. A young girl who looked into the camera in a clear-eyed way, not quite smiling. A girl with pale hair and a look of graveness and dignity and a soft, young mouth.

"Hmm," he said.

"My sentiments exactly," George said thickly.

"Read the letter, dear," Wilma said in the soft voice of command.

The letter said the expected things. Much in love. Arranged our leave at the same time. Suzy had no family. Decided we'd be married here. Flying to Washington first and then up to see you. Should arrive Saturday the twenty-third. And it was near the end of the letter that Ben read a line that gave him a twinge of alarm: "Could be I have had enough of foreign parts. But we'll talk about that when we see you all."

One dead-weight Delevan on the executive payroll of the Stockton Knitting Company was quite enough. It would indeed be unfortunate if Robbie thought that, because of his name and his inheritance, he could ask that a place be found for him. A well-lighted place with short hours, handsome salary, and pleasing title.

The bride had added a postscript to the letter: "Dear

Robbie's Family—I'm nervous as a bride. Robbie says
that's to be expected. I want you to know that we're very
happy, and I'm looking forward to meeting you all at last.
Robbie has told so much about you that I feel as if I
know you already. All our love—Suzy."

"That's a sweet note from her at the end, isn't it?" Bess
said warmly.

"She sounds like a good addition," Ben said. He liked
the look of her handwriting. It was not peculiarly slanted,
nor tinted, nor affected. It had a look of decision.

He left them talking and planning, and went into the
house. He stopped in the kitchen and floated two ice cubes
in bourbon in an old-fashioned glass and took the drink to
his bedroom. He was glad he hadn't had to finish the
warm martini. He sat on the edge of the bed, waiting for
the ice to chill the bourbon. The window was open and he
could hear them talking out on the terrace, the sound of
the voices, but not the actual words. The voices had a
summer sound. Already there were insects in the fields.
The birds were making a great racket these mornings.

He heard his daughter laugh. Clear young voice of
seventeen. Clean and young and fresh. Gay enough and
sad enough to break your heart. There was nothing more
miraculous than a daughter of seventeen.

Lately all of them had seemed like strangers, except
Ellen. He wondered if Ellen would grow up to be like his
own mother. Whenever he thought of that long-dead
woman, that was the phrase he used. His own mother. A
private person, not shared by the rest of the children of
Big Mike.

He remembered his own mother as being tiny and crisp
and tidy and always laughing, and with a smell of soap
when she hugged him, which was often. Soap made of
flowers and the cakes were oval and lavender in color and
when they were new and crisp, there were flower patterns
on them. It was a big old house, but she had filled it for
him. She died when he was ten, and then that aloof
stranger in the house, his father—Big Mike they had all
called him at the plant—had married again, two years
later, married a woman who was tall, young, elegant,

poised, dignified. As aloof as his father. It had taken Ben many months to learn that her cool poise and dignity had concealed a dull, frightened and conventional mind. When he had learned that, she ceased to awe him, and he began to love her, and she responded with starved affection, for there was very little love or warmth in Michael Delevan, and the big old house had been very cold after Ben's own mother had died.

When Ben was fourteen, the second wife, Elaine, had borne the twins, Alice and Quinn, and they had grown into tall, poised children, of fine, lean, almost arid construction, full of themselves and their quiet games. Robbie was born eight years later. Two years after that, when Ben was twenty-four, Elaine had died. Ben had gotten there in time. She died with simple poise and dignity and only Ben had seen the fear that was sharp and thin behind placid eyes, only Ben had felt the odd strength, the frantic strength of hands and nails, strange in one so wasted. Her name had been Elaine and it had suited her.

Twenty-six years ago she had died. And though Michael Delevan had never seemed to be emotionally involved with her, had seemed to accept her as a convenience in his house, he was not the same after that. He lasted a year and, in dying, he sprung the trap that snapped shut on Ben. The twins were eleven. Robbie was three. There was the plant and the job and that was where he went. It was that simple.

Often it seemed to him that Elaine had been his wife, that the others were his children. Quinn and Alice, now thirty-six, were their mother's children. Her tallness and reserve and odd pride. Robbie seemed to have a bit more of Big Mike in him. And the very reserve of the twins had seemed to drive them into the arms of extroverted people. Alice, married to George Furmon. And Quinn marrying warm and husky Bess who, at thirty-five, made Ben think of haymows and milkmaids.

From Alice's restrained and antiseptic body George Furmon had acquired the twins, happy, energetic, uncomplicated boys of thirteen who had been bundled off early to camp this June, and Sandy, the ten-year-old girl, she of

the grave energies, the solemn absorptions. Yet from
Bess's warm sturdy body Quinn had achieved no issue.
The only child was her child, David, the odd one. A
crazy, tragic, runaway marriage when she was seventeen,
and David born when she was eighteen, so that he was
seventeen now, the same age as Ellen. Strange David, full
of ancient despair.

No, there could be no room at the plant for Robbie, if
that was his intention. Not with the dead weight of Quinn
Delevan on the payroll as vice-president. It was a blessing
that George Furmon had his contracting business and did
well at it. The Stockton Knitting Company was too enfeebled to carry much on its back. It irritated him, very
often, that they could not or would not understand. When
they thought of the plant at all, they seemed to think of it
as a sort of inexhaustible General Motors, Junior Grade.
They did not know how truly precarious was the Delevan
security and way of life, so delicately balanced on the
keen edge of his daily decisions.

He drank half his drink and undressed and carried the
rest of it into the bathroom. It was curious how impossible
it was to tell them the true state of affairs. Ben is worrying
again. You know how he worries. They thought that
because it had always been there, making money in
greater or lesser amounts for the family, it always would
be there. And if it slipped fatally and he lost it, and it fell
and smashed, they would all stare at him in fear and
accusation and say, "Why didn't you tell us how bad
things were?"

He stepped, dripping, out of the shower and finished his
drink, sucking the sliver of ice that remained until it
dissolved on his tongue. His mood was brightening a bit.
A drink and a shower could always do it. If Robbie
wanted to stay around, maybe George Furmon could be
talked into taking him on. George, of all of them, was the
only one who understood about the plant. On the other
hand, George, for all his expansiveness and his expensive
personal habits, was not known to throw money away.

Half-turning as he reached for his towel, Ben caught an
entirely unanticipated glimpse of himself in the full-length

mirror set into the inside of the bathroom door. It was not pleasant. His was indeed an unlovely nakedness, male frame softened by the years and the offices and the luncheons, until the belly was suety and the thighs raddled and the haired breasts matronly and the buttocks flaccid, with only the shoulders remembering the look of drive and power. He looked at himself with disgust. You felt like a man, and then you saw something that should go in a waddling run across a vaudeville stage being beaten around the ears with a bladder.

Where did it all go? The good years and the taut muscles. "Ben, you mustn't run up and down the stairs that way!" And all the times of walking in the night and singing aloud. All the quickenings, now buried in grossness, in the staleness of the body. He turned away from himself. Now you can stop looking. It is left there in the mirror. Now you deceive. You hide it all behind tailoring and fabrics. So far from the body. Today the bright fabrics are our new skin. A new sort of animal that walks the world, wide and stately and full of ponderous dignity.

He rubbed the back of his hand along his jaw and decided not to shave until morning. He put on baggy gray slacks he loved, and a clean plaid shirt in lightweight wool. He went to the window and looked out toward the terrace. George and Alice and their Sandy had left, and so had his own two kids, Brock and Ellen. His half-brother, Quinn, still sat there, relaxed and slim and brown and handsome, holding a highball glass moodily in both hands, elbows braced on the chair arms, while Wilma talked with Bess. Ben refilled his glass in the kitchen. Two more cubes and a generous amount of bourbon. He went out. The sun was gone. It was dark under the trees. Birds made settling-down sounds in the elms. He sighed as he sat down.

"Tired, dear?" Wilma asked. Stimulus and response. He would sigh and she would say that, precisely that. Last time. Next time. Marriage seemed to be largely a Pavlov experiment on a more intricate scale.

"Little bit," he said, giving the equally meaningless response.

"Feel guilty," Quinn said, "getting out for a round of golf on a day like this. Had to do it though." He yawned hugely, mouth cavernous behind the carefully unkempt mustache, that British colonial mustache which went with his terse, rather abrupt manner of speech.

Yes, Ben thought, you had to do it all right. Who was it this time? The second cousin of the brother-in-law of the county tax assessor? Your reasoning gets more remote every year. "How did it go?" Ben asked.

"I had something going on the back nine and then I blew up on that dog of a seventeen. Came in with five over par."

Bess was hunched forward in her chair, her expression serious. As usual, she had a curiously rumpled look. She was always shining clean, but oddly disorganized. She was a big, strong-bodied, high-breasted woman who seemed to be always pulling and wrenching at her clothes. They never seemed to fit, always too tight or too loose in the wrong places, slips showing, sweaters coming out of skirts, heels coming off shoes, straps breaking. She seemed to be in continual stubborn conflict with her clothing, unable to subdue it. She had too much pale brown hair of a texture so silky that it would never stay the way she wanted it.

For a long time after knowing her, Ben had wondered how a woman who always managed to look rumpled could emit such a strong flavor of desirability. She seemed so utterly unconscious of her body, so perfectly willing to collapse into any posture regardless of how unflattering it was. And then it had come to him that she was one of those people to whom nakedness is a natural state. She was tight in her skin, resilient with health, uncomplicated as a puppy. He had felt an amused and pleasant desire for her for a long time, and he was certain she was unaware of it, and equally certain that nothing would or could ever come of it. The advantage was that it always made him feel good to be near her. He liked her and knew she liked him. Sometimes he had a strong urge to smooth back that glossy brown hair and, perhaps, scratch the nape of her neck.

Eighteen years ago she had run away from Sarah Lawrence and married a wild and improbable young man named Carney, a black Irishman, a brawler, a laborer, a poet of sorts. Three months later, in Philadelphia, he took violent exception to a comment about his bride, a comment made in a place to which he never should have taken her. He did mighty damage and walked out with her, walking casually, taunting them, laughing low in his throat, walking a dozen feet before someone threw a knife into the back of his neck, dropping him in the quick spineless death which is a bull ring art. She came back to her father's house, wearing a disturbingly vacant smile, her emaciation accenting the first evidences of pregnancy. She was eighteen and Quinn was nineteen when David was born. They had been playmates. Quinn, for perhaps the first time in his life, felt needed. The families approved the marriage. Not only did it seem sound emotionally, but it looked like a healthy move for the Stockton Knitting Company. Bess's father's firm had weathered the early depression years very well, but not so well but that both firms could not benefit from a merger. The difficulty, Ben discovered later, resulted from the very thoroughness of the audit which had to precede any merger agreement.

Not long after the marriage, while the audit was in process, her father went home from the office in the middle of the afternoon and drew a hot tub and opened his wrists with a single-edged Gem razor blade and drifted peacefully out of life, listening to the afternoon game on the bathroom radio, lasting long enough, perhaps, to hear the Yankees pile up a substantial lead in the bottom of the fifth. His badly depleted stock interest in his own firm had to go on the block to cover his speculations, and the interests which took over control wasted no time in moving everything movable to a low-wage area in the back-woods of Tennessee where, ever since, they had profited mightily.

Ben heard a note of uncertainty in Wilma's voice as she said, to Bess, "Well ... I suppose if Alice did volunteer ... but I do think we *ought* to have them stay here with us."

"She can do it so much easier, Wilma," Bess said. "She's got that cute little guest wing George put on last year, with the little terrace and private bath and everything and the little stove-refrigerator gadget for breakfasts. Newlyweds don't want to be right in the *middle* of the family. That's the way they'd have to be here or at my house. Besides, she's got Mrs. Bailey to help and the cleaning girl that comes three days a week. You *heard* her say she'd be glad to. And the twins are away."

Ben knew Wilma enough to sense the relief behind her hesitant words. "All right. I mean, I guess it's all right. But let's not let Alice do any entertaining for them. That's our job, Bess. She's doing enough just having them there."

Bess stood up and stretched and yawned. She put her hand on Quinn's shoulder. "Come on, honey. These people want to eat." Quinn unfolded his lazy length out of the chair and set his empty glass on the tray. They said good night and walked away through the late dusk toward their house.

Wilma banged glasses on the tray and said in a low voice, "I wish that once, just once, she'd at least carry stuff into the house after one of these parties that just happen. I want the chance of at least telling her not to bother. I even wish I had the gall to not offer when we have a drink over there. I do, though. Every time. And she says sure. Honestly, Ben, sometimes it makes me so *damn* mad."

"She just doesn't think about it, I guess."

"At her age she ought to start thinking about it. I guess it's a good thing Robbie and Susan won't be staying with her. Susan would be working her head off."

"David might make it difficult."

"I guess he would make it difficult." He picked up the pitcher and shaker and followed her into the house. She turned on the white amphitheater glare of the kitchen lights. She turned to him as she put the tray down. "You better do something about those cushions. The dew has been heavy these nights."

He walked out and collected the canvas cushions off the wrought-iron chairs and put them on the shelf in the pump house. He bent over, grunting a bit, and touched the grass with his fingertips. It was a bit damp already. He was far enough behind his own house so that he could see through the trees the lights in Quinn's house and in George's. There was a dim trace of color in the west, a dull orange, low to the horizon. He lit a cigarette. Day is done and the Delevans are in their nests and all of us have gotten through this one. Fifty is a time when you think too much of all the things that can happen. Twenty is a time when nothing can happen.

Turning, he could see through the kitchen windows, see Wilma walking back and forth. She was a stranger in a tricky stage setting. Suburban matron. The billowing breasts and the rigorously girdled waist and hips, so that she seemed balanced in a rather topheavy way on the legs which for some reason had remained as slim and smooth and unblemished as when she had been young. She used some sort of blue tint in her white hair, and it was carefully sculptured, looking in that light as cold and rigid and planned as marble. There were two deep lines between her eyebrows. And a compressed look about her lips. He had heard her described, quite often lately, as a handsome woman. Perhaps it was the way her features were cut. A certain bold clarity.

And he suddenly felt ashamed because he had looked at her so coldly. What right had he to indulge himself in a critique. Both of them had changed in the same slow way, the same terrifying day-by-day way, so that the faces in old photographs became the faces of strangers. A strange girl in a muddy print, looking out with shyness, and the young man beside her—that fast walker, that fast talker, that one who bounded up stairs and sang and knew a thousand things and told of them well, and perhaps too often. There had been a thousand things in the world and a thousand risks to take gladly.

It was, he thought, like a network of tunnels. A thousand choices. And the next year five hundred choices. And each year the choices were fewer and finally one day there were featureless walls on either side of you and nothing to do but keep on going forward toward your inevitable death, hoping only that you would be given as much time as possible, and not too much. Hoping that it would not end in pain. Hoping that it would be as right and good as it could be for both of you. He saw this very clearly, and for a moment it was like that time of awakening in the night and suddenly knowing the answer to everything. But as you try to grasp it, it slips away and down and back into the sleep you have left behind you. The idea seemed good and then it was gone and he stood there, feeling the evening dampness, looking at his wife in her kitchen, feeling his hunger for the evening meal, feeling the faint edge of the liquor. A man standing on his land.

There could have been other tunnels. Other roads. Maybe one that would not have dulled the shyness of her, the awareness. A life of more simplicity, without all this jangling, these tin noises and twistings. A place where he could have been a hard, brown man with outdoors in his eyes and the gift of quietness and long thought. . . .

He smiled at himself. Plow jockey. Peasant life. Cottage with a dirt floor, mulled wine, and potato pancakes, for God's sake.

You started with a woman and she was magic and she was mystery and that was the way it was supposed to be. And then you grew into each other and learned each other so that what had been high adventure became a comforting, a warmth, a reassurance of existence. Good gal, you can say. Contentment, you can say. But, oh, where did the shy one go, the shy wild one of all the awareness, of magical blue vein on porcelain breast, who loved earth under her hips, eyes strained shut against sunlight. She went to the same place, Ben, as did that great walker and talker and dreamer of a thousand things. They look out of the old muddy prints and they are still together. Every tunnel is right and every tunnel is wrong. Choice is immutable.

"What in the world are you doing out there, dear?"

"Thinking, I guess."

He went into the kitchen, blinking at the lights. "Kids around?"

"Ellen had a date. They picked her up while you were showering. Brock's in his room."

"Who did Ellen have a date with?"

She put her hand on his arm. "Darling, listen to me a minute. Please try to be nice to Brock tonight. Just try. You don't know how it is for me, you two sitting there like wooden dummies. I'm right in the middle. You know, you just can't keep on treating him like a criminal for the rest of his life."

"It seems to me that that particular label was applied in a very accurate——"

"Ben!"

"All right. All right. I'll try. Who did Ellen go out with?"

"Thank you, darling. Oh, she went out with the Schermer boy again. In the jeep. There was another couple. I think she said they were going to the drive-in movie."

"You *think*!"

"Don't bark at me. Goodness! Look, aren't these nice chops?"

He said they looked very fine indeed and he mixed himself another drink and carried it into the living room, aware of her silent disapproval. He turned on the television. A grave man sat behind a big desk with his hands gently folded and looked Benjamin Delevan directly in the eye and said grave sensible things about people and nations. Apparently the most sensible thing that could be said about nations was that every effort must be made to alleviate the tension in the family of nations, and the tension seemed inevitable. If you looked at him while he said it, it seemed to make sense. If you thought it over, it made no sense. But they didn't want you to think it over. They wanted you to look at the next item. The next item was a grinning shot of the President as he boarded a plane. Then there was the man at the desk again. And then a clock that said Calcutta under it, and then a crowd of dark people in white pajamas waving illegible signs and hollering, and then a toy airplane crushed against an artificial mountain. Ben sipped his drink. The grave man spoke about the product which sponsored his services. He spoke with greater gravity than before. He went away and there were little line drawings of people knocking on a bar and singing about beer.

Benjamin sat and sipped his drink. The program made him feel curiously diffused. One Ben sat there. One contested a robot on Gilman Hill. A naked one stood inside the bathroom mirror. One still sat in the office silences. And there was one out on the grass, standing on his land, standing in a circle painted in white on the grass. He frowned and wondered what in the hell that circle meant.

Chapter Two

Brock Delevan was glad when the dinner hour was over and he could get up from the table and go back to his room and be away from them. This dinner hour had been bad in a different way. He could not decide which was worse—the sour silence of other dinner hours, or the false cheer of this one, with the old man's conversation sounding as if it had been lifted, complete and shining, from the fillers in the *Reader's Digest*. The conversation could not have been more forced, even if there had been a microphone suspended over the table, a television camera aimed at them. Dinner with the happy Delevans. *Sorry, folks, Ellen could not be with you tonight, but turn to channel thirteen tomorrow at this same time and—*

It made Brock want to bang his fist on the table, bouncing the dishes into the air. He had guessed at once that his mother had spoken to the old man about it. During the joyous hour she had looked both pleased and uncertain.

Brock kept it under control and said that he thought he would read and went to his room and shut the door. He had not been holding his breath, but when he heard the click of the door latch he had the feeling that now he could take a deep breath. He moved mechanically, taking LP records at random from their cardboard envelopes, stacking them on the spindle of the player. He turned the record player on and turned out the light over the bed and stretched out. The volume was low, so low that the bass was like the slow, deep pulse of someone who lay beside him in darkness. The trumpet sounds were thin, far away, like summers at the lake when you were little and in bed and they were dancing across the lake, over at the pavilion. The only light in the room was the tiny light of the dial on the player. It was good to have the lights off in the room. When they were on, you could see the kid stuff. Framed high-school pictures. The football enameled white with the score painted on it in red. STOCKTON—14, SYRACUSE HIGH—13. A sleek gray model of a PT. A yellow highway sign that said DEER CROSSING. A lot of kid stuff that some other Brock Delevan, some smug untroubled kid, had collected and stuck in the room. A punk kid. A high-school wheel.

He lay there and waited for it to happen to him, knowing that it would. It was not pain, but it was like pain. It was like a time long ago, when he had been little and very sick, and faces had loomed over the bed and gone away, faces that were too big and sort of twisted looking. It kept coming then, a pain, and it came like a red light down a track, like a train that made a noise too loud and then faded away, but was on a circular track so it would come back.

It came then, as the pain had come long ago, a great wave that made him tighten his fists and lock his throat. Not me. It didn't happen to me. Not a thing like that. I'm Brock. Remember me? They looked at me with pride. Pride kept me warm. It gave me dignity. So I shamed them and the pride is gone. Why? That was the thing. Find out why I did it. How could I have done it?

And so it was necessary to go over it all again. An old ritual. A nightly searching. A going back and looking for clues. Because you could not accept a flat statement that it happened because that is the way you are. There are the good guys and the bad guys. All your life you are sure you are one of the good guys. And then this.

They hadn't even let him stay at the University long enough to take the exams. He would have made a mess of them. So perhaps it was a good thing to have gotten out of them. It was funny how that first year, the freshman year, had gone so well. The grades had been pretty good. He'd made the basketball squad and been pledged to a good fraternity.

The trouble had started in April. There was a good smell of spring that last April. Clear days, warmer than they should have been, and the sort of lazy air that made you feel as if you wanted something without knowing exactly what you wanted. It was the crazy season. You couldn't learn anything out of the books. People took all the class cuts they could afford. People pulled kid tricks or got in fist fights for no reason. And the girls looked good. They looked wonderful with that warm spring air teasing their skirts, and wonderful the way they walked arm in arm and giggled and looked back at you.

He met her on an April afternoon. He had a two o'clock lab. And he walked right up to the door of the lab building and turned around and walked away. He knew he would have to make up the cut. But it was an afternoon when you *couldn't* spend two hours in there in the stink, setting up an experiment, making the dull notations. He dropped his lab book off in his room in the fraternity house. The house was deserted. His feet on the staircase made empty echoes. He walked for a time, feeling free and guilty. He went into a campus beer joint, a cellar place with steins and mottoes and sawdust. He hooked an elbow on the bar and he drank and felt a curious mixture of listlessness and excitement. The place was narrow and there was a row of rustic booths across from the bar. He saw her sitting there alone. He could tell that she wasn't one of the coeds. It was the way she was dressed, and she looked a bit older. She was using the straight pretzel sticks to make designs on the table top. She wore her black hair long, and it swung forward as she leaned over the table and every once in a while she would comb it back with her fingers. She was small and trim and dark and she looked blue. He watched her, with that feeling of inevitability and excitement growing inside him. He had some more beers and it was like remembering the time the other kids had jumped off the garage roof into the snow and he had waited a bit too long before jumping, and stood there, frozen, the others taunting him until at last he had shut his eyes and jumped.

All she could do, he decided, is give me a real chill job, so he carried his beer over and stood by the booth, hoping he looked casual and relaxed, hoping the tautness didn't show, and when she looked up at him blankly, he said "Know the match game?"

She looked up at him, unsmiling, and he saw that she was not quite as good-looking close up. Her cheeks were a bit roughened and pitted with scars of adolescent acne, and her pallor had that faintly waxy look of Latin women. He guessed she was maybe twenty-five. He was glad he'd changed to his good sports jacket when he dropped his lab notebook off at his room.

"I've played," she said, looking amused.

"Play you for a beer?"

"Sure." He sat across from her. They played with the pretzel sticks. She won. Her lipstick was dark red and she had applied it a bit carelessly. She wore a frothy white blouse, a dark, severe suit. Her purse was big and red and she wore no hat. He realized she was a little bit high. Her eyes were very black and very alive, and her small face had a pertness to it, a triangularity which, with its overtones of coarseness, excited him.

Her name was Elise, and she said Brock was a nice name and she asked him if he was a senior. That made him feel good. He said he was and he told her he was twenty-one and she told him he was just a kid, which annoyed him because she seemed to be laughing at him.

"What do you do, Elise?"

"I'm a singer. I sang at the Golden Room for a while. Singing and pantomime. But it was like this. There was this fellow. He used to go wherever I was singing. And always trouble. That was him. Always making a stink about something. You know the type guy. It got me fired a couple times, him and his big mouth, so then the booking agent, he didn't want to handle me anymore, and that makes it tough, trying to get something on your own, so in between times I've been working at waitress work. It's hell on your feet. This last place I was at, it's the Tavern Chop House. They got good steaks and it's I guess three blocks from here. There's a lot of college trade. You ever eat there?"

"Twice. Maybe three times."

"Artie, he's the manager, he's a little louse, believe me. All the time he's got to get his hands on you. Well, brother, did I ever tell him off, so here is Elise again. Unemployed as usual."

She made a face. She looked so small. It made him feel protective about her. She talked sort of tough, but her voice had such a whispery husky quality to it that it seemed to give everything she said a special meaning.

"The hell of it is," she said, "I got me a little studio apartment right near the restaurant so it would be handy. What I ought to have is a car. You got a car, Brock?"

He had to say no and it made him feel inadequate. They sat a long time and talked and he bought her quite a few beers. She said her name was really Mrs. Archie Berris, but she used her maiden name Elise Lewis on account of he was killed overseas. Brock said he was sorry about that and then there were tears in her eyes and in his too, and they felt closer. Yet not close in the way he could be close with someone from his own background. She made him think of a girl he used to watch in high school, a pretty Polish girl who wore cheap, tight dresses, who looked wise and knowing, who was the entrancing subject of conversation of his friends. He had not dated her. He sensed that this Elise was much the same sort of person. From a more forthright world. Being with her like this made him feel both shy and sophisticated.

"Brocky, you hurl a lot of big-sized words around. You going to grow up and be a professor?"

"I'll probably go into the family business. It isn't exactly exciting. But that's what I'll probably do."

"What kind of a business?"

"It's a textile mill. My grandfather started it. It used to make a lot of money. It hasn't made so much for a long time. My father and my uncle run it."

"My God, I had a girl friend worked in one of those in Alabama. She quit it on account of it drove her nuts not knowing what the weather was. It hadn't any windows. All air conditioning and artificial light and a coffee break in the morning and a coffee break in the afternoon and they gave her uniforms and so on and I said she was nuts but she said she had to work in a place where you could look out and see if maybe it was raining— What'll we do for food, Brocky? I'm empty like a bass drum."

They left the place. Standing, she was a little taller than he had expected her to be. Long-legged and a little broad across the hips. She held his arm tightly and walked in stride with him, her dark hair bouncing against her shoulders, red purse swinging. He thought of how the evening might end, and it made him feel weak and dizzy. One moment her coarse vitality would make him feel weak and trapped—caught in something beyond his depth. And the next moment he would feel strong and possessive and excited.

"Honey, I bet with those shoulders you play football, do you?"

"Not at this place, Elise. I used to in high school, but they've got guys they pay to play. Coal heavers. Gorillas."

"I had a boyfriend once used to play pro ball for a truck company. He was real punchy. He was a tackle and they were for always hitting him on the head."

They ate in a small dark Chinese restaurant and she said, "I love this gunk, but it don't stay with you. It kinda goes right on through and you're hungry all over again."

And in the dark spring night, back out on the sidewalk, she clung to his arm, swaying a little and her voice was lower and huskier and she said, "I bet you don't think I'm a singer at all. I bet you figure I was throwing a big snow job."

"I believe you, Elise."

"You know what you're going to do, Brocky boy?

You're going to come up and I'll put a record on and I'll show you I'm a singer, see."

It was a narrow building, crowded in between stores. The street door wasn't locked. They went up three flights of stairs, and the air in the stairwell had a musty flavor. Her room was small, with a vague smell of laundry and dust. It had a kitchen alcove, a small bathroom with noisy plumbing. The studio couch where she slept was not made up from the previous night, and by the head of the couch, beyond the rumpled pillow, cigarette butts had been squashed out on the varnished floor beyond the edge of a dark-brown rug. He felt sick and hollow inside. There had been girls. A very few. Back seats of cars. Blankets under the trees. Once a back hallway. But girls. Not women.

They drank what was left in a bottle. She had a record player and she put on a blues record and sang along with it, slurring her way into the notes, snapping her fingers, swaying in exaggeration of the mannerisms of torch singers. In the dim lights of the room she had a feral, overpowering look. He wanted to leave and he couldn't think of any way to get out of it without looking like a fool, like a fool kid. She had sort of taken it all for granted.

She made him sit and watch her sing and then she came over to him and kissed him hard and turned off the floor lamp near the day bed. It was different than ever before. It was a kind of delirium, and a devouring, and a sense of evil.

He awoke and the two windows were gray and the light was in the room, insipid on the litter and the spilled clothing. She was asleep, breathing heavily through her mouth. He was on the outside and he slid out with great caution. He looked at her as he dressed. She was on her side, one arm high, showing the dark patch of armpit hair, one breast like a sagging white gourd. She was a stranger he had never seen before. A strange woman, and in that light she looked forty.

He had his door key and he got into the fraternity house without waking his roommate, and managed to wake up when the alarm went off after nearly an hour's sleep. The night with her was like something dreamed. In class he felt like something dead. Through the drone of the lecture he would think of her and something would turn slowly in his stomach and the backs of his hands would prickle. It was a nauseous excitement.

He went back to the beer joint that afternoon. He knew he shouldn't. But he had to go back and on the way there he told himself she wouldn't be there.

She was in the same booth and she was looking directly at him as he came through the door. She wore the same suit but this time her blouse was yellow. He felt ganglingly awkward as he walked to the booth. He knew he was blushing.

"You snuck out like a mouse or something, Brocky," she said, and he wanted to shush her because her voice was too loud.

"Had to make morning classes, Elise."

She reached across the table and held his hand strongly and said, "We had fun, Brocky. We had fun, didn't we?"

"Yes."

"I don't want you should think I'm like that. I mean that I'd do that with anybody."

He wished she wouldn't talk so loud. "I don't think that."

"It's on account of it was you. Cute Brocky. With the shoulders."

He wished he could stop blushing and that she would let go of his hand. And the day became a replica of the previous day. And it was at her place, his arm around her, that she said, "You're going to think I'm awful when I tell you something."

"What?"

"Archie, he wasn't overseas. He isn't dead. I wish he was but he isn't. He's a seaman. He's on an oceangoing tug. Right now he's down somewhere in the Caribbean. They're hauling some kind of dredge down there. He's a genuine bastard, Brocky. He goes away, he thinks I ought to lock myself up and wait for him or something. I should be dead or something all the time he's gone. I got to have fun, don't I? This time, and he's been gone seven months now, he doesn't send a damn nickel. How do you like a guy like that?"

"But when will he——"

"You relax, honey. He won't be back for a long time. Now you kiss Elise. Kiss her nice. There. That's my boy with shoulders. That's my good boy. Do you like this, darlin'? Do you?"

The April days were like that. The April days and April nights. She had taken him down with her into some dark place. Nothing else mattered. Classes were vague things. They talked about work he did not understand. He dozed often. He prepared nothing. He moved through a world that was like a dull dream, moving each day closer to that single vivid reality of her body. He knew she was a liar. He learned she had never sung. He knew she was sloppy, ignorant, opinionated, dull of wit. But that did not matter. It did not matter what mind or spirit went with that practiced body. Each day was time that must be gotten through somehow, because the hours led inevitably to her bed in the musty room. Sometimes they would cook there, and he would buy food and bring it to the room. She was an indifferent cook. She liked to have him bring a bottle.

His allowance, compared with the average, was generous. But he soon found that it was not nearly enough. She didn't have any money at all and she wasn't working. He had to give her lunch money. And on May first she had to have thirty-five dollars for the rent on the tiny, shabby apartment. She kept needing things. Stockings. A new bra. Repairs to her wristwatch. A pair of shoes. When she wanted something and he could not provide it, she became sulky and she wouldn't let him near her. He knew precisely what she was doing. He raised money in every way he could think of. He wrote home for money for imaginary textbooks, for a fake dental bill, for new shoes. He started selling his possessions to other students, hocking things at a pawn shop, borrowing from the guys in the house. At first it was easy to borrow. A five here, and two dollars there, and a ten-dollar bill from his roommate. Then they started making excuses and he could borrow no more. He knew they sensed the change in him. He felt as if he were falling through space toward the inevitable smashup. And it didn't matter.

He cut so many classes and did so poorly in classwork that he had to have an interview with his faculty advisor. He promised everything with great sincerity, trying to cut the interview short because Elise was waiting in the usual place. Everything was going to hell, but it didn't matter. He thought that he might get a chance to crack the books just before exams and squeak through somehow. His watch was gone, and most of his clothes, and that helped a little, but June first came inevitably closer and with it the need for another thirty-five dollars in one chunk. He didn't want to think beyond June first. He had a vague idea of getting a job there in the city during the summer so that they could go on as before. Elise began to ask a bit nervously about the rent, but he told her he knew where he could get it.

It wasn't until nearly the last day that he remembered Marty. He wondered why he hadn't thought of Marty before. During his freshman year he had been required to live in the dormitories with a roommate selected by lot. He had drawn Marty Greenshine. At first he hadn't liked him at all. A strange guy, older than the others. Serious as a judge. And bright. Disconcertingly bright. And Marty always had plenty of money. After a time he had learned that, behind all that seriousness, there was an off-beat sense of humor. An obliqueness. Marty would have the money. He had heard Marty was still in the dormitory, in one of the single rooms. He stopped at the gate office and checked the number. Number 312, Lowman Hall.

It had been a long time since he had been in one of the dormitories. He went up to Marty's door and knocked. He remembered that it had been a little after twelve when he knocked on the door. And a bright, good-smelling day because it had rained in the morning and the whole world was washed clean and new. He could hear some guys playing catch down in the quad, *pock* of ball into glove. And somebody singing somewhere, in a deep resonant voice, a trained voice. When there was no answer, he started to turn away and then tried the knob. The door opened. He saw Marty's clothes laid out neatly on the bed. He remembered Marty's habits. Marty would put his robe and slippers on, lay his clothes out, and then go down the hall to the shower. He checked the closet and saw that Marty's wooden clogs were gone. Marty usually spent a long time in the shower room. He looked out the window. Maybe Marty would be sore that he hadn't been over to see him. Maybe Marty would go off on one of his queer stubborn streaks and refuse to lend the money. Or maybe Marty had heard that he had been borrowing from everybody.

The more he thought about it, the more positive he became that Marty was going to say no. His hands felt wet and he dried them on his handkerchief. He began to get sore at Marty. The little bastard would say no, all right.

It wouldn't hurt to make a quick check and see if Marty was flush enough to spare the cash. Just a quick check.

He remembered going to the bureau and the way the top drawer creaked a little as he pulled it open. Marty always put his wallet in there when he went to the shower room. Brock took the wallet and opened it and saw the wonderfully crisp sheaf of bills. Marty liked new bills. His hands felt shaky. He thumbed through the bills, counting the three twenties, a ten, a five, and four singles. He took the three twenties out and started to put the wallet back. He hesitated, then opened it again and took out the ten. Seventy dollars. Marty certainly didn't need it. Anyway, he would pay it back. Mail it to Marty in a plain envelope after he got the summer job. No harm done.

He felt a sudden need for haste. He opened the door and looked down the hallway. It was empty. He walked lightly and quickly toward the staircase. He glanced into one of the rooms as he went by. The room door was open. A boy sat at a desk and glanced at Brock. The guy looked faintly familiar. But, hell, he'll never remember me. Marty won't even know when he lost it. He was only two blocks from Elise's place when he realized that the bills were still folded tightly in the palm of his hand. He stopped and, with great casualness, transferred them into his wallet, sliding them in beside the single dollar of his own. He'd promised Elise, hadn't he? What the hell could you do? You couldn't go back on a promise. Marty would never miss a lousy seventy bucks. Anyway, he was going to get it back, wasn't he? It was just a loan.

So he had given Elise forty dollars and she had taken thirty-five of it down and given it to the wife of the building superintendent and come back upstairs and they had gone to bed, he with greater eagerness than ever before, as though in this way he could blind himself. Later it rained again. They made toast of stale bread and ate it with jam. In the evening they went out and ate well and went back to her place. Every once in a while he would think of Marty. And he would feel angry with Marty. He stayed with her all night and missed his first two classes, and went directly from her place to his eleven o'clock class without textbook or notebook.

At eleven-thirty a man came in and tiptoed to the front of the hall. The lecturer frowned at the interruption. The man whispered to the lecturer. The lecturer checked the seating chart and Brock saw them both look directly at him. His heart seemed to make a wild, fluttering leap within him.

"You're excused, Mr. Delevan," the lecturer said.

Brock got up. He walked down the aisle and followed the man out into the corridor. "What do you want me for?"

"You're wanted in the office of the Dean of Men, Delevan."

When Brock walked into the office, he knew it was all over. He had fallen through the air for a long time and this was the shock of landing. His faculty advisor was there, and three members of the student council, and Marty, and the boy who had glanced at him as he had passed the open door. They kept glancing at him and looking away nervously.

The Dean of Men said quietly, "This is a serious matter, Mr. Delevan. I shall ask you a question. Did you go to Mr. Greenshine's room yesterday at about a quarter past twelve and, without Mr. Greenshine's knowledge or consent, remove seventy dollars from his wallet while he was taking a shower?"

The words came from far away. And so did Brock's voice when he answered. He tried to talk about a loan, but it sounded weak and silly and strange. He couldn't put it into words. It was a Thursday. They made him wait in another room. Then he was called back in. The others had left. Just the Dean of Men was there. It was a Thursday.

"I've placed a long distance call for your father, Delevan. It will save time if you listen to this end of the conversation." The dean was a mild-looking man with a soft voice. "You may sit down."

The phone rang and he picked it up. "Mr. Delevan? May I speak freely about a personal matter on this line? This is Hardy, Dean of Men. All right. I am most sorry to tell you, sir, that yesterday your son, Brock Delevan, stole seventy dollars from another student here. He has been expelled as of noon today. No, sir, there is no doubt about it. He is here in my office and he has admitted it. No, sir, there is no chance of a mistake or a misunderstanding. The student involved does not wish to press any criminal charges. He will be satisfied if the money is returned. Do you wish to speak to your boy? I see, sir. I understand. I'll tell him. Yes, sir. Good-bye."

He replaced the phone gently on the cradle. "Your father will arrive in the morning, Delevan. He will give me the money and I will see that Mr. Greenshine gets it. You can meet your father here in my office at ten o'clock tomorrow morning. Do you have enough money for a hotel room?"

"I can stay at the house until . . ."

The dean shook his head. "I've seen this happen before. I don't think you should stay at the house. I don't believe they would let you stay there in any case." Hardy looked intently at him. "Why did you take the money, Delevan?"

"Do I have to answer questions?"

Hardy stood up. "That will be all."

Brock walked to the fraternity house. One of the fresh-man pledges stepped in front of him just as he got inside the door, blocking his way. The freshman looked scared. He did not speak. He held his hand out, palm up. After a moment Brock understood. He took off his pin and put it on the outstretched palm. The pledge pointed to a corner of the hallway. Brock saw his two suitcases there, his topcoat and overcoat on top of them. He went over and picked them up. The pledge stood, holding the big front door open. Brock felt the silence in the house. He sensed that they were all back, out of sight, listening. Maybe they wanted him to cry like a baby. He stopped in the door-way, turned around and yelled, "Good-bye, dear brothers! Good-bye, you dull bastards!" The pledge slammed the door hard as he walked down the steps.

Elise had known that he had classes and a lab that would take him until four, and they had agreed to meet in the cellar beer joint at four thirty. He walked to her place and carried the two suitcases up the three flights. He still had thirty dollars in his pocket. It would buy a pair of bus tickets. The old man could wait around the dean's office for a long long time. They would get out of this crummy city. Take a new name. Call themselves husband and wife. Get jobs. In a few years this would all seem far away.

He set the suitcases down and he had his hand lifted in order to knock when he realized that a strange noise was coming from inside the room. For a moment he could not identify it, and then he realized that it was the familiar and hideous sound of the springs on the ancient studio couch, a rhythmic surge and creaking, too well known to him, too well remembered. "Elise!" he yelled. "Elise!" and his voice cracked on her name, the way it used to long ago when his voice was changing.

There was a sudden silence in the room. And he thought of other answers. Someone else was in there. Or she was doing some kind of exercises. Or her husband had come back. The silence continued. He put his ear against the door and thought he heard whispering. He banged on

the door. There was no answer. And he remembered
something he had seen in a movie. He backed up a little
and swung his leg up and stamped his heel hard against
the door, just above the lock. Wood ripped and the door
went open so easily that he lost his balance and fell to his
hands and knees, just inside the doorway. He raised his
head stupidly and looked at them there. It was like a dirty
picture that had been passed around in high school a long
time ago. It was Elise, and it was a squat, brutal man he
had seen several times on the stairs in the building, or
standing in front. He had always nodded at Elise, and
Elise had told Brock that the man drove a taxi. It was all
gone in that moment. It was just a dirty picture of somebody he had never known. The woman made a thin
sniggling sound. The man yelled at him to get the hell out.
He pulled the door shut. He felt a great calmness. He
picked up his suitcases and the two coats and went down
the stairs with even, methodical tread. Down in the lower
hallway he had difficulty opening the door. One of the
suitcases banged against a doorframe. It spilled open and
everything fell out. He knelt and repacked it carefully. He
saw that they had put his dirty laundry right in with his
fresh clothing. He felt calm and far away and it shocked
and surprised him to feel tears running down his face, to
stick his tongue out the corner of his mouth and taste the
salt.

He checked in at a small hotel near the campus. It was
still afternoon. He undressed and went to bed. When he
woke up, it was daylight. He did not know if he had slept
an hour or a week. He phoned the desk. They said it was
a little after nine in the morning. After his shower, he
shaved. It seemed wrong that he should still be wearing a
Delevan face, a face bearing the clan resemblance, eyes
that tilted down at the outside corners, shelving brow, the
high-bridged nose, the heavy mouth, an expression elu-
sively whimsical.

He got to the dean's office at precisely ten. His father
was there. The old man said evenly, "Hello, Brock."
"Hello, Dad." "Wait in the hall, Brock." "Okay."

He waited in the hall a long time. The old man came

out. He didn't look at Brock and he said nothing. Brock fell in step beside him. Once they were out of the building the old man said, "Where's your stuff?"

"In a hotel room. The Cardinal Hotel. Three blocks up Thompson."

"I know where it is."

The old man did one strange thing. He stopped short near the quadrangle. He stopped and just stood there and looked at the kids walking by. Classes were changing. Girls with one arm hugged around a stack of books. Sweaters with letters. The old man stood and gaped at them as though he had never seen college kids before. Then he started walking again. They went up to the room. The old man said, "I left Greenshine's money with the dean. Do you owe any money?"

Brock had the list in a small notebook. The old man sat at the desk. Brock read off the names and accounts and where the guys lived. The old man copied them all down and totaled the figures. Ninety-six dollars and fifty cents.

"Have you hocked anything?"

"My watch and some clothes."

"Give me the tickets." Brock took the tickets out of the back of his wallet and gave them to the old man. He stood up. "You wait here. I'll redeem this stuff and pay those boys back."

"I got the addresses. You could send them checks. That would be all right."

"I'll pay them in cash."

"But it would be a lot easier to——"

"I know that. I know that."

"I don't get it, Dad."

"I wouldn't expect you to."

The old man was back by one o'clock. He had a suit box tied with string. He took the wristwatch out of his pocket and handed it to Brock. Brock strapped it on his wrist. He remembered that it had been the big high-school graduation present. He even remembered the box and the way it was wrapped and the card. The old man had a funny look. He went into the bathroom and shut the door. After a little while Brock heard him being sick in there.

He thought of the bad time the guys probably had given him. They had no reason to do that. The old man hadn't done anything. Brock called through the door, asking if he was all right, if he could help. The old man said no in a strained funny voice. Brock sat on the bed. His father was in the bathroom for a long time. He looked pasty when he came out.

He planted his feet and stood in front of Brock. "What was it? Gambling?"

"No sir."

"A girl?"

"Y-yes."

"Get her in trouble?"

"No, I didn't."

"You wanted the money, then, so you could give her a big time."

"I . . . I guess so."

"Sleeping with her?"

"Yes."

The old man stared at him expressionlessly. "Every damn thing in the world. Every damn thing. Every damn chance. Now a thief. A stinking filthy sneaking thief."

"Wait a minute, Dad. I——"

"Oh, shut up. I hope that she was the best lay since Cleopatra. And it would have had to be a thousand times better than that to make it worth what you've done to yourself, what you've done to your mother and to me. Love doesn't come that high, kid. There's too much of it around. Pick up your stuff. We've got a flight to catch. And don't open your damn mouth."

The old man had never spoken to him that way before. He had never used that kind of language. He was glad his father hadn't seen Elise. That would have made it worse. But he didn't see how he could feel worse. It couldn't ever get any worse than those minutes when he was at the foot of the three flights of stairs putting things back in the suitcase, knowing the two of them were up there in her room. . . .

Now he lay in darkness in his own room and he heard the faint buzzing and knew the records had ended some time ago. He got up in darkness and reversed the stack and started it over again. School was out now. Next year they would come back and they would talk about him in the fraternity house. And maybe the next year they might remember him and talk about him too. And then nobody would remember any longer. He saw himself in Marty's room. They talked about moments of decision. That wasn't any moment of decision. There hadn't even been any thinking. Just taking the money in an automatic way, as though he were dreaming. If you could find any moment of decision, it was that moment when he left the bar and walked toward the booth where the strange girl sat. Or maybe the moment he had turned away from the lab door after walking all the way over there.

He saw himself in Marty's room. A little automatic toy figure about four inches high standing there opening the top drawer of a toy bureau. Why? Like a sickness. As if he hadn't been there when it was happening. One day in high school one of the guys had worn a trick ring. You held it up to the light and looked through a little hole and you could see a naked woman. April and May had been like that this year. Like standing in a crowded place while people shoved by you, but you didn't notice being jostled because you stood there in the middle of the sidewalk looking through the little hole in that ring, looking at that naked body, that woman-body, that only clear and real thing in the world, while all the rest of the world was just people shoving by you, going no place in a hurry, wanting to push you out of the way.

He wondered who would pay her rent on July first.

The summer was ahead. He knew they expected him to do something. To make some sort of decision about himself. He knew that he was expected to get some sort of a job and work hard and try to get into the fall session somewhere. But it made him tired to think about it. He wanted to stay in the room and keep the music low and keep going over April and May, trying to figure out what had happened to him. There were good guys and bad guys. Could you be a thief from the very beginning and not know about it? Would you steal again? He wanted to be alone. He wanted something that was broken to begin to heal. But it didn't heal. It stayed broken.

He knew that Ellen had heard some of the talk. Enough so that she had guessed the rest. He saw it in the way he would catch her looking at him, a pinched look in her eyes, a flatness in her stare, a look not of hurt, but of appraisal. They had passed, long ago, from the embittered warfare of childhood into a relationship of pride and trust, a sense of maintaining a united front. And now it had become something else. All gone now, the shrill yelling as the brother broke into the clear and went up and up, hand reached for the wobbling ball, framed there against the autumn afternoon, shadow lanky in late cold sun, and a hero had died. Meat had spoiled, and the flesh turned sad, and the eyes turned inward to look at the pitilessness of what might have been.

It was the death of dreams that mattered. Those slow dreams that are used to bring on the true dreams of sleep. Taking the long walk from the bullpen to the mound in the bottom of the ninth, and the bases are full of Yankees and Mantle is up, standing expressionlessly aside but watching closely as you take the warm-up pitches, and the stands are muttering *who is he who is he,* and others say *a kid named Delevan they brought him up from class A for the pennant race and they say he's got stuff* and then you are ready and Mantle steps in with that blocky face and the big back flexing and you let it go for *steeeeerike* so blazing fast he doesn't even twitch and *steeeeerike* again and on the last one he swings in desperation too late and then the next hitter gets a tiny piece of one enough to send it spinning crazy off to your right and you pounce and make the play at the plate so it is two down and the stands yelling and the manager looking like he would cry and they put in a pinch hitter who bangs one foul but just barely and you steady down and burn one by and then break his back with the floater and that's the game and the series.

Now you come up and the big back flexes in that power swing and you turn and watch it out of sight over the roof of the left-field stands.

There was the dream where you floated down through the tropic sky and pulled the shroud lines and landed like a cat and cut the chute loose and buried it and that night moulded the plastic explosive to the bridge trusses and hid while the train burst in red fatness.

Now they stand down there and look up and as you swing close enough the finger tightens on the trigger. . . .

Your putt stops short of the hole and you watch Player tap his in.

You walk down the dusty street, spurs jingling in cadence and fingers hooked and ready, but you are a bit slow and lead spanks dust out of your shirt and later they all come out of their hiding places and look at your body there in the road, and they congratulate the hero.

You are dead in the dust there because there are new heroes.

Your bags have been packed for you and they took back your pin and the tables are stacked and the Chinese lanterns folded away and now they are tearing down the bunting while tired musicians pack away the tarnished brass horns.

So there is nothing much to do anymore. It is a good thing to lie alone in the dark room with music not quite audible. Then in the darkness you can savor the stink she left on you. Inhale it deeply. Finger the marks she left on you. Remember her teeth and her softness. Roll in the sourness of her, as a dog returns to filth.

Downstairs are the strangers. And they listen to the distant anguish of television. Here you are, on the hill of the Delevans in the middle house, your face clan-marked, and yet you are no longer one of them.

The records stop and this time you do not stir. You touch the plaster beside you. It is rough and cool. There is time to go over it all again. And then maybe it will be time to sleep.

You walked right up to the door of the lab that April day and then, for no reason, you turned around and left. And if you go over it enough times, there will be a time when you walk up to the door of the lab and pause . . . and shrug . . . and walk in.

Chapter Three

Fremont is a very old street in the city of Stockton.
It had been very narrow at one time, a street of big
Victorian houses, sitting tall and narrow and secluded, like
spinsters thinking quietly of what might have been. There
had been iron fences, and the quiet metal deer under the
elm shade, bird-spattered and noble. There had been
money on that street. Money from the lumber mills, which
chewed and chased the good hard woods all the way from
the valleys back up into the faraway hills—so that each
year the money was less. But it had been invested in
heavy parchment, embossed and engraved, with red seals
and gold seals and bits of silk ribbon, testifying to a share
in the interest of the old Commodore Vanderbilt, of the
shifty, mercurial Jay Gould. Money in railroads, in textiles, in steamships.

But the wars came and they were fought, and the giants
died, and for those on the street a good world crumbled
quickly away, leaving the great houses which had been
built with the conviction that they should last through
eternity. Behind all the silly scrollwork, the fan windows,
the pretentious turrets, the stone and the beams were
sound and true and good.

The street was widened, and widened again. It was a
good route to the heart of the city. The street widened like
a stone river until the sidewalks touched the steps of the
old houses. The metal deer and the iron fences were gone.

Now there are not many of the old houses left. There
are supermarkets there, and a great metal river of traffic
flows endlessly by. There are many gas stations, and there
are green-and-yellow city buses that *chuff* at the corners
and grind away. It is a street of people who are strangers

to each other, because no one stays long anymore. The few old houses that are left have been cut up into apartments and into furnished rooms. There is no dignity left in the old houses. The new partitioning is flimsy. The lawns are gone and the trees are gone, and the houses are naked to the traffic. In the houses shrill voices saw at the nerves of children, television screens flicker as the trucks roll by, men leave in surly humor for the swing shift.

Quinn Delevan, as he ate dinner with Bess, was constantly aware that on this Wednesday night he would go down to Fremont Street again, down to the girl who waited for him. They ate together in the breakfast booth off the kitchen, and he had asked his usual meaningless question about David, and she had answered as always, "He took his dinner out to his studio."

They ate and she talked a great deal, talked about Robbie and his new bride, and she ate as she talked and he wished for a dining room table of baronial proportions, so that she could sit at one end of it and he could sit at the other, and then she would be muted by the distance, reduced to life-size. In the booth there was no escaping her. When he was quite small, his mother had read him the story of Jack and the Beanstalk. It had made a horrid impression on him and caused many nightmares. The giant would grab him and hold him in a big damp fist and, grinning, lift him slowly toward the big wet red cave of his mouth and he would wake up screaming. Now it often seemed to him that he had indeed married a giant. She talked *at* him. She directed herself at him, talking of trivialities with such a dreadful energy that the very burst and flow and torrent of her in that constricted space, under the bright light, seemed to shrink him, dwindle him, dry him to a dusty husk. She was a movie where you had to sit too far forward. The whites of her eyes were blued with the health of her, and her white teeth chewed, and the red membranes of her mouth were busy, and he would get a dazed dizziness by looking at her, so that her head would seem to be the size of a bushel basket, all glistening and bobbing and chomping and making loud

sounds at him that he could not quite understand. The
torrents of her washed and buffeted him.

Sometimes he would realize, almost with a feeling of
shock, that she was, after all, a woman of just slightly
more than average size. She was five feet eight inches tall
to his six feet. She weighed one hundred and forty as
against his one seventy. Those moments of realization
would occur when he happened to stand beside her, as
when they stood at church, or when he saw her clothing
on a bed or a chair. A shoe, a bra. In such moments he
guessed that it was her sheer health and energy that made
her seem so vast at other times. Early in their marriage he
had played the part of the aggressor, and Bess had accepted a frequency based, after the first month of marriage, on his lesser energies. But by the third year of their
marriage the roles had become reversed, and even though
he felt that a certain amount of masculine pride and honor
was thus sacrificed, he was glad to be rid of the burden of
decision. As her needs were stronger than his, and due to
her persistence, once she was the aggressor, his energies
were reduced after a time to the point of impotence. This,
added to the reversal of roles, troubled him to the extent
of seeing a doctor, though he waited a long time before
taking that step. If his relations were shameful, they were
at least private. Only he and Bess knew the true state of
things. He waited until he went on a business trip and
then he picked the name of a doctor out of the phone
book and made an appointment, giving a false name.

He realized later that he had been fortunate in the
choice of doctors. The man was sallow and quiet and
wise. When Quinn Delevan faltered, the doctor drew him
out with carefully casual questions so that Quinn betrayed
far more of himself than he intended.

At last he was finished and he sat back, sweating. The
doctor turned so that he looked out a large window across
the city. "Would you say, sir, that you have been torturing
yourself with suspicions of a ... repressed sexual devia-
tion?"

"I guess I have, Doctor."

"That is nonsense of course. You feel lacking in masculinity because of your wife's strong sexual energies. You hear your friends talk in locker rooms, in smoking cars. Tales of great prowess. You begin to think you are unique. You suspect that your marriage relationship is ... unhealthy. Uncommon. Nonsense! You would be surprised. In many marriages the male is the aggressor. In many others both partners assume that role almost alternately. And in a great many the female is consistently the aggressor, the more active partner. That is the way it should be. But out of pride and out of lack of knowledge, you have forced your own response to her until she has literally exhausted you." The doctor smiled. "It is the privilege of the passive partner to say no, as many wives have learned. You are too tired. You are not in the mood. This is most easy. Above all, do not think about it too much. You have been doing that. Because your own marriage relationship is divergent from the popular ideas of married love, it does not mean that it is either unhealthy or abnormal. I will stop being professional for one moment and express a certain personal envy. You are a fortunate man, sir. When you go home, I want you to sit quietly with her and tell her that you came to me and tell her what I said. It will make it better for both of you, because she may be as uninformed as you were." The doctor walked him to the office door and smiled broadly and said, "Above all, do not be impressed by those men who wink and brag. They are the very ones least likely to possess the sexual prowess they talk about."

When he got home, he could not make himself tell Bess about the visit. But it had helped him a great deal. Because of the advice given him, they were able to find a new rhythm of adjustment. But always there would come the dark nights when she would be at him, a relentless rubbery vastness about her, a giant eagerness that wrenched at him with a smothering strength until she sighed off into a placid mound of sleeping warmth, leaving him aged and bitter and dry, lean and devoured in the night.

But now it was all changing. Now there was escape, delicately and carefully contrived, and the awareness of it made the booth seem less cramped, made the avidity of her casual conversation easier to bear. He looked at his watch and frowned.

"Oh, darn it, dear! Do you have to go out tonight?"

"It's Wednesday," he said, faintly accusing.

"That meeting again. I forgot about it. I wish you could give that one up, dear. You never seem to be home anymore. What darn good does it do for you to keep going to that meeting?"

"Political fences. Part of the job. We have to stay on the right side of the city and county fathers, Bess. One little hike in assessment could hurt a lot."

"Well, Ben seems to be able to spend his evenings with his family."

"He puts in more hours at the office than I do."

"Sometimes I think he takes advantage of you, Quinn. I really do. You're *so* decent about it."

He slid out of the booth, picking up his plate, cup, and saucer and carrying them over to the drainboard of the sink, feeling within him the curious division of emotion that her words gave him. A guilt-shame balanced pleasurably on the slick edge of intrigue. Wanting her to say more to bring on the self-punishment, and at the same time dreading it.

"I shouldn't be too late, honey," he said.

"I think I'll start on the new curtains for David's studio. That monk's cloth is drab, sort of. And yellow will be cheerful. I forgot to tell you, dear, when I used your car yesterday and put the gas in it, the man in the station said all that clicking is valve springs or something like that. Maybe you ought to take it into town tomorrow and leave it at the garage. Don't you think he'll like yellow?"

"What?"

"You weren't listening again. The curtains for David's studio. They say yellow is a cheerful color."

"That sounds fine."

He went to the bedroom and retied his tie, took the new shaggy sports jacket from his closet, and slipped it on. There was a coiling and shifting of excitement in his middle, cyclical-like hunger pangs, and when the spasms were most taut, they shallowed his breathing. He looked at himself in the mirror and was gratified to see that nothing of what he felt showed in his face. He looked mildly back at himself, lean and brown and bored and casual. When he went back to the kitchen, she was rinsing the dishes and placing them in the dishwasher. He put his hand on her shoulder and she turned around and he kissed the corner of her mouth. She gave his tie a quick adjustment and tilted her head a little and looked at him and said, "You look very nice, dear. Don't be too late, please. And see if you can stay out of those card games after the meeting like last time."

"Sure. But don't wait up if you're tired, honey."

After he was out of the house, he stopped in the driveway and lighted a cigarette and looked for a moment at the stars. The studio windows were lighted. It was beyond the garage, about forty feet from the back door of the house. He thought of David in there, and he hunched his shoulders a bit and walked quickly to his car and got in and turned around and drove out the length of the driveway, pausing by the rural mailbox, then turning toward the village, the heavy convertible dropping swiftly down the twelve-degree grade, falling smoothly down through the night by the lighted windows of the old houses on the hill. He turned toward Stockton and felt good that it had been so easy this time, and felt slightly querulous because it had been so very easy, felt a contempt for Bess for making it that easy. They did not know—not one of them knew—how great had been the change in him in the past few months.

Yet perhaps Alice, his twin, suspicioned an emotional change. Their emotional involvement was intricate, beginning in the shared womb, evolving through the slow days of childhood, so that without conscious thought, with no exercise of logic, with nothing observable, she could yet sense change, the information transmitted along channels unknown to the untwinned and only suspected by the twinned. It had always been that way. A wordless knowing. And lately he had gone out of his way to avoid being alone with her. This was a physical reaction she could observe and he knew she had. But awareness of change had antedated his caution. She would never ask. He knew that she would never ask because they had always known what the other one was willing to talk about.

Yet he was afraid he would tell her. Not because she was his twin. Because, rather, of the wish to have someone know about it. Someone who would do nothing. Perhaps the way a man will brag of a successful crime to someone who is a known criminal. Not that Alice had ever erred in this way. But being twin, she shared guilt.

"Alice, I am having an affair with one of the girls in the mill."

Not even one of the office girls. A mill girl. He would say that and Alice would not see Bonny. She would see some crow-voiced wench or rolling haunch and brows plucked to thin lines and too much makeup. Or maybe she would see Bonny without being told, and know how Bess and David were a part of it, making it happen.

Making it happen in such a strange way. There had always been, for him, a quickening male excitement in going out there where the looms roared and clattered, where the factory girls called shrilly to each other over the continual din, moving with practised sturdy swiftness, deft and sweaty, with knowing eyes filled with promiscuous insolence, daring him to take closer notice of buttocks and breast. It always made him think of a peasant village where the magpie girls worked the clothes white on river-bank rocks. They managed to bring to these dingy clattering floors a flavor of gossip and intrigue and speculation and body awareness.

One day in March he had left his office where sleet was crinkling against his windows, and he had gone restlessly to wander through the narrow aisles where the girls worked. It was late in the afternoon, and nearly dark outside. He saw a girl he had not noticed before. She was waiting for the checker and a new setup. There was a slimness about her. A daintiness and the wilted look of physical tiredness. He walked slowly. She did not see him. She stretched then as he came near her, and she yawned, fists next to her ears, feet planted wide, arching her back so that as he watched her the shirt she wore pulled free from her slacks and he saw in the shop lights the smooth miracle of her young waist, the downy spinal crease at the small of her back, and there was about her, poised there, the breathtaking perfection of ancient statues, of sun-warmed marble. She stretched the long, young muscles and, poised there, turned her head, and he had stopped, looking at her, so that she looked directly into his eyes six feet away. Her eyes were dulled with tiredness, and her mouth was yawn-stretched. Then her eyes changed and she stood utterly still, as he did. It seemed like a very long time. She turned hastily away, tucking her shirt into her slacks, her cheeks darkening, looking down then. He moved on along the aisle, seeing nothing else, feeling as though he had been blinded by her. Her face was very young. The weariness told him that she was new, that her body had not yet conditioned itself to the demands of the working day.

Back in his office he kept thinking about her. There was an excitement in it, and he told himself that there was no harm in learning more about her. It became a game, because he could not ask any direct questions. The next day at closing time he stood by the bulletin board near the time clock for her production floor. He pretended to be reading the notices on the board. The noise of the equipment began to diminish at five. It faded rapidly. Within a minute there was nothing left but an almost stunning silence, a single whirring that died away. Then, as though to replace the production sounds, the babble of the girls increased in volume. There was a tinny banging of locker doors, and shrill laughter, and heels clamped hard against the floor, and snapping of compacts and purses. They filed behind him, snatching cards, inserting them in the clock, the soft bell of the clock ringing constantly.

They talked as they walked behind him, and he sensed that some of them, glancing at him, talked more quietly, and some of them raised their voices to a higher pitch. ". . . I don't see what the hell he's got to kick about if I ask you to come along. . . . You never tasted such glop and she calls it Chinese cooking for the love of . . . and told me I ought to stay off my feet . . . so he says to her look I can get a job anytime I feel like it and she says then why . . . then they marked them down again and I figured it was the last markdown so I . . . don't be so damned late like last time, you hear. . . ."

And out of the corner of his eye he saw her coming along alone, and he was very aware of her as she passed behind him and he turned his head just enough the other way so that he saw her hand take her time card. Second row, third slot down. He turned further and watched her put the card in the out rack, the same slot, and go through the doorway.

They were all gone and he heard the last of the fading voices. He took the card out of the slot. His fingers trembled and he turned it toward the light. Bonita Doyle. She was probably called Bonny. Bonny Doyle. He liked it. It seemed to suit her.

The next morning he invented a weak reason for looking at the files in the personnel office. Unobserved, he took out her big yellow card and studied it. The picture of her in the upper left-hand corner was poor. She was twenty years old, and five feet six—she had looked taller— and one hundred and ten pounds, and her physical condition was perfect, and she got a high mark in manual dexterity, and her intelligence was good enough so that she was marked for on-job training beyond the requirements of the job she was hired for, and she had two years of high school, and before this job she had been a waitress for Blue Ribbon Restaurants, Inc. for ten months, and she had been born at Frenchman's Lake, a small town he vaguely remembered as being up in the hills, up in the resort section of the Adirondacks, and in case of accident please notify LaRue Doyle, 14 Orange Avenue, Bakersfield, California. Relationship—Bro. He turned the card over and saw that her local address was 60 Lefferts Avenue. And she had been with them ten days.

After he was back in his office, he made up sour little histories. She had a boy friend about twenty-three years old, a vet, who clerked in a supermarket—a dull young man of the bovine type who loved her very much indeed and they were both saving money toward the marriage.

In spite of the very delicate and very lovely configuration of her face, she would be supremely dull. She would buy confession-type comic books, and she would have one of those little record players and a collection of sweet-and-low records, and she would have a whole collection of sticky pet names for her bovine friend.

He told himself that he was a stable and well-adjusted thirty-six, and it was a bit too early for the reputedly dangerous forties. And he told himself he couldn't possibly get acquainted with her without the whole damn mill knowing about it, snickering behind his back at this lurid spectacle of this mustachioed chaser of mill girls, this Eros-smitten executive, this deviant Delevan.

But he found Lefferts Avenue and drove down it and found Number 60 and noted its shabbiness and the smeared window signs which told of furnished rooms to rent.

Counterbalancing the sour case histories he made up there were the warm bright dreams. And those dreams sent him walking in the mill, walking by her station as often as he dared. He knew that she had become aware of him and of his interest. She showed that by her intent preoccupation with her routine task when he was near, by the faint coloring of cheek and throat, by a certain self-conscious awkwardness of movement.

He learned more about her. He learned that she walked back and forth each day and he learned the route she took. Yet he did not quite dare take the next step. Yet knew that he would take it. Soon. Knew that he had to. Knew he was being driven by something more involved and ornamented than a simple lust for the girlness of her.

And there came an early evening near the first of April when he left the parking lot as the factory girls were leaving. It had been unseasonably warm and there was a line storm moving on the city, yellowing the western sky, muttering with the first untried thunder of the year. He started to drive home. The first fat drops spattered the asphalt, thrummed on the canvas top of his car. He saw how it could be and he turned recklessly and bulled his way back through traffic, intersecting the route she took.

He looked for her, imagining how she would look running through the rain. And he nearly missed her. He caught a glimpse of her, standing in the doorway of a small store. He braked quickly and the car behind him yelped in surprise and indignation before swerving around him. He backed up when he could and opened the door on her side. The city was dark with the rain. He touched the horn ring and saw her look rigidly in the other direction, purse hugged in her arm.

"Bonny!" he called and saw her start and stare toward the car and knew she hadn't recognized him, knew she could not see him clearly. She took two slow steps out into the heavy rain and then scampered across the wide sidewalk and then stopped, half in and half out of the car, looking at him with recognition and uncertainty.

"Get in before you drown," he said.

She got in with that young awkwardness and pulled the heavy door shut, and with it shut he could smell the wet fabric of her. She laughed in a thin nervous way and, sitting far forward on the seat, said, "I'm getting your car all wet." Her voice disappointed him a little. It was thin, childish, a bit nasal.

"That doesn't matter."

"How did you know my name, Mr. Delevan?"

"I guess I heard one of the other girls talking to you. Something like that."

He started the car up. She accepted his answer. She moved her legs a bit, with a sort of slow caution. She still held her purse hugged tightly against her. He sensed her uneasiness, her shyness. This, after all, was an executive. One of the owners.

"You turn left at the next corner, Mr. Delevan, and then——"

"I know," he said, speaking before he thought. And he waited for her to ask him how he knew. She glanced at him quickly, but she did not ask.

He pulled up in front of the rooming house. The rain was beginning to diminish and he was afraid he would lose her without having said anything. She put her hand on the door handle and he felt despair. And then the rain suddenly increased again. The dash lights glowed green. The wipers swept back and forth. He could not hear the motor. They were shut in a small private world in a dark city and the rain hammered the canvas and the steel, and the cement around them.

"Relax. Wait until it lets up a little."

"I don't want to hold you up. I'm wet anyway."

"I'm in no hurry. You're not as wet as you'll get running for the porch."

She took her hand slowly from the door handle. "All right," she said. She leaned back tentatively. Her voice was small.

They sat there and he felt the silence between them grow into an electric and monstrous thing. He did not dare turn and look at her. He did not know what to say. She sat in stillness. He felt ancient, helpless, grotesque, soiled. The rain slackened again and suddenly it was gone, dragging a white curtain down the street and away into the east. She slid forward and opened the car door and turned toward him and said with quaint formal courtesy, "Thank you very much, Mr. Delevan, for——"

He put his hand on her arm, quickly, and shut his fingers hard on the thin aliveness of that arm under the bulky damp wool of her coat, and the quickness stopped her words with a small gasping.

He looked at her then and her eyes shifted away and he said, "I've got to see you again, Bonny." He cursed his own clumsiness, knowing that this would invite down upon him a twittering coyness, an alarmed coquettishness. He released her arm quickly. And she turned and looked directly at him.

"Why?" she said. It was a child's question and she gave it the gravity and dignity children have.

"I don't know. No, I mean I wish I knew. I keep walking into the mill just to see you."

"I thought that. I thought you did that. I wasn't sure. But I pretended that was what you were doing."

"I just want to see you again."

"It's not right. I mean it's something I can pretend, Mr.

Delevan, and that doesn't hurt anything. Just to pretend. To make up things. But it shouldn't happen for real."

"I'll come here tomorrow night and I'll park down there beyond the streetlight. At eight thirty. I'll wait for you right there."

"Don't. Please don't. It makes me feel almost sick inside. No, not sick. Dizzy inside, sort of. Please don't, Mr. Delevan."

"I'll be there tomorrow night."

"I won't come out," she said. And she got out quickly and swung the door shut. He watched her go up the steps and into the shabby house. She did not look back. The next evening he lied to Bess and drove to the city and parked where he said he would park. He arrived a little before eight thirty. He left his parking lights on. She did not come out. He had kept away from her in the mill that day, staying close to his office. She had not come out by nine o'clock. He decided to wait fifteen minutes more. At nine fifteen he said he would give her until nine thirty. At nine thirty he said five minutes more. At twenty minutes of ten she pulled the car door open and slid in beside him and yanked the big door shut and she was crying. He did not speak to her or touch her. She sat there and he felt her sadness. He felt as if they were both involved in tragedy not of their making, like passengers on a plane that falters inevitably toward a wide wild sea.

The tears ceased and she leaned back. In the faint light her face looked thin and white. "I wasn't going to come down."

"I know."

"I saw the taillights. I pulled the shade down. I walked and walked in my room. Then I would look and tell myself each time before I looked that you would be gone. But you weren't. And the last time I was afraid you would go and I ran."

"I shouldn't have been here. I shouldn't have waited so long."

"How long would you have waited?"

"I don't know, Bonny. I don't know."

"Drive someplace, Mr. Delevan. Please. I don't want to stay here. It keeps making me feel like crying."

He drove slowly out of the city. She wore a perfume that was too heavy for her. It did not suit her. He drove on back roads he had never seen before. And after a long time he began to talk to her, not looking at her, just talking as though he were alone in the car and he had to tell himself what he was and what he had been. All of it, all the continuing knowledge, never before admitted even to himself, that he was dead weight in the firm, that a large area of him was dead. And there were the dreams of things you would do, and found you had waited too long, and there were the sterling resolutions that always seemed to degenerate into a sort of mild and meaningless futility. The words went on and on, draining thinly out of him. He talked to the night and to the girl's silence, his voice growing hoarse as the words exhausted him. And with a complete despair he realized that even here honesty was denied him, that as he tried to explain himself and what he was, a sly censor kept coloring the facts and dreams, adding dramatic highlights, spicing the hopelessness, so that the dusty plots became drama, and drama became a tool of seduction. He was the adolescent lover who combats his girl's indifference by inventing a unique and fatal disease for himself, selling himself so heartily that, in self-pity, his tears become genuine.

He stopped at a crossroads and trained his spotlight on the road signs and found an arrow that pointed to Stockton sixteen miles away. He felt weary and disgusted with himself. Ashamed of contrived emotions. What had all this meant to the silence beside him? An embittered complaining bore, whining about his life. She could tell her girl friends about it. It would be a fine story, particularly if she had any gift for mimicry. They could all giggle.

"I'll take you back," he said, his tone dulled.

"Please stop a minute," she said.

He pulled over in the darkness and turned the car lights off. "Dandy evening for you, Bonny. Maudlin. A cheap movie."

In the darkness she moved to him almost harshly and

her cold hands went flat against his cheeks and she put her lips hard against his and turned her head back and forth as she did so, so that her mouth was ground warmly against his and his hands found the long fine line of her back. Then she pulled his head down a bit and kissed his eyes, her lips releasing the tears of self-pity, and she murmured, "Quinn—oh, Quinn darling—oh, Quinn honey." And lips and murmurings and the giving warmth of her tuned the drama of self just a bit higher so that the harshness of his first sob was almost completely genuine to him, and even as he tried to believe in it, something inside him was cool and sneeringly disdainful of this method which won her so easily and so completely.

When it was over, he assumed a gruffness, a colonial manner of understatement, saying, "Dreadfully sorry. Didn't mean to crack up like this."

"I'm glad you did. I'm glad I understand you now."

And now the promise of ultimate victory could be neatly countersigned, so he said, "I hope you'll let me see you again."

"Of course . . . Quinn."

"Even though we both know it's wrong and we shouldn't."

"It's too late . . . for shouldn't, I think. When, Quinn? When?"

"Not tomorrow night. I have to go to a dinner party. The next night? Eight thirty."

"Yes," she said. "Yes, Quinn. I like saying your name. I like to hear you say my name."

"Bonny."

"I never liked it before. Now I like to hear you say it."

He drove her back. This time she looked back from the lighted porch, made a small gesture of parting, a furtive wave before she was gone into the house darkness.

The next time they were together they talked and they kissed often, and they laughed and there was fondness in the laughter. And a new fierceness in the kisses. And the next time after that he drove her thirty-five miles from Stockton and she made a small protesting sound in her throat as he turned in by the sign that said CABINS. The lights there were dim. A fat woman asked for five dollars and she gave him a key wired to a piece of wood a foot long and told him where to go. Bonny sat far over on her side of the front seat of the car. He drove up across dark ruts and parked by the cabin. One lighted orange bulb hung over the door of the cabin. He went around the car and opened the door on her side. She sat there. "Quinn. Quinn, should we?"

"I need you, Bonny." His voice trembled. He held his hand out to her. She gripped it very tightly with thin cold fingers and she got out of the car still holding his hand, not speaking again. He made the key work and the door creaked open. The place smelled of dampness and linoleum and it was colder in there than outside.

He found the light switch and turned on the overhead bulb and she stood looking down at the floor and whispered, "Please turn it off." He turned it off. He kissed her. Her lips were dry-cool and her body trembled.

"Has it ever happened before, Bonny?"

"Y-yes. But not like this." Their eyes were used to the orange light from the outside bulb. It was against the two windows, like a distant fire.

"Let's skip it," he said, his voice pitched a bit too loudly. "Let's skip it, Bonny."

She pushed at him. "Don't look at me. Look out the window." He turned his back to her. He heard the quick fabric sound of her undressing, a muted chattering of her teeth, a creak of springs and a sharp intake of breath as she slid between the icy sheets. He looked at her then. Her head was a darkness on the far pillow, her face turned to the wall, her thin body lost under the lumpy spread. He undressed quickly and slid in beside her. He warmed his hands against his own body. He reached for her. She was far over, against the wall. He found the soft, secret, concave place of her waist, his hand large enough so that the ring finger and little finger were up-canted by the swell of her hip while between thumb and forefinger he could feel the rigid delicacy of the rib cage, feel the rib cage swell and subside with her quickened breathing. He sensed the resistance of her, a stiffness that was an amalgam of fear and shyness. He moved a bit closer to her and waited a long time and their body heat slowly warmed the sagging, musty bed. She shuddered and then he felt her body soften, and she turned toward him, turned into his arms, her whole body flattened against him, all the silk of her and all the urgency of her exploding against his heart.

When they floated at last to rest from the places of the dark movings, the slow searchings, the quick findings, when they glided and slid down and away from that bright high place of final breaking, and her head was on his shoulder, mouth inward, breath a small moist furnace on his naked chest, he ran his fingertips down the gracile line of her cheek with a feeling of awe and wonder, and with a brute pride of conquest.

Then, in the orange night, for the first time, she talked of herself, talked in a voice contented and far off, a voice like cat purrings. He liked listening to her. He would hear only the sound of her voice for a time and not the meaning and then he would catch the sense of the little stories she was telling. For a time he resented her tales of herself and did not know why, then realized he resented her having had any previous existence. He rather wanted her to be something he had created in the moment of first awareness of her, with no past but that which he formed with her. She was a person beyond his own self-considerations and once he had learned the reason for resentment, he was able to listen to her and even take pleasure in learning her.

It was about her father, ". . . killed when I was four. I don't remember much about him. They say he was big. I remember him as big, the way the house shook when he walked. There was Irish in him, and French-Canadian and some English I think, and some Mohawk Indian. His grandfather had been a trapper and guide, up near Saranac. We all lived in the house at Frenchman's Lake that his father had built. When I was ten, twelve, fourteen, around there, they were still talking about the way he died. They talked around the stove in the store in the winter. He was topping a big tree. They do that, climb up and saw the top off so there is just a straight stick standing that they use to fasten the cables to when they use the donkey engine as a sort of hoisting engine. He had his safety belt around the tree. He sawed and as the top started to go, the stub split. It expanded inside his safety belt. They used to tell how he screamed twice and then there was silence and then he gave a great laugh and he was dead."

And her mother, ". . . was pregnant and LaRue, that's my brother, he was six and I was four. One time she had cooked for the camps. She turned our house into a restaurant. She looked sort of weak, but she could work twenty hours a day and sing while she worked. She named it Doyle's Pinetop Restaurant. It was a long time before it made any money at all. In the winter we'd get the local trade and hardly break even, but in the summer with the cottages and the camp grounds full, we'd make money. I quit high after two years because she started getting too tired and I had to do more and more of it. Then two years ago some people wanted to buy us out but Mom didn't want to sell. We borrowed money from the bank and had a big addition put on and hired more girls for the summer trade. Then a year ago a big restaurant firm came in and put up a big chain restaurant on the corner diagonally across from us, with a big parking lot and everything. I think that's what killed her, but they said she had been sick for a long time without admitting it. She worried so much. LaRue came back for the funeral. We couldn't get enough business to keep the place going. The bank took it over and it was sold to meet the mortgage thing for the addition, but it didn't bring much on account of the new place being so close. After it was all settled up, LaRue and I got four hundred dollars each. I didn't want to stay up there. I mean working all those years and then nothing. We lived off it, but it had been hard. So I came down here and got a job as a waitress. Then one of the other girls quit and came to work at the mill because the pay is better. She said I should try it and after a while I did."

And about herself, "Me? Gosh, I don't know. I guess I was always sort of shy and funny. I couldn't walk down the road without thinking people were looking at me and talking about how skinny my legs were. And it was awful forcing myself to leave the kitchen and go out on the floor and wait on strangers when I was old enough. I liked it best to go off in the woods alone. I love the woods. Then I was always pretending. You know, making up kid games. I was a princess and a wicked witch had changed all my subjects into birds and animals. When you stand still for a long time, they stop being afraid and come out. Red squirrels, porcupines, and beavers working. The best was finding a fawn once. All flattened out and hardly breathing. They don't have any scent when they're little. I hid where I could see. After a long time the doe came and got him out of there and pushed him along. He wobbled on his legs."

She talked and then she yawned and so they left, dressing in the darkness, going yawning to the car. They went back once, but it was not a good place even if it was the first place. They talked and they decided they both wanted a place where they could be safe and alone together. She solved that for them. She found a ground-floor apartment in the back of one of the old houses on Fremont Street. The apartment had its own private entrance. They came nearest to a quarrel when he insisted on being permitted to pay at least the increase in her rent. And she was shy about accepting presents—the little radio, the silver bracelet, the perfume which was lighter in body than what she had been using, and thus was better for her. . . .

Now he drove swiftly to the city, eager to see her again, trying to forget all the implications of this intrigue, trying to think only of her and of tonight. It was odd how she was the one who thought up the little devices which protected their deceit. He had paid to have her telephone installed. The desk man at the club had been appropriately bribed. Should anyone phone him at the club, the desk man would say he would have Mr. Delevan call back. And he would phone Bonny's unlisted number and give Quinn the message, and Quinn would phone from there.

And it had been Bonny who insisted on his parking behind the gas station a full block away, and taking the short cut through the alley to her private entrance.

The gas station floodlights were off, just the night light

shining inside. He parked and walked down Grant Street
to the alley, and through the alley to the scrubby lawn,
and across the lawn to her narrow walk, to her private
door. He tapped on the door and she opened it, smiling,
and he closed it behind him and took her in his arms.
Then he held her off at arm's length.

"New blouse?"

"It's the white one. I dyed it."

Now it was a pale blue. It brought out the subtle golden
tints in her skin, and it was good with her hair. Now that
the warm weather had come, she had started taking the
sun outside her door, behind a low concrete wall that kept
the wind from her. The sun streaked her hair, making it
pale at the temples. It was coarse hair, alive, and he had
seen it crackle blue in darkness when she drew a comb
through it. There were little folds of flesh at the outside
corners of her eyes that gave them the illusion of slanting
down. Unplucked brows were a furry brown. Her
cheekbones had a massive look, too heavy for the fragile
jaw.

"It's a good color for you, Bonny."

One lamp was on in the room. It had a black metal
shade. They sat on the day bed and he held her hand,
content to be there with her, feeling safe and warmed in
this place, as though a door closed gently in his mind,
shutting out everything else. The hooded light slanted
across her hand as he held it. He turned her hand over,
examining it carefully. Though when her hands were in
motion, they gave an impression of grace and fragility, at
rest they had a thickness about them, a short-fingered
thickness. Those hands were as surprising to him as her
feet. Her feet were short and broad, a bit puffy across the
instep. The rest of her had a patrician elegance that con-
tradicted the peasant cast of hands and feet. The skin of
her body was so fine-grained as to be almost textureless.
Her bones were small and straight. With his fingertip he
traced the faint blue lines of the vulnerable side of her
wrist, then kissed the palm of her hand.

This was overture, and they made love together with all
the symbols and rituals that had become dear and neces-

sary and familiar to them. Afterward, there on the studio couch he lay on his back and she was beside him, propped up on one elbow, talking down at him, and he saw how the lamplight made good shadows and highlights on the long elegance of her body, on the princess figure, that figure that was as controlled as a line drawing. He ceased to hear what she was saying and, reaching out a hand, he touched the highlighted line that swept from her armpit to the slender waist, creased by her position, then up and over the ivory hip and down to the warm socket of the back of her knee.

She moved back a bit from him and stopped talking and he knew it was because he was looking at her. She did not enjoy his look. She suffered it because she knew he liked to look at her. It had taken a long time to overcome her modesty to this extent. He knew it made her uncomfortable. And the fact of her discomfort increased his pleasure in looking at her merely because it was such a strange contrast with Bess who, from the very first, had padded about with all the naked and sexless poise of a men's shower room.

Moreover this girl could sense his mood and adjust quickly to it. Bess crashed blindly through his moods like a movie he had once seen of an elephant eating its way through a cane field, munching in heavy pleasure as the feet came down on the green shoots.

Behind Bess were the schools and the money, the cotillions, the student cruises, the country clubs. Theoretically she had been groomed carefully and expensively for life and marriage. But it seemed that somewhere the pattern had become so complicated that a certain primary function had been lost—the function of pleasing a man. Somehow men, to Bess and her set, had become Dagwoods, the Boys, poor dear helpless creatures to be harassed and chivvied into a weak form of conformity with what they— the Wives—considered the proper pattern for living. Bonny however seemed to have an instinctive awareness of her function. It gave her a timelessness denied the legions of women named Bess. She could have functioned in this special and dear way in any era, never patronizing or condescending.

"What are you thinking about, Quinn?" she asked.

"Us. As usual."

"Is it good? As usual?"

He pulled her hard against him and said, against her hair, "What are you getting out of this, Bonny?"

"Everything, probably."

"Why don't you quit the job?"

"And do what? Just hang around here all day. Gee, I'd go crazy."

"But what do you want of me?"

She pulled her head away and gave him a surprised look. "Just for you to come here. Isn't that all right?"

"And when I can't come?"

She snuggled close again, sighed. "Well, then I just wait until you can. That's all."

He felt a stubbornness that was like anger. He knew he should let it alone. Leave it at that. Be grateful it was like that and relax and be warmed by her. But he was being driven along by a stubborn search for complications, a need to make things difficult.

"It doesn't make sense. God knows it doesn't. I'm thirty-six. You're twenty. You're only a little older than David. There's not a damn thing in this for you."

"Let me decide that. Right now is enough."

"Is it? Is it, Bonny? Maybe *I* want to think ahead. Maybe this isn't enough for me."

Her fingertips found his lips. Her head was buried against his shoulder again. "Hush, Quinn. Hush."

"I was never alive before. I was frozen—sterile. Now I feel alive. It's in the way I look at everything. Everything has more form and color. The people and the streets and the places. I never looked at them before. And I keep asking, what the hell does she see in me?"

She lifted herself up again, a small frown appearing, self-consciousness forgotten. "Well, you know I've thought about that, sort of. At first I just liked the way you look. Sort of tired and confident, like in the ads. Then you talked that night and I found out you were sick inside.

And needed warming. Needed me. Like I could be a stove where you could get warm. I wanted to help. Like when I was a kid. Forever finding sick birds and things and putting them in boxes with cotton and on the back of the stove to be warm. I guess I just wanted to give. And that is what I like. To give to you so that you're well now, on the inside. And you see I love you now, too. So that's what I see in you. And don't start asking and asking about why I love you, because there aren't any whys for that. You just do."

"And you actually, honestly don't want any more than . . . just what we have."

"Oh, more would be nice, I suppose. It would be nice to be together all the time. But we can't, so we can be happy with what we *can* have."

"I could divorce her."

"No!"

"Why such a violent reaction? Why not?"

"I just don't want to talk about it. Just no." And she got up quickly and walked away from him, out of the cone of light, the long legs, the milky flex of hips, carrying herself in a constrained way because she walked naked in front of him. Then she was in the far shadows, a long, pale blur in the darkness of the room.

He said, carefully, wishing he could stop his own mouth, "Maybe you get so violent about it because *you* don't want to be tied down that definitely with a man nearly twice your age."

And she used a voice she had not used before. A voice with toughness in it. "Why don't you leave it alone? You're getting what you want, aren't you? It isn't costing you anything. Just leave it alone."

"Don't talk like that, Bonny. I don't like the way it sounds, you talking that way."

And her voice was tired. "It's late. I think you better go."

As he dressed he thought of what she had said and how she had said it. And he could not deny the little surge of relief within him when she had so flatly discarded any idea of divorce and remarriage. This life was now very comfortably arranged. With her each day had a new and special flavor. If she loved him and if she was satisfied with the relationship, then no one was hurt. He told himself that it was a decent impulse that made him bring it up. Fairness to her. Yet he knew that he had brought it up only because he had known her response beforehand, and tonight had felt a nagging need to hurt her—just a little. Had she accepted the idea, he knew there was no need for panic. He could keep inventing delays indefinitely. Sometimes he felt a little sick when he thought of what she could have been. There had been no way of knowing. And he might have placed himself in the hands of a greedy little tramp. So it was luck.

As he laced his shoes he had a sudden odd feeling of loss. He had hurt her tonight. And would hurt her again. Each time it would be a bit easier. And each time would rub off some of the magic. He wondered why he had this compulsive desire to create tension between them. It seemed, in one sense, to be a stepchild of the exaggerations of bathos he had employed on that first night, on that first blind drive. Perhaps it was only because she was something he could use and, in using her, avoid the usual consequences of such use, and so wished to relegate her to the single function of the body, destroying all emotional overtones. The taker and the giver. A relationship with its inevitable shadings of cruelty, born of contempt, of domination.

He was dressed and she turned more lights on. She wore a dark blue flannel robe with a full skirt effect under the wide white belt. Her eyes looked tired.

"I'm sorry, Quinn. But we'll keep on having trouble like this if we try to plan anything."

"But you see, darling, it makes me feel guilty. That's why I strike out at you. You're getting so little. You're so right for a kind of life where you'd have a home, kids, security."

"I'll worry about what I ought to have. I don't want you to think about that."

He put his hand on her slim shoulders. In her slippers

without heels she seemed very tiny, looking gravely up at him. He kissed her. "Okay, Bonny."

She smiled. "When will I see you again?"

"It isn't good. My kid brother is coming this weekend with his bride. As far as I can tell, it might not be until next Wednesday. But if there's a chance to make it sooner, I'll walk by you and give you the sign."

"I'll be here, darling," she said, close to him, her face against his chest, the top of her head under his chin. He stroked her straight back, wanting her again, enjoying the strong feeling of wanting her again.

"I hate to leave," he whispered.

She pushed at him. "Go home now, Quinn. Go on. It's late."

He looked back at her just before he closed the door. She stood watching him, almost without expression, her face the ancient face of woman, timeless and passive. He closed the door quietly. All the stars were high and far away. The night was cooler. He walked slowly to his car, pausing and searching the night sky when he heard the distant whispering rip of a night jet. But he could not find it against the stars. Her satisfaction had been complete and evident this night. He walked more quickly, squaring his shoulders, taking longer strides, thumping one fist against his thigh in rhythm with his walk.

There was no reason why it couldn't go on for years. Not if they were careful, discreet. She shouldn't start to fade even a little for at least six or seven years. Perhaps longer than that, because her bones were so good. A nice safe arrangement. Sometimes Bess could be talked into taking a trip down to New York by herself. Shopping. Maybe go with a girl friend. Then he could move right in with Bonny. Buy some things and keep them there. Liquor, razor, pajamas. She could take time off from the job. Say she was sick. Like a honeymoon. Stay right there with her. She could cook.

There certainly was no point in worrying about the rightness or wrongness of it. She was there, like a dollar bill on the sidewalk. If he hadn't seen it, somebody else would have. Some dull clown. This way it was better for her. And she said it was enough for her. So it was enough for both of them.

He drove home through the night feeling good, tapping on the edge of the steering wheel in time to the late jazz on the car radio. He felt big and whole and wonderful.

And the sickening depression came without warning, came climbing up out of his belly, moving black across his mind. No reason for it. None. He stamped the gas pedal. The trees began to swing toward the car and then jump past him. The motor settled into a high note of strain and he leaned forward trying to see beyond the reach of the headlights.

He did not see the car come up behind him. He heard the siren over his own motor sound and glanced in the rear-vision mirror and saw the red spot on top of the car. He slowed down, feeling sweaty and shaky. He pulled over onto the shoulder still moving fast enough so that his car bounced and swerved before he halted it. The police sedan pulled diagonally in ahead of him, the siren dying into a low growling and silence. They both got out quickly and the nearest one had his revolver drawn and ready.

"Out!" the cop said. "Move!" Quinn got out. "Turn around and put your hands flat against the car." He did so, feeling like a fool. Quick hard hands slapped him, took his wallet. One of them carried the wallet out in front of his car, looked at it in the headlight brightness.

"You Mr. Delevan?"

"Yes, I am."

"You can turn around, sir. You got treated this way on account of when we come up behind you and clocked you at ninety-three, you started to pull away. That's a silly thing to do, Mr. Delevan."

"I didn't see you at all."

"That's a hell of a big red spot we turned on."

"I'm sorry, I just didn't see it."

"I hope you won't get sore about us handling you this way, Mr. Delevan. You were in one hell of a hurry. What's the idea?"

"I was late. The road was empty. I wasn't thinking."

The two policemen stood there uncomfortably, facing

him. The powerful motor of their cruiser made a bubbling
sound. A truck went by, pulling wind behind it.

"I'm glad to see you're so much on the ball," Quinn
said.

"Keep it down below sixty, Mr. Delevan. Good night,
sir." They hurried to the cruiser, banged the doors shut,
and left. Quinn got slowly into the car. Exhilaration was
gone. Depression was gone. He merely felt tired. He put
the car in the garage, pulled the door down. The studio
lights were off. Bess had left a light on for him. He drank
a glass of milk, turned out the lights and went to the
bedroom. She was asleep. She made a soft whistling sound
with each inhalation. He undressed without awakening her
and got into his bed. Farm dogs were barking on faraway
hills. A diesel hooted in the valley. He turned on his side.
The nervous sweat of his encounter with the police had
given his body an acid smell. Take a shower in the
morning. Take the car in and leave it at the garage. Ask
Bess when the brown dacron was due back from the
cleaners. Buy blades. And get a dozen Medalists in town.
They don't carry them at the pro shop. Got to work on
that slice. Lucky break hitting that tree on the eighth and
bounding back onto the fairway. That's a funny sound she
makes when it's right for her. Sort of a whimper. He
rolled onto the other side. If she'd stop that damn whistling, it would be easier to get to sleep.

Chapter Four

When the porter pushed the button that sounded the
buzzer inside Roomette 8 of Car 801 on the advance
section of the Commodore Vanderbilt, eastbound, at ten
minutes of eight on a Thursday morning in June, forty
minutes outside of Stockton, New York, the occupant of

the roomette, Thomas Marin Griffin, awoke immediately and was immediately aware of his precise location in time and space. He answered the porter at once, pinched the shade latch, and slid it up. The fields were June-green, gently rolling, sprawling ripe in the morning sun.

Griffin slid the mirrored door open, backed against the zippered curtain, and slid the bed up so that it banged and latched itself into the wall. He moved with a deliberate precision that gave him a look of slowness, yet he accomplished all routine tasks with an astonishing quickness because there was no waste, no blundering, no pauses.

Trains and the roomettes on trains pleased him. It was stainless, functional design. The train rode on straight rails. You knew where the rails went. Air travel did not please him. There was a formlessness about it. In the air you were given no privacy, no steel place in which to work. At forty Griffin could have been a youthful fifty, or a tired thirty. He was of middle height, and weighed within five pounds of what he had weighed at twenty. His hair was very black, and though it was a heavy growth that gave his forehead a narrow look, there was a lusterlessness about it that made it seem wiglike, unreal. His skin was very white, with a look of transparency. His eyes were a pale gray-blue, meaningless as marbles. There was a look of Irish about him, a suggestion of the black Irish in the jut of blue-shadowed chin. And a look of remoteness and dedication. There was something priestlike about him. Only the most unimaginative were ever at ease with him. He seemed always to be watching and condemning. He wore dark clothing, subdued neckties. He should have been invisible in any crowd, and yet he never was. He was always noticed. And many people speculated about him. And they were nearly always wrong.

After he had shaved and dressed and closed his suitcase and unzipped the green curtain, the train was ten minutes out of Stockton. He sat with his briefcase on his lap, opened it, and took out a Manila folder. He looked at the balance sheet of the Stockton Knitting Company. SK stock was not listed. It was not offered for sale. With Delevan ownership of the stock, the firm was under no obligation to make their financial affairs a matter of public record. Griffin had gone to considerable effort to construct this balance sheet, and the accompanying profit and loss statement. He knew they were inaccurate. And he knew the inaccuracies were most probably minor.

When he felt the train begin to slow down, he closed the briefcase. The conductor hurried down the aisle announcing the stop at Stockton. Thomas Marin Griffin put on his hat and waited a few minutes, then walked down the car after the porter had taken his suitcase forward. He stepped down onto the morning platform, tipped the porter, picked up his suitcase, and walked through the big gloomy bad-smelling station, past the golden oak of the scarred benches, the grubby marble. The hotel where he had stayed before, the Brigadier, was just three blocks from the station. He walked swiftly, carrying the heavy suitcase with ease. His reservation was in order. There was a bulky Manila envelope from the office. He sent the bellhop up to the room with suitcase and hat. He took his briefcase into the dining room, opened the envelope after ordering his breakfast. Miss Vidranian had arranged things the way he liked them. Letters and memorandums in increasing order of importance, so that the top letter was almost, but not quite, within the range of Miss Vidranian's authority to have handled herself. He went quickly through the stack. He set some aside for dictation. On others he wrote marginal comments to guide Miss Vidranian in answering them herself. His pen had a very fine nib, and he used jet-black ink. His writing was small, angular, precise, unanimated—and very fast. The last item in the group was the unopened envelope containing the confidential information he had requested from Credit Search on the Delevan family. He was glad it had arrived. He decided he would read that in his room.

When he had returned to the room, he unpacked quickly, placing the small dictation machine on the desk. He did his long distance telephoning first, then, adjusting the small flexible belt in the machine, he dictated answers to three of the letters Miss Vidranian had sent and dictated memos on two of the three phone calls. She had enclosed

a Manila envelope addressed to his office. Before he sealed
the two flexible belts, the memos, and the correspondence
in the envelope, he placed a call to his own office.

"Good morning, Mr. Griffin."

"Good morning, Miss Vidranian. I'll mail the correspondence back to you this morning. I just finished handling it. Anything special this morning?" His voice was
soft, polite.

"A Mr. Henry Parks phoned from Washington. Mr.
Tomlinson has approved the container project. Dr. Garsh
is anxious to see you again. There's nothing else of any
importance."

"If Parks phones again, turn him over to Gary. Wire
the Acme people about Tomlinson's approval. And phone
Dr. Garsh and tell him I'll phone him when I get back to
town. Have you got that?"

"Yes, sir," she said, and sounded a bit upset that he
should have asked. Of course she got it. And in addition to
her notes she would have a tape of the phone call in case
there was any question in her mind.

"Good-bye," he said, and hung up before there was
time to hear her response. He sealed the envelope and
placed it beside his hat.

Then he opened the Credit Search envelope. He had
requested a detailed report. Intensive coverage. For such
reports—and they were expensive—Credit Search supple-
mented the information on file and brought it up to date
by either sending their own people or employing local
agencies for an on-the-spot survey. Following the theory
that a person's credit is influenced by many other factors,
their investigations were often quite personal. And Credit
Search had had three months to do a thorough job.

Griffin scanned the report and then read it more slowly.
When he folded it back into the envelope marked for his
personal attention, he had inadvertently committed large
portions of it to memory. The report contained many
factors which could be considered favorable to his plans.

He phoned the Stockton Knitting Company. He asked
for Mr. Benjamin Delevan. A young-voiced girl requested

his name. In a few moments Mr. Benjamin Delevan was on the line.

"Mr. Thomas Griffin? Is that the Griffin of Thomas Marin Griffin Associates?"

"Yes it is, Mr. Delevan. My office was suppose to have arranged for an appointment with you today. I find there has been a slip-up. I wonder if you could fit me in. I know it's an imposition."

"Just a moment, please."

Griffin held the phone with monumental patience. Delevan came back on. "Would quarter of eleven this morning be convenient for you, Mr. Griffith? Good. I'll be expecting you then."

Later, on the taxi ride out to the Stockton mill, Griffin remembered the revealing change in the tone of Benjamin Delevan's voice. It was something that happened more frequently these days. It is pleasing, yet handicapping, to be well on your way to becoming a legend in your own time. He remembered a lunch in New York, a dark upstairs place, expensive, with the very best of food and service, and the heavy half-drunk voice from the neighboring table.

"That Griffin son of a bitch. That sly bastard. Never know what he's up to. Know what, though? Whatever he does, it comes out like Fort Knox. That Associates outfit of his is turning into a holding company, that's what it's doing. You read that thing they had on him in *Newsweek*? What the hell was it they called him? The doctor for sick corporations. Okay, so he does help, but the bill is too high for my taste. He does business for a stock-purchase concession. Offer him cash sometime and I bet he'd laugh in your face. I happen to know for a definite fact, see, that that stone-faced character has cut himself a piece of some of the fastest-growing outfits in the country, and furthermore . . ."

The man with Griffin had been painfully embarrassed. But Griffin was sorry the noisy man had lowered his voice. There could have been useful information. It was too bad people thought of him that way. It made them difficult to deal with. Suspicious of his motives.

Griffin had tried the corporate world from the other side of the desk. And at twenty-seven had become an executive vice-president of a Michigan corporation that manufactured fork-lift trucks and special conveyor equipment. And had been bored. And had known that it was the wrong way to climb—if you wanted both money and power. This was better.

When he walked into Delevan's office, he sensed the wariness. The girl who had let him in closed the office door behind him. Benjamin Delevan came around his desk, shook hands. There was wariness there and, confirmed by his investigations, considerable shrewdness.

"This is a pleasure, Mr. Griffin. I've heard a great deal about your work. Sit down, please."

Griffin sat down and put his briefcase beside his chair. He said, "This is my third visit to Stockton this year."

"I'm disappointed that you didn't stop in before. Or at least let me know you were in town. I could have gotten you a temporary card at the club and——"

"I'm not much of a one for clubs, Mr. Delevan. I'm comfortable at the Brigadier."

"Well-run, that hotel. Old-fashioned, but they do things right."

"That's my impression too."

"Is there something I can do for you, Mr. Griffin?"

Griffin inwardly admired the way Delevan handled himself. No questions about the other trips. "There may be, Mr. Delevan. I have a client-firm. Varnen Textiles. They've gotten themselves into a spot of trouble. They are prepared to accept my recommendations as to the way to get out of trouble. I'll have to tell you the situation. I'd like it to be confidential."

"It will be, of course."

"They built the new Tennessee plant four years ago. Woolens on a large scale. Bad timing. You know the picture in woolens, of course. Short runs. The plant isn't suited for that sort of thing. They want to make a switch to a synthetic. They've made a licensing deal. If their production people try to feed synthetics in with the woolens, it is going to make the expense of operation too high. New equipment will be needed. It would imperil the woolen production. They don't want to do that because they need the income from woolens." He saw the sudden awareness in Delevan's eyes, quickly hidden. So he said, "Do you have any guesses now?"

"Do you want us to contract to plug gaps in their line?"

"I'm afraid Varnen wouldn't play on that basis. They have to control the manufacture of their own lines. When I took them on as a client-firm they had the idea of building another plant, smaller, more flexible, for the shrinking woolen line. In Tennessee. I investigated it and ruled that out."

"Would you mind telling me why?"

"Expensive. A lengthy operation."

Delevan leaned back. His face was still. "You recommended they buy a mill in the North."

"I recommended that they retain me and let me and my people look into the possibility of buying a mill in the North. Someplace where there would be a trained labor pool, an existing plant, a flexibility of operation, a backlog of existing business. You have those things right here. Plus some desirable brand names, old names in the field. I am not a salesman, Mr. Delevan. I have told you your own advantages first. There is another side to the coin. This mill is not big enough. You have quite an obsolescence problem. You have been modernizing slowly but too slowly. A recession of any duration would give you serious problems. You deal in high-style items, with the appropriate percentage of net for such risk, but you have been consistently outguessing the market. Your speculations in inventory have been, unfortunately, necessary. And fortunately successful. I do not think the mill could pass a rigid safety inspection at the moment. It is too much of a one-man operation. Too much depends on your judgment. I admire your shrewdness, Mr. Delevan. You have done remarkably well with an operation which ignored normal maintenance and modernization for far too many years. Those are the handicaps."

"You don't make us sound very desirable, Mr. Griffin."

"There are other factors. The place would have to be

enlarged. The room for expansion is there. And I have
been assured by your Chamber of Commerce that they are
eager for expanded business in town. So eager that they
will cooperate with the county and city governments and
get a good break for Varnen on property taxes. I was in
Washington a few weeks ago. They are aware of the
difficulties in the textile industry. Construction costs can
be written off very quickly. Varnen would start shifting
woolen production up here as soon as feasible. Existing
equipment would be moved into the addition to this mill
from the Tennessee mill."

There was silence in the office for a short time. Delevan
smiled a bit wearily and said, "This company is family
owned. You have no idea of our financial situation at the
moment. I fail to see how you can do all this . . . conjec-
turing without knowing at least our net worth here."

Griffin opened his briefcase. He took out the folder
containing the financial reports. "This information was
gathered from various sources. Some of it may be way out
of line, Mr. Delevan. You might glance at it and see how
far off we are."

Benjamin Delevan studied the reports. He ran a pencil
down the columns of figures. He smiled a little bitterly as
he handed it back. "You people are damn thorough."

"We have to be."

"I suppose you have an offer all ready, too?"

"Just a general offer. Varnen has already obtained permission from the SEC for a new stock issue. I won't go
into all the details of the split on common stock outstand-
ing. It would come out this way: thirty thousand shares of
Varnen Textiles for the thirty thousand shares of Stockton
Knitting. It is estimated that market value would stabilize
about twenty dollars a share. So it would be a share-for-
share trade. As your stock is not listed, it is worth precisely what you can get for it. A share-for-share trade, in that
case, would obviate a personal tax problem. Over the past
ten years Varnen has paid an average of six point two
percent on common stock. It is a healthy operation, Mr.
Delevan."

"Even with this trouble they seem to be in?"

"By becoming a client-firm they took a long step toward getting out of trouble. This plan I have suggested to you is only one of the plans I have in mind. It wouldn't be wise to have only one alternative."

"What would be my status?"

"You would be given a one-year contract with a bonus provision as production manager of the Stockton lines."

"And after that?"

"Varnen has their own executive-training program. They would want you only during the changeover. I checked the recorded copy of your father's will. You have ten thousand shares. And the three children of your father's second marriage have the balance split equally among them. I should think you would all be . . . reasonably comfortable. And you would avoid the risk of a liquidation of this operation at a sacrifice."

"How about the other employees here, Mr. Griffin?"

"Varnen would keep the labor force and add to it, and retrain the lower-level supervisory personnel. All the rest would come from Varnen, or be hired locally and trained in Varnen methods."

Delevan shook a cigarette out of the package on his desk, offered one to Griffin, who shook his head. Delevan leaned back in his chair and lighted his cigarette. "Assume that I would go along with it. That's no indication that the rest of the family would."

Griffin, for the first time, was disappointed in the man. "Come now, Mr. Delevan. It's quite apparent that you get their approval on anything you recommend."

"Would the Varnen stock be voting stock?"

Respect returned quickly. "No, it would not. But the dividend picture would be identical with the voting stock."

"It isn't something that can be decided here and now, Mr. Griffin."

Griffin latched his briefcase. "I realize that. But there is a need here for more than the usual speed in making a decision. The Varnen situation deteriorates from week to week in the Tennessee plant. Today is Thursday. I will have to know by next Wednesday."

"What if we should agree, and then Varnen turns down your recommendation, Mr. Griffin?"

For the first time Griffin smiled. It was a suggestion of a smile and it faded immediately. "That's a very remote possibility."

"And if we make a counteroffer?"

"I learned long ago, Mr. Delevan, that I am inadequate in a bargaining situation. It is a form of gambling. I do not gamble. In situations like this I am impartial. I make the best possible offer for both parties concerned. You can employ some disinterested party and have an audit of the situation made, if you so desire. But I am afraid that would take too long."

Delevan's sudden grin looked oddly boyish. "This beats me. Things like this are supposed to happen with about nineteen people around a table and a bunch of corporation lawyers telling everybody what to say. It isn't supposed to be like this. One man and one briefcase."

Griffin stood up, unsmiling. "The conference method is a grossly overrated method of doing business, Mr. Delevan. Final authority usually rests with one person. You have that authority. So do I, in this matter. I prefer to work alone. Some people consider that a weakness of mine, an inability to delegate authority and responsibility. But it suits me. I'll leave my card with your secretary. It has my office phone number on it. I will be in town until nine o'clock tomorrow morning. You can reach me at the Brigadier if you have questions you didn't think of this morning. Please phone my office when you reach a decision. They always know where to reach me."

Delevan stood up. "Could we have lunch together?"

"Thank you, no. But I would like your permission to walk through the mill."

"Sure. I can have one of the——"

"No thank you. I can find my way around. I've studied a floor plan."

Delevan stared at him. "If you don't mind my asking, just where in the hell did you get a floor plan?"

"You had one drawn up for the Loomarite people as a basis for their making an estimate two years ago."

"What gives them the right to turn it over to you? I'm not annoyed. I'm just curious."

"I'm a director of Loomarite, Mr. Delevan. Thank you for your time."

"Just a minute. What's the next step if we should agree to the proposition?"

"I'll make a recommendation to Varnen. Then their attorneys will meet with yours to establish the routine. When the papers are signed, they'll send up a plant manager with staff."

Griffin left Benjamin Delevan's office. He felt that he had handled it adequately. He had caught Delevan off balance, and had given an impression of great organization, of monolithic power behind him. It would be very natural for Delevan to feel subconsciously that the situation had been taken out of his hands. And it was of comfort to find Delevan a man who looked tired and unwell. Delevan carried a heavy load. The fact of its being a family firm added an imponderable factor of sentimentality. Except for that one factor, he sensed that he had won. But he did not trust factors which could not be measured.

It took him forty minutes to see all he wished to see. The employees gave him sidelong curious glances. But visitors were common in every plant. They came from federal, state, and local agencies. They walked about and looked and made requests for reports. Each agency attempted to increase its own size and importance. Thus many of the requests became quite strange. And the overhead costs of industry went up—with whole sections of the offices engaged in making reports which bore no relationship to the efficiency of operation. Thus the cost of the goods manufactured went up. And taxes went up, in order to pay the salaries of the field men who went about conceiving and demanding ever more intricate reports and surveys. It was a destructive spiral that Griffin was well aware of. An inevitable result of the police function of government insofar as industry was concerned. And so he knew that his visit through the mill was unlikely to start rumors.

From time to time he stopped, and, seeming not to see any special thing, saw everything. Like the captain of many ships and many years who walks on a strange vessel while she is at dockside and knows at once what her response will be to heavy weather. And this was an old ship. She had come close to foundering too many times. She had rolled and shuddered in heavy seas.

When he turned and left, he knew all he had to know.

When the door closed beyond Griffin, Ben Delevan sat down behind his desk. So that was Thomas Marin Griffin. Creature of many fables. And not at all what he had expected. You deal with many men and learn the many little ways in which they can be moved and turned and twisted. It is a primary function of the executive mind to be able to detect which way any man can best be controlled. After many years it is a function which becomes automatic. And thus it was shocking to Ben Delevan to meet a man who presented such an absolutely featureless surface. There was nothing to be grasped or triggered. He was as remote as a distant line of hills, and as immediate and personal as death. You sensed at once that he was a tool without handles. The coldness seemed to extend from his eyes down to the bottom of his soul. It was, Ben realized, the personality you would expect in a professional assassin. The man could not be bought or bullied or kidded or hurried or delayed. Yet with all that coldness, the man was not as impersonal as a machine. Not when he radiated that strange force. A force and hardness that was as immediately noticeable as any physical deformity.

Ben could not imagine Griffin laughing aloud, kissing a woman, casting a trout fly. He was as perfectly designed for his function as a scalpel or an axe. He was a symbol of the facelessness of the great corporations, and a symbol of this new era of management.

Ben realized that his own self-confidence had suffered an alarming decline. Compared with Griffin, his own thinking and functioning were fuzzy, erratic, emotional.

Griffin would never operate by hunch. He would never have to.

He looked down at his scratch pad and saw that he had doodled some chubby dollar signs. He tore the sheet off and made a quick computation of his own personal net worth. Equity in insurance policies. Fair valuation on house and land. Savings and investments. Conservatively, seventy-five thousand. Add two hundred thousand worth of Varnen stock. And a one-year contract. Then what? House of glass and tile and cypress on a Florida bayou? ... My name is Ben Delevan. Yes, I was in textiles. Ran a mill up North. Family outfit. Sold out to a big firm. Moved down here. You can't beat this sunshine. No, sir. We had our roots sunk deep up there. Family firm for generations. So we cut those roots right off. Right off. Man can get too infatuated with his own traditions. Job would have killed me by sixty. Down here I'll live forever. Man has to think of himself sometime. Doesn't he? Wouldn't you say he had to? No, sir, you couldn't get me back in that rat race. Not for a million bucks.

The job could kill you. It was a monstrous task, fighting the creeping neglect of two generations. Little by little he was gaining. Bit by bit he had been pulling manufacturing costs down through a modernization program that crept as slowly as a glacier. Griffin was right, though. A recession would set the whole thing back. They were still not competitive in the market. For the last two years he had had a very good man in New York. He was paying him well. They were getting a better share of the high-style fabrics, and the shopmen were performing miracles with the antiquated equipment to turn out the desired weaves, to deliver on time. High style meant risk and a consequently bigger margin. The bigger margin meant that more could be plowed back into new looms, into new attachments for old looms, into shoring up rotting floors, pointing up flaking brick walls, improving factory lighting. A Stockton fabric had always meant something. Maybe it could mean even more. . . .

And yet he was so damn tired. Most of the time the old mill seemed like a big debacle tottering along on its inevitable way to complete chaos. So damn tired. He went out of the office, nodding blankly at the new girl, forgetting to tell her where he was going. He went down the old corridor to the old-fashioned board room. The shades were drawn and the air was dusty. He closed the door behind him and walked to the head of the table and sat in the ornate oak chair. Benjamin Delevan, President and Chairman of the Board of Directors—Grandson of the Founder—Past President of the Stockton Rotary Club—Member of the Board of Governors of the Stockton Club—Chairman of the Board of Admissions of the Oak Dell Country Club—Deacon of the First Presbyterian Church of Clayton—Husband—Father—He who with Childish Faith always stays in the pot with a Pair of Sixes— He who can never remember a bawdy story or tell it properly. . . .

So very damn tired.

Every reason in the world to accept the offer. But he felt a dulled urge to block it. And wished he knew why he felt that urge. Maybe it was a stubborn pride that came from making something run when there were so many reasons why it shouldn't, kicking it along, prodding it, outguessing the fat-cat competition, carrying the whole scheme and plan of everything that concerned the family, carrying it all on plump tired stubborn shoulders. A horse in a worn harness, so used to traveling this known road that it distrusted all others. There had to be more reason than blind habit for this reluctance. He would have until Wednesday to see if he could find the reason. And if that was all the reason there was—then accept.

He got up and the big chair tilted and came back down hard on its front legs. He pulled the shade away from the window frame and looked out at the mill. As always, the metal ventilators on the roof looked to him like the woman on the Dutch Cleanser cans. He heard the sound of the mill. It was not like the sound of the heavy industries, where metal was shaped and ground and peeled and polished. Those places sang deep in their chests, with counterpoint of the tortured molecular scream. His mill, at a distance, had a hissing, clittering, rushing roar, thin-voiced, feminine.

He was a small boy. He sat beside his father and they rode down to the mill in the big car. He heard the sound of the mill. And wondered if it was like the sound ships made when they moved before the wind under full sail. The men who worked for his father always laughed down at him from their tallness and made jokes with him. He sat at a table in his father's office while his father worked, and he drew pictures of ships on the big yellow pads of paper, the kind of paper you only saw when you went down there with your father. And they had come into this room and he had sat in the ornate oak chair at the head of the table and pretended it was the captain's chair and this was the dining room of a great ship.

There were more pictures on the walls now, but the room had not changed. He walked slowly around the room, looking at the pictures in the dimness, not wanting to raise the shades. Pictures of forgotten company picnics. Of the company booth at an exposition. The Columbian Exposition. Somewhere among his things there was a fifty-cent piece from that exposition. His grandfather had worn it shiny. Next to that picture was one of himself, younger, trimmer. 1944. Accepting a scroll from the Quartermaster General. And then a picture of his grandfather, that beaked pirate face with its flamboyant mustache and look of amusement.

"What did you get out of it, you old bastard?" Ben asked softly. "What did you get out of it?"

The original Benjamin Delevan was family legend. He had taken the rewards of his own shrewdness in tra-ditional earthly fashion, lifting the flounced skirts of the eighteen hundreds from Atlanta to Paris, drinking brandy from Buffalo to Silver City in Jim Fiske's private car, and once winning a reputed five thousand dollars from Fiske by guessing at a distance of fifty feet the exact circumference of the most meaty part of the calf of a dancer in New Orleans. According to the legend, Fiske underestimated. He had founded the mill and it had profited and he made it his life to spend that money in the

ways that pleased him best and those ways were both
ribald and expensive. He got all that out of it, and in the
end he got the hillside plot and the tall, granite marker
and the name of Delevan carved deeply enough in the
tough stone to last ten thousand years.

The world had changed. Laughter was no longer
Gargantuan. It was marked with acid. And the world was
full of gray faces this year. Men walked with an awareness
of defeat.

At the door of the board room Ben turned back and
looked at the face of his grandfather again. "You wouldn't
have liked it," he said quietly. "You wouldn't have liked
it at all." And went out and closed the door, closed it with
a ceremonial carefulness typical of headwaiters and under-
takers. At other times of crisis the shabby old board room
had restored him. Today it had little meaning for him.

When he got back to his office, he found the new girl
had gone to lunch. This irritated him out of all proportion
to the severity of the offense agaist the code. His face felt
hot. He sat at his desk. She had left letters there for his
signature. He read them. He found two small errors that
could have been corrected with an erasure. But he
checked them so heavily with his pen that the stub point
caught in the fiber of the paper and spattered droplets of
ink out toward the margin. He realized at once that he
was being spiteful and childish. But it was too late to
repair that particular bit of damage. He could not imagine
Thomas Marin Griffin doing a thing like that.

Chapter Five

Alice Furmon stood in the kitchen doorway and
watched her husband plod heavily out to the big
green car. He turned and grinned and waved, slammed

the car door and swung in a fast circle and was gone. She
was left with the faint aroma of the cigar he had lighted
after his hasty lunch, left with the fading sting where he
had given her a lusty affectionate slap as he left the
kitchen.

It was hard to remember the man she had married
fourteen years ago, when she was twenty-two. There had
been almost a Viking look about him, and the clear strong
lines of his big body had made her feel almost faint when
she had looked at him. He had been tender and humble in
his approach to her, making her feel fragile, delicate, and
adored. They had been able to talk, back in those days.
Really talk. There had been so much he didn't know, and
yet he seemed anxious to learn. It had made her feel good
to think that she could get inside that warm slow mind
and teach him perception and awareness. He had been
twenty-four then, an ex-college-athlete, working for a
construction firm, making an extra fifty dollars every Sunday playing tackle on a pro football team. She had
graduated from college that June, and she was living in
the big house in town with Ben and Wilma and Brock and
Ellen. Brock was five then, and Ellen three. Quinn and
Bess were living in an apartment, and David was two.
Robbie was fourteen and away at preparatory school that
fall.

The big house in town had been sold for a long time. It
had been a gloomy pile of reddish stone, and Alice
remembered how it matched her mood in that strange
vague summer when there was all of life ahead and no
idea of what could or should be done with it. Quinn had
gone apart from her into another life when he had married
Bess. Ben and Wilma had their own full existence. The
silences of the big house, the rusty scrape of tree limbs on
the roof edges, the long high hallways—all had given her
a curiously disembodied feeling, a haunted sense of
drifting out of control. She would see herself in
unexpected mirrors, tall and silent and slow.

There had been a few friends that summer. A pale,
dandruffed boy who had recently discovered Kafka. And
a fat, pimpled girl who brought over the music of

Hindemith and Stravinsky and laboriously pecked out passages on the out-of-key piano in the old music room. They sat often on the floor and they talked of many things that summer in the house coolness while the street baked.

She had gone one afternoon to the club with Ben and Wilma and the kids to swim in the newly opened pool. George Furmon had come into her life that day. Thor-muscled, splendid. Like a roof tilted to let sunlight in. His employer had brought him there that Sunday afternoon.

They were married in November. It was a big wedding at church, a reception that brought the old house alive. She was a virgin bride, filled with all manner of clinical knowledge and emotional ignorance. She remembered the dry chittering sound of the rice as it fell from her undergarments onto the tiled floor of the bathroom of the hotel in Montreal. He had been tender and gentle with her. He had known many women. Yet in the dark moment of consummation all the tremulous desire he had awakened in her was obliterated by the nightmare panic, like the dreams of childhood when some great beast had gotten at her, panting and straining. She knew she had disappointed him. And, out of her clinical knowledge, she knew that this phase of marriage had to be right. And she knew what was expected of her. During the honeymoon she tried. And at times she found fleeting moments of an electric pleasure which tantalized her because they were like a coin that is seen frozen in sidewalk ice, visible, but impossible to grasp. At last, with a histrionic ability that startled her, and a sense of shame and deceit, and yet with the determination that she could at least give him this much, she pretended to achieve that which he desired for her. In that way she trapped herself, for in his joy he no longer practiced the restraint she had not known he was using. And he wanted her and took her very often. He was a virile man, and their days and nights seemed to be full of this meaningless action which pleased him, full of her stylized response, so that she felt physically beaten, dazed, too worn and weary to recapture even those moments of incomplete pleasure she had been able to achieve, whereas George appeared to gain in strength, in virility, in need.

Two months after they came back from Canada, she found she was pregnant. The twins, Michael and Richard (named for her father and his) were born three weeks before their first wedding anniversary, and she had enjoyed the final months of pregnancy because they meant a respite from George's needs. On their anniversary night she found that she was once again trapped in her role. And she found then that George did not require evidence of her pleasure each time. Cooperation sufficed. The ersatz frenzies were used less often and she learned, in self-disgust, that she was more inclined to pretend participation in his joy when there was something she wanted of him. A coat, a hat, a trip, a pair of shoes.

Sandy was born when the twins were three. By the time she was eighteen months old, it became evident that Sandy, like Mike and Dick, was distinctly George's child. Aggressive, extroverted, muscular and very active. It seemed to her as though the very pallor of her own contribution to the uxorial act had in some way suppressed the potential contribution of her own genes—as though she had acted merely as receptacle and incubator. She loved them. George adored them, spoiled them. Her discipline was cold and certain and predictable and fair.

At times she found it difficult to remember or believe that she had given birth to these three brown noisy ruffians. In fact, their birth had seemed to leave her body unmarked. She had been unable to nurse them. At thirty-six she was slender, lean of hip, with the half-formed breasts of a young girl, with something cool and withdrawn and unaccountably virginal about her.

George and the children had filled all her days and nights, until this summer. In the early years, before Sandy was born, Ben and Quinn had made the proposition to George. Build us our homes on Gilman Hill. We will give you advance payments. Enough to get you started. George had jumped at the chance. Alice knew her brothers had done it to help. She knew they had done it a bit dubiously. But the houses were good. Before they were finished, he had other jobs. It was a full year before he was able to begin their own house. It seemed to her that almost from the first day he was in business for himself, she had lost him, that little of him she had once owned.

But the children left little time for introspection. George had changed so slowly she had not seen it. Now, with the twins away, with enough help so that she had leisure, she was seeing him all over again, making the inevitable comparisons. He was a stranger she lived with. There was no real talk. No good talk. He came home tired. He played with the kids. He needed his drinks before dinner, his drinks after dinner. He read the paper and the trade magazines. He watched certain TV shows, mostly sports telecasts. He kissed her with genuine affection. He smacked her bottom frequently, with lusty good humor. He smelled of cigars and good rye and wool. He was solid and powerful, but his belly was vast, and he was often short of breath. She wondered if he ever really looked at her. A man's man. A straight-flush, panatela, daily-double, locker-room, membership-badge man. A good provider, a man of even humor, a generous man. Henry, meet the little woman. Al, here's a picture of my three kids. Took it down on the Cape last August. . . .

He bellowed in the shower. He liked French cuffs. Every year he tried to start a vegetable garden. He bought a lot of insurance. He played catch with the twins. After dinner on spring evenings he would sort fishing tackle, clean his reels. He told funny stories and then laughed a bit too loudly at them. And he was somebody who came over into her bed with gentle hands and lusty frequency and hoarsely whispered endearments, with stallion ardor which would alter so abruptly into the long sigh, the slowing lungs, the inevitable first snore. He had a snore which awed the children and seemed to rattle windows.

This stranger she lived with. She wondered what in God's name was wrong with her this year. Her eyes had started to see again, and she had preferred the country of the blind. She stood at the kitchen door, looking at where the car had been. Sam, an old man made of roots and sweat and leather, trudged in trance behind the power mower, walking on the pool-table smoothness, following the bow waves of chopped green, a green with a strong smell of childhood.

Back in the house she could hear Mrs. Bailey teasing Sandy in a sugary way to take her nap. Alice turned and called through the house. "Sandy!"

Complaint turned into obedience. "Okay, Mom."

She could see Ben and Wilma's driveway, an edge of the terrace. A jeep wrenched and coughed into the driveway and stopped, throbbing like an indignant insect. The horn made a small humiliated beep, and Alice heard Ellen's yelp of acceptance. She came into vision, walking across to the jeep, tennis racket in frame swinging from the loose wrist, can of balls in the other hand. She wore white shorts, very brief, very starched-looking above the lovely golden legs, wore a fire-red halter, wore a dark-blue cap with a long bill. She climbed into the jeep in a leggy way. Alice saw the Schermer boy grasp the bill of the cap and yank it down over Ellen's eyes. The jeep poised, swiveled, and was gone, coughing and banging as it went down the hill, leaving the afternoon in sudden silence while Sam squatted and prodded at the blades of the still mower.

A sudden hot fierce wave of envy of the child startled Alice. She felt as though she had never laughed.

Behind the property were the birches, formal as children's drawings. Beyond them the slow hills, squared off in the block fields. Alice went to their bedroom, changed to walking shoes, to dull-red corduroy slacks. She had a great many pairs of slacks, preferring them high-waisted in cut, knowing she looked well in them, knowing that the best clean lines of her body were from the indent of waist down the long, taut, slim line of her hips. It had hurt her and puzzled her when George said he didn't like her in pants, so she tried never to wear them when he was around. She put her cigarettes in one pocket of the red-and-white-checked shirt, and her lighter in the other.

Mrs. Bailey came from Sandy's room. "Going walking again?" she asked, pleasantly enough but with obscure accusation.

"Sandy was up late last night. Keep her in bed until at least two thirty, Mrs. Bailey."

"Yes, ma'am."

She left and she walked on the shoulder of the road, away from the village. She settled into the steady swing of her walking, liking the feel of the flex and pull and clench of her muscles. She turned and looked back and saw the three houses set white against the green. Sam was marching again, in his geometric pattern. The next time she glanced back, a curve of the upwinding road hid the houses. She turned left on a familiar dirt road. It climbed steeply. The dirt was damp-packed but not muddy.

She walked hard and fast, so that when she reached the high crest of the hill, she was winded, sweating lightly. There was an old stone wall in the shade, beyond the ditch. She stepped long-legged across the ditch and squirmed up onto the wall and sat there and lighted a cigarette, shifting until the hollows of the rocks fitted her more comfortably.

What is going to become of me?

Though the question was inevitable, it left a bad taste. There was too much bathos in it—too much of an aroma of self-pity. Pollyanna should count her blessings. And know they were not enough. And sense also that the world this year was full of silly, sighing women who fingered constantly the superior texture of their souls and yearned for an appreciation and understanding denied them.

But it was a question which she could not ask of herself down there, down in that white house that George had built. What is going to become of me? She had asked that same question before, long ago, in the old house in town in that empty season after she had come back from college. That unreal time in the old house. But she had known then that something was waiting for her. Something wild and wonderful, as yet unknown. So it had been a good game. What will become of me? This is my life and now I am ready to step into it. Exhilaration in the question then. But not now. Now a question that is dry and withered. This was the life I stepped into and now it is not enough.

Does that make me a malcontent? Do I think life should be a skyrocket thing, all thrills, chills, and shudderings of ecstasy? All unbearable joys? Sweats and swoons and hysterias? Surely that must be immaturity. Like the bride who believes that every breakfast will be like the husband-and-wife breakfast shows—without the commercials. Am I like this only because there is more growing up to do?

This can't possibly be enough. This can't be all there is. *Remember* this season smart hostesses will be keeping hors d'oeuvres piping hot over the cheery charcoal glow of a genuine Japanese hibachi. *Try* for that exciting touch of madness by wearing unmatched earrings and see who will be the first to comment. *Do* use an ice cube in a saucer as a stamp moistener when sending out those scads of invitations to your next really important party. *Watch* those smart gals this season who don't begin to fray at the edges because their drink—and they are sticking to it—is vermouth on the rocks. *Be* bold and merry by sewing an ordinary hardware store bolt and latch to the new dark blouse. *Respond* to the needs of your community by being active in at least two worthy fund drives each year. *Use* one of our tape recorders in your home as an aid in correcting your own voice level.

There has to be more.

More than the rancid joke wheezed into your ear on the dance floor at the club; more than the overboldness of the hand of the man who sells insurance and is named Chester something; more than the tiresome sexual gossip of the bridge group; more than the bitching about the cost of help, the price of meats, the way salesclerks don't seem to *care* anymore.

But what do you substitute?

A dream of yourself in a cold-water flat devoting your life to some unsung young genius? Or hurrying down the dim corridor to where the postoperative patient is calling you? Do you want to be a fiction story in a slick magazine?

A loving husband, a nice home, healthy intelligent children. Mrs. Bailey to do the drudgery. Why couldn't it be enough? If the sexual adjustment had been better, would it be enough? She could not guess. This was an unreal year. Full of a lost restlessness.

She thought back to the best time of her marriage. When George was just getting started. How they'd spread out drawings on the floor and sit and argue. "No housewife is going to like that arrangement, George."

"Why the hell not?"

"Now don't yell. The way you have it, she'd have to walk just miles more than she should have to."

And then the slow change in his face as he studied the drawings again. "Hmmm," he would say. And sketch the change. Then ruffle her hair.

That was good. But it did not last long. Not when there were three small children and no help. Not after George began to get more work and began to gain confidence.

She sat on the shaded rocks of the old stone wall, her face still and withdrawn. No longer was there any sense of excitement or anticipation in any of her days. When she awakened in the morning, it was with an acceptance of the day ahead and a full knowledge of what it would bring. George, in his own way, had gone away from her. There was no talk anymore. There was nothing to say anymore. George accepted her as a part of his home, as a quiet mechanism that supervised the efficient functioning of the home aspects of environment.

She knew that her mind was good. But this was a problem too vague to handle. Directionless discontent. A small ship adrift, guided by no wind, no stars, ripe for some unknown tempest. There was always the suspicion that there *should* be nothing else. That this was what people had. Only this. Symptomatic of the times. An aloneness. A disease of "now" when all values had become diffused. As one of Mr. Gibbon's Roman ladies, on the slave-made patio, hearing, without interest, the far roars of spectacle in the amphitheater.

It was not diversion that was needed, but purpose.

The disease of "now," searching for purpose. Looking in all the wrong places. In the PTA and the League of Women Voters and the Little Theater and the Garden

Club and the Auxiliary of this and that until the voices of all the women in all those places began to sound distressingly like a chicken yard. And then they would look— those others—for another purpose in the discreet code, the sly, kitchen kissings, the knowing glance, the engineering assignation—cold and glossy as a helical gear, measuring safety against mutual trust. And the other ways out, the spot of watercolor, the bit of sculpting, the book review. Trying them all meant an eventual confusion of activity with meaning, a part so thoroughly overplayed that everything became drawing-room farce.

But there had to be more. It was quite clear that there should be more. Otherwise you were unused. You were something that stood in a corner and rusted.

Life could not turn out to be like one of those endless rainy days of childhood—Mommy, I'm tired of myself—a listless wandering through the dull rooms where there was nothing to do. No dolls to dress, no books to color. Mostly there was no one to talk to.

Here I am, she thought, sitting on a damn wall, feeling sorry for myself. About to break into big sobs of self-pity. In disgust she swung her long legs around and over the wall and dropped to the other side and took the path that led down a briared slope to the open pastureland. She walked slowly in the sun on the uneven ground and closed her mind to everything but the sensuous warmth of the June sun, the relaxed flex and pull of the long muscles of her legs. With a fresh cigarette in the corner of her mouth, she jammed her hands deep in the pockets of the slacks, spreading her fingers flat against her thighs, feeling the alternate tightening and loosening of either leg, head bent, hair brushing crisp against the back of her neck, focusing inwardly upon a body-awareness, summoning up such a formless eroticism that after a time she felt a tingling of breast, a false and hollow excitement under her heart.

She had read widely. And she knew the clinical psychological explanation of this body-excitement she was able to induce in herself. It was, the books said, such a clear evidence of sexual immaturity. An indication that the individual had never progressed far beyond the status of self-love, that infantile first awareness which should have progressed through a brief period of homosexual longings to the mature status of heterosexual love. And the books said that the self-love status could be indefinitely prolonged if the individual during that period had a strong feeling of emotional insecurity.

So, with that evidence, it was easy to say that this discontent was an evidence of immaturity, sexual and emotional. It was too easy to say that. And thus excuse everything—including the inadequacy of the physical relationship with George, including a social coldness, including nameless fears, and the hidden shyness, and this sick excitement she could generate in herself, an excitement which sometimes, in shame and loathing and desperation, she would build to a bitter and lonely and conscience-stricken climax, swearing each time that it would never happen again.

She quickened her steps, swinging her arms, looking about her, thrusting her mind away from herself, and in that way came to the far side of the pastureland to where a line of trees divided the pastureland from the cultivated field beyond, and where the old wire of the patched fence ran deep in the grooved places of the bark of the trees.

The field beyond was tilted and blackly fertile, with June-green rows of something tender and young thrusting up from the dirt. A yellow tractor made a throbbing sound in the stillness and she saw it on the far side of the field, the man stripped brown to the waist, watching carefully as he cultivated the new greenness. She stood in the screen of trees and watched him, and she could smell the warm rawness of the dirt. She knew that his name was Harker. She had seen it on their rural mailbox at the small farm beyond the crest of the hill of the dirt road where she had sat on the stone wall. She knew he drove a rattly old gray pickup, and he had waved to her when he had passed her during her walks, after stopping that one time to ask her if she wanted a lift. Walking by the farmhouse, she had seen small children in the sun, seen a stocky young woman hanging out clothes. She stood and watched, enjoying the colors of the scene, yellow of the tractor, brown of his broad young back, dark of the field, paleness of the new growth.

Spring grass grew high and lush in the field beyond him, and as she watched, she saw the woman coming from the direction of the unseen farm, thigh-deep in the new grass, wearing a blue dress, carrying something. She angled toward the moving tractor and then the man saw her and the tractor stopped, the throbbing sound stilled. He swung down and walked across the rows and met her at the edge of the grass, standing tall beside her, and Alice saw him take a handkerchief from the hip pocket of his jeans and wipe his forehead. They were too far away for her to hear their voices, but she thought she heard the high note of a woman's laugh. They stood close together and it wasn't until he tilted his head back and drank that she realized the woman had brought him something to drink, knowing perhaps that the day had grown warmer and he had brought nothing with him. They stood there for a time and she saw them both turn and look down toward the farmhouse. Then the man turned to look across the field and Alice moved quickly and instinctively back beyond the protective trunk of one of the larger trees.

The man had his arm around the woman's waist and they walked a short distance into the deep new grass, and Alice did not understand until she saw them stop and saw them melt down then, into the grass, and she could not see them at all. A bird sang valiantly over her head. She looked across the field at the silent deserted tractor, at grass bending in the gentle wind. She felt hollow. She had never seen anything remotely like what had happened. She felt on the verge of some strange, wide truth. It was not that there was a coarseness or a casualness about what they had done. It was the inevitability of it, a peculiar rightness to it, so that it touched her deeply. She was ashamed of having been there to see, yet glad at the same time. She wanted to cry. They were over there, nested in green tall grass, sun-warmed, and performing a wild, warm, outdoor act of love. She stood outside some warm place and looked through glass. There was a peasant directness to it, like in old stories of the countryside of France. And a great humanness to it, beyond class or strata.

And she realized that what was strongest in her was a vast and desperate envy of that woman who had so frankly accepted, who knew in such an uncomplicated way what can be done with love and a warm June afternoon, who perhaps had known down there in the farmhouse kitchen and, with inward flutter of excitement, had brought him a drink he did not need, because the world smelled of spring, filling her body with its strong demands.

It made Alice feel silly and shallow and decadent, a neurotic ghost of a woman without loins or breasts or truth. She stood with the bark of the tree harsh against her forehead and, feeling a tickle, watched a red ant run frantically along her wrists.

She tried to mark the imagined scene with evil, and could not. She tried to re-create disgust of all such scenes and memories and imaginings, and could not. For the scene beyond was function, and her function also, and the stocky woman her sister, and in function there was no place for fear or withdrawal or shame, no place for a muted acceptance, no place for blank endurance.

After the earth had turned a little bit, and the red ant had run home to tell of alien horrors and the bird had flown to sing from a distant tree, the man sat on the tractor seat and the woman walked to where the grassy hill slanted down. When only her head and shoulders could be seen, she turned and waved at the man, a quick wave in which there was a certain shyness. The man did not wave back. He sat and watched the place where she had disappeared. Then he started the tractor and watched the new growth with care. And moved along the field.

Alice walked back the way she had come. She crossed the pastureland. She though of herself and how she was, and she thought of that woman and how she was, and she thought of the two lives, lived on the two sides of that same hill and suddenly, with little warning, she was physically sick. Something wrenched and turned inside her, and she stood, bent forward from the waist, feet spread, weak with the helpless spasms of nausea, choking and emptying herself on the pasture grass. It took a long time and when it ended, she felt like a wraith. She turned to where she had seen a brook, and found a small pool where the water moved black and slow. She sat on her heels and dipped a Kleenex in the cold water and bathed her face and eyes. She lay flat and drank from cupped hands and rinsed her mouth. She stood up and used a damp Kleenex to wipe off her spattered shoes and the bottoms of the slacks. She felt lightheaded.

By the time she clambered across the stone wall, the strength was coming back to her. Her body, chilled by the sudden unexpected sweat, began to feel warm again.

She walked down the rutted hill, thinking back to the Alice who had sat on the wall in shallow discontent. The reality of what she had seen had done something as yet undefined. It had torn something loose, released something long suppressed.

She walked slowly for a time, trying to rationalize what had happened to her, trying to poke and pry and finger, trying to lift the edges of things and feel what was underneath. Then she realized it was something that should not be dissected, dismembered, spread apart, and held down with little pins. If something had happened, it should be accepted on the levels of instinct. Maybe all her life she had tried too hard to understand herself, had tried to gauge and measure and weigh each little reaction, seeking a better understanding of self, yet seeking it so intensely that every reaction became suspect, that each flutter of instinct was chilled by appraisal.

Accept that something has happened, and do not try to find out what it is. Stop being so bloody sober about yourself. Maybe if you stop thinking, it might be possible to become a woman. Something which feels rather than thinks. Something to be joyfully bedded in spring grass, eyes tight against the bright hot sun, rejoicing in the strength and sureness of him who takes you thus.

Something cool and hard had been ripped out of her, leaving a feeling of softness and vulnerability. So leave it at that. She walked more quickly down the slope, her heels hitting hard so that she felt a jounce of breast and buttock.

There would be little harm in trying to accept it on the unthinking basis that the woman in the field had accepted it. To let it be something that happens. Too many years of trying to intellectualize pleasure. So that it was a coin-glint, frozen in ice, unattainable.

There could be another way. To imagine greenness, and the movement of grasses, and bright, hot sun and broad, brown back. To think of green things growing. Perhaps, after fourteen years, it would not work. After cheating both of them for so long, it might well be too late. But it was nice to think that perhaps it had all been inadequate merely because she had been too tense with the desire to make it adequate, too intellectually objective, standing apart from it and watching herself rather than merely ... being.

As simple, maybe, as that long-ago time of the riding lessons when she could do nothing right. That little man with the leathery face bellowing at her. Elbows in! Watch your hands! No, don't saw on the reins! Now your feet are wrong! Around and around, knowing she would never, never get it right, hating the great meaty horse and the stink of the place and the violent little man. And deciding one day that it would be the last time, that she would not be bullied into coming again, and thus ceasing to care what the little man yelled. And, on that very day, suddenly getting the posture and rhythm of it right, very suddenly, knowing what she should do, feeling control and mastery of the horse, flushing with pride and excitement as the little man stood grinning, turning slowly so that he faced her as she made the circuit, yelling, "Now, girl. Now that's it, girl. Now you look like something, girl."

Could the answer be that simple? Could it be that I have bitched everything up by assigning too much significance to it, by dwelling too long on the dark patterns of Freud, by acquiring little emotional knots and twitches and uncertainties?

Maybe I have learned too many wrong things. Maybe it

is just something that is physical and a function and you start from there and try to do it physically well, and accept it as a thing that you do with your body when you are a woman.

She reached the curve in the paved road and from there and for the rest of the way down the slope she could see her house.

She swung along, her stride long, the cuffs of the slacks whipping her ankles. She decided that she would take a hot bath and then dress in something frothy and silly.

And she realized that for the first time in a long, long time there was within her a quickening sense of anticipation, a feeling of being quite alive. And she resisted the habitual desire for self-analysis, the need of poking and prodding at herself to determine the cause of well-being.

This time she would accept it without question.

And she was humming softly as she went into the house, letting the screen door hiss and close softly behind her.

Chapter Six

Brock, reading in his room, had heard the sound of the jeep when Clyde Schermer picked Ellen up. After the jeep noise had faded down the hill, he found that he was reading whole paragraphs without getting any meaning from the words. It was a science-fiction novel by Simak, a writer who was usually able to capture and hold his full attention. Ever since disaster, he had found more pleasure in science fiction than in any other sort of reading. He guessed that it was because it went so far afield that there was little in it to trigger unwanted memories. There were no beer joints on the outlying planets. No deans and no small apartments.

He stubbed out his cigarette in the bedside ashtray, slapped the book shut, and laid it aside. Afternoon sun made a pattern on the throw rug near his bed. Ellen had said at lunch that she was going to the club and play tennis. He thought how it would be there, on the sleek asphalt courts. And he wondered what shape his racket was in. He got slowly off the bed and went to the closet and brought it out. He unclamped the brace and took off the plastic cover and tested the gut against the heel of his hand. It was taut, and the *pong* sound was satisfying. He cut the air with it a few times, forehand and backhand. If he went over to the club, maybe somebody would have some smart crack. Word would have gotten around. Brock was tossed out. Some kind of a jam. But he felt restless. He wanted to use his muscles. The room was fine, but you could stay in it only so long. He changed to tennis shoes and went out into the hallway and stood there for a few moments, then shrugged and went downstairs.

His mother was in the study working on the books of one of the organizations she belonged to. He leaned against the doorframe, bouncing the racket against his bent knee. She looked up at him, half-frowning, and then smiled. "Going to the club, dear? I've been worried about you not getting enough exercise."

"Thought I'd go over there if there's any way of getting there."

"I think Bess is home, dear. Why don't you ask if you can use her car?"

"I should have gone with Ellen. I didn't think quick enough."

"She should have asked you."

"Maybe she got tired of asking. Okay, I'll ask Aunt Bess. See you later, girl."

"Have fun, dear," his mother said absently, turning back to the club books.

As he approached Quinn and Bess's house he heard the busy humming of a sewing machine. He went to the kitchen window and called, "Yo, Aunt Bess!"

"Brock? Come on in. I'm in here."

She was at the sewing machine, working on some

yellow material, wearing the glasses that always looked incongruous on her, somehow. Brock had always liked her, had always gotten on well with her. He liked the way she looked. So big and alive.

"What do you think of this color, Brock?"

"Nice color. What's it going to be?"

"New curtains for David's studio. Sort of cheerful, huh?"

"Nice."

"He's very aware of colors, you know."

Brock felt uncomfortable, the way he always did when the conversation was about David. It wasn't as though David was any sort of actual blood relation. But he was in the family. And he certainly was an awful creep. A real weird item. It was tough on Bess and Quinn, the trouble they'd had with him. It made him feel guilty about how little he'd done lately.

"I've . . . I've been meaning to stop over and see him."

Bess nodded. "I wish you would. He likes you, Brock. He could show you the model of the Roman galley he's been working on. It's really quite nice. Mr. Shelter has been working with him on history, you know. I'm sure David would like to show you."

"I guess I'll go take a look, then. Or is it nap time?"

"No, he sleeps right after lunch. I can go out with you."

"No, it's okay. I'll just take a look in. Say, you using your car today? Any chance of borrowing it?"

"I won't need it at all today, Brock. You can have it this afternoon and this evening too, if you'd like."

"Just this afternoon will be fine. Thanks, Aunt Bess."

"The keys are in it, dear."

The sewing machine started again as he went out the back door. He put the racket in the car and then went over to the studio. The door was open. He looked through the screen and saw David sitting at a long table, working at something.

"Hey, Dave!"

The boy started violently and scrambled up out of the chair and peered toward the door. "Easy, guy," Brock said with that forced joviality he used when he was around David. "It's me. Brock. Can I see the ship? Your mother told me about it."

"Sure. You can see it," David said in his blurred, stumbling voice. Brock went in, smiling broadly. God, the kid was a creep. A huge guy, but frail-looking. Skin like paste and all those pimples, and the eyes all swimmy-looking behind those thick lenses. The room held the banana-oil stink of airplane cement. Brock had heard his mother and father talking about it many times. They thought David was the way he was because of what happened to his father when Bess was pregnant, getting killed that way with a knife. Apparently that Carney had been quite a guy. Funny that a strong woman like Bess and a rough guy like Carney must have been should have had David. But he was a Delevan now because Quinn had adopted him legally.

Even as a little kid, David had been odd, but it had seemed to get worse as he got older. It wasn't that he was stupid. Mr. Shelter said that David was bright. But you would certainly never know it. Not the way he acted. Everything scared him. Nothing about him was completely right. He'd spent half his life in bed with serious illnesses, one after the other. The few times they'd tried to send him to school, the other kids had made his life a hell on earth. He quivered and shook when you tried to talk to him. God knew what would become of him. The "studio" had been built for him on the advice of the psychiatrist. Something, Brock remembered, to do with security—the emotional security of having a place of his own where he could lock the door. At times he had fainted dead away when introduced to a stranger.

"This it?" Brock asked too loudly. "Say, this is real good, Dave. This is a good job."

"It's a Roman galley," David said.

"There's a lot of work there. I guess I wouldn't have the patience to do all that work."

"They rowed it with oars. There were a lot of them and they were chained to the benches and they rowed it."

It was one of the longest sentences Brock had ever

heard him say. He looked at David. The hair grew low on his forehead and was combed straight back. The glasses frames were mended with tape. Bess said that David carried on long conversations with Mr. Shelter.

Brock knew of the years of Mr. Shelter's teaching, of his efforts to gain David's confidence, but even so, it was hard to conceive of David carrying on any long conversation. The boy seemed eternally trapped in some rigid, frozen world of his own, tense and speechless and frightened, denying communication with those around him, imbedded in inexplicable fears, like a housefly under an upturned glass. With uncoordinated body, blurred speech, faulty vision, David was, Brock thought, like one of those aliens in the science-fiction stories, a visitor from a far galaxy who would never comprehend the works of man.

"Well, I just thought I'd stop by and say hello," Brock said, backing gratefully toward the door. "Sure is a nice ship model."

David swallowed audibly and moistened his lips. His face had a sudden twisted look, eerie and unpleasant. "Cuh . . . cuh . . ." he said, his mouth working oddly.

"What?" Brock asked, his hand on the screen door latch.

"Come again!" David blurted, his face turning crimson. Then he turned away from Brock so that he faced the wall.

"I'll do that, Dave," Brock said, and fled. He had sensed the agony behind David's invitation. It was something Mr. Shelter had doubtless been drilling into him. A courteous invitation. One of those little phrases you say so easily. Come again. Come back and see me. And almost utterly impossible to David. Because somehow it was allied so closely with the social block.

They had looked for brain damage and found none. It was, they said, some genetic imbalance at the time of conception.

When Brock got back to the car, Bess was standing beside it. "Was he glad to see you?" she asked anxiously.

"You know, he asked me to come again."

Her face lighted up. "He did! Oh Brock, how wonderful! You will, won't you? He *does* like you."

"I'll try to see more of him, Aunt Bess. I . . . I haven't wanted to see much of anybody lately."

She touched his arm. "I know. Don't let 'em get you down, Brock."

"I'll try not to, Aunt Bess."

She looked up at him with a crooked grin. "You're getting too damn big to go around calling me Aunt Bess, boy. It makes me feel ancient. How about just plain Bess from now on."

"Bess."

"That sounds better."

"It's hard to say."

"Thanks for visiting David."

"And thanks for the car . . . Bess."

They grinned at each other in quick understanding. He got in and backed out of the drive. Her car was a small business coupé, a tan Plymouth which had been purchased used. He tested brakes and acceleration on the way down the hill into Clayton.

The Oak Dell Country Club was on the old Stockton road, six miles from Clayton. It was on a knoll, a long, characterless, red brick building which had been made attractive by the ivy, by careful plantings and landscaping. Beyond it were the tailored fairways of the eighteen-hole golf course. Down the slope to the left were the tennis courts and the big swimming pool, with a separate bathhouse and locker rooms.

Before the depression of the thirties, Oak Dell had been very exclusive and very expensive, with membership limited to one hundred men. But the dues had dropped substantially and there had been a great campaign for new members, a great many new members, just in order to keep the club from going under.

Some of those whose wealth had not been too sharply diminished by the depression started a new club, far off on a back road in the hills, but they retained their Oak Dell membership because it was a good place for kids, and the golf course was the best in the area. The food at the club was inexpensive, rather tasteless, but very abundant. The chef, a club fixture, simplified his duties by depending too much on steam tables.

In the late 'thirties, with the idea of providing additional revenue, five guest cottages had been erected off to the right of the club beyond the caddy house, so close to the fairway of the first hole that heavy wire mesh was needed to protect those vulnerable windows from the effects of a screaming slice. The guest cottages had proven popular with those members whose houses were so small as to make house guests more of an irritation than a pleasure, and who did not wish to put them up at a hotel in the city. "We'll put you up at the club." It had a nice sound, and the guest cottages were pleasant, though rather meagerly furnished and equipped. That did not matter, as the people in the cottages could eat all their meals except breakfast at the club, and walk down the road a quarter of a mile for a bean-wagon breakfast if they so desired.

When Brock turned in between the squat brick pillars of the entrance, he looked first at the big parking lot and saw about thirty cars parked there on this Thursday afternoon. He knew that most of those would be the cars of golfers and thus both pool and courts might be fairly empty. This pleased him. He parked and walked around the clubhouse and down the slope toward the tennis courts. There were four asphalt courts, looking blue against the surrounding grass, freshly and crisply lined. Two of the courts were in use, two games of singles, and one figure sat on the grass watching the action on the near court.

He walked down the slope with an exaggerated nonchalance, feeling conspicuous. It seemed these days that he had to imitate the person he used to be, and that he had forgotten exactly how to do it. He saw that Clyde Schermer was playing Ellen on the near court. Bob Rawls was on the next court over, playing against a girl Brock did not know. And the girl sitting on the grass watching was, of course, Norma Franchard. For the past six years, starting right after the last year of junior high, whenever you saw Bob, you looked around for Norma and there she was. Now they were both in Cornell, both in the first year, the same class as Clyde Schermer.

Ellen, gathering herself to serve, turned and waved her racket at Brock, smiling as though she were glad to see him. Norma, hugging bare knees, turned and grinned up at him. "The little lost one! My favorite hermit. Why haven't you been up and about, Brockie?"

She was a small, dark girl with black, shining eyes, and she had a deep tan for so early in the summer. Brock eased himself down onto the grass beside her. "I've been studying up on women, kid."

"For them or against them?"

"The jury is still out."

Clyde finished a sweaty point, gathered up the balls, and wound up for his big serve. "Set point, darn it," Ellen called. She braced herself. The big serve hit hard and fair and she couldn't get her racket in front of it. It hit her knee and went almost straight up into the air. She rubbed her knee and glared at Clyde. "That does it, oaf."

"You're the one told me not to play pat ball with you," he said, grinning.

They came over and sprawled on the grass, breathing hard. Ellen lay spread-eagled, her eyes closed against the sky glare. Clyde braced himself on one heavy elbow, close to her, looking across her at Brock. "Where you been hiding, boy?"

Brock wondered how much Ellen had told him. Or if she had told him anything. Ellen had always been vibrantly loyal. "Resting up, I guess. Reading and so on."

"Reading," Clyde said. He made a sound of disgust. "I've cracked enough books this year to last me forever."

"They make you muscle boys read down there in Ithaca?" Brock asked.

"Short words," Clyde said. He picked up a handful of the thick grass and sprinkled it on Ellen's bare midriff.

"Cut it out," she said, and brushed it off, not opening her eyes. He sprinkled more on. Ellen opened one ominous eye, then brought her leg up fast, stamped a tennis shoe against Clyde's thick shoulder and shoved hard, rolling him back and away from her. She sighed and closed her eyes again. Brock, looking at her, thought how nicely and sweetly she was built, those tenderly rounded brown legs, the young breasts snug in the halter. When he looked at her and thought of her as a woman, it made him feel strange. He didn't want anyone looking at her like that. Clyde or anyone. It was a funny queasy feeling to think of Clyde looking at her and wanting her. To stop thinking about them that way, he turned and watched Bob Rawls playing the strange girl.

She had a sure, unhurried way of moving. She managed to be in the right place every time. He saw that her tennis had been worked on. She had a lot of power. She had Bobby's tongue hanging out. She was a tallish, ginger-headed girl, angular but well-built, and she wore yellow shorts with big, black buttons down the side and a white halter. She kept driving Bob back with a big forehand, then cross-courting him for point after point.

"Who's the new beast?" Brock asked Clyde, keeping his voice low.

"She's staying with her mother at one of the cottages. Betty Yost. Pretty hot. She took me six-four, six-one. They're guests of the Trynors'. California beast."

"I thought it looked like that brand of ball. Anybody play me?"

They said they were too pooped at the moment.

Bobby pushed one too weak and too high and the ginger-head moved in like a big cat for an overhand kill so hard that the rebound took the ball over the backstop.

"Game and set," Bob Rawls said. He trudged around and got the ball and tossed it toward the net and then came slowly off the court with the Yost girl. Bob was a tall, thin, wiry boy, sandy-blond, with colorless brows and eyelashes, and at this point he looked sulky. He said hi to Brock, then introduced Betty Yost. Betty sat down and Brock sat down again beside her. Bobby had collapsed beside Norma.

"Who in the world do you usually play with?" Brock asked the new girl. "Billie Jean?"

"She's way out of my class. I have been on a court with

her twice. It's humiliating. I'm not even good enough to give her a warm-up game."

Brock noticed that her breathing had quieted quickly. She looked neither warm nor ruffled. When she smiled, she squinted her eyes and wrinkled her nose. The nose was short, and her eyes were big and a funny shade of lavender-blue. He liked the color of them. She had freckles to go with the ginger, blond-red hair, but not a redhead's complexion. The freckles were darker spots against a smooth, even tan. Her long legs were very, very special, he decided.

"Six-two, six-love," Bobby said disgustedly.

"Gosh," Betty Yost said, "I *ought* to play pretty good tennis. I've played all year round since I was about five years old. And it's a big thing in Southern California. I can swim and play tennis and that's all. Take Ellen here. She can do both of those and play golf and bowl and ski and ice skate and play basketball and softball."

"But I don't do anything really *well*," Ellen said.

"Why should you, unless you want to make a living out of it?" Betty asked.

"You could make a living out of tennis," Clyde said.

"Oh, no! I didn't work at it hard enough. And I can't cover enough court. And I guess . . . I don't care enough about winning. You have to have a certain psychology about it. It has to be your life."

Brock sensed that they liked her, accepted her. And that was a bit unusual. The group was usually cold to newcomers. Betty seemed to have an air of maturity that the others didn't have. He wondered how old she was.

"Want to give me a lesson too?" Brock asked.

She looked at him. "Well, one set."

They went out and volleyed for a time. She put a surprising amount of weight on the ball. It came over as heavy as a baseball, and his return had a tendency to hang and float when her drives resisted the overspin he tried to put on them. She asked him if he was ready. They volleyed for serve and he won on a fluke that crawled along the tape and dropped in.

He went doggedly after everything. Time after time the

game settled into long booming volleys, base-line stuff that was hypnotic. They each held their serve until it was six all, and then she broke through his service and took her own to win the set eight-six. Brock was glad she had consented to only one set. He had played hard. His knees trembled and he had a heel blister and he was soaked with perspiration. It shocked him that he was so out of condition. He tried to control his panting as they came off the court.

"That was fun," she said. "Let's play again. Not today though. Six sets is all I can handle."

"One set is all I can handle, I guess."

They stretched out on the grass. The other four went out for their usual clown set of mixed doubles.

"I like your sister, Brock," Betty Yost said.

"She's a good kid."

Betty sat up. "I don't want to sit here all sticky. How about a swim?"

He called out to Bob Rawls. "How's chances of borrowing swim trunks, Bobby?"

"Number twenty-one. It's unlocked. Take the red pair, hey?"

"Thanks." He turned to Betty, standing beside him, tall enough so that the crown of the ginger head was just a shade above the level of his eyes. "See you at the pool, then."

She headed off toward the cottages on the other side of the club. He watched her go. Slim, straight-backed girl, with a sort of pert, jaunty look about the trim little backside of hers under the yellow denim of her tennis shorts. He saw how it might make a lot of sense. She was fun. No involvement. A lot of exercise. A few laughs. He liked her voice. A nice fuzzy edge to it. He could get in shape, get a tan, have somebody to be with when he was asked to go out with the others. He wondered how long she was staying.

He found the locker and the red trunks. He left his sweaty clothes on a bench, took a fresh towel from the rack outside the shower room and went on out to the pool, highly conscious of his winter whiteness. Small children splashed and bickered at the shallow end of the pool. Some young wives he knew by sight though not by name played bridge at a metal table under a striped umbrella. "*Rudy!* Stop splashing Marie. You *hear* me? Joey, you let Sonny have the ball if he wants it. You've had it a long time. Rudy, if you *don't* behave, you're going to have to come out of there *this minute*. Do you hear me? *Joey!*"

He dropped the towel, padded out on the low board, took two long steps, bounded high, hit the water a bit too flatly. The water made his broken blister sting. He swam two lazy lengths of the pool, avoiding the little kids. He hoisted himself up onto the apron and saw Betty Yost coming. She wore a strapless one-piece suit, a tight, tubular affair in pale blue that looked as if it were made of velvet. She moved just a bit awkwardly as he waved at her and watched her approach. She spread out a big yellow towel, put sunglasses, sun lotion, cigarettes, lighter and magazine beside it, then took a quick run and slanted off the side of the pool. She bobbed up in front of him, hair darkened and pasted to her head, making her look boyish.

"I needed that," she said.

"Best grade of water, girl."

"Race?"

"One beating is enough for one day, Betty."

"Coward!"

"Okay, then. Four lengths?"

She climbed out lithely. "Done." They started at the deep end, gripping the edge with their toes. She counted. She was in the water with a flat racing dive while he was still in midair. He gained on her all the way down the pool, but her turn was much better, and he was back where he started. He gained on the way back and made a slightly better kick turn. He got to the third turn a few feet ahead of her, but she more than made it up on her return. On the last length, at midpool, she was a shade ahead of him. He used everything he had left, which was not very much, and sensed when he passed her. He hit the end and grasped the edge of the trough, wheezing and gasping.

She was beside him, laughing. "The winnah! Now we try the high hurdles."

"High hurdles. I can't even climb out of the pool."

She eeled her way out and bent over and offered her hand. He took her hand, braced himself, and flipped her over his head into the pool behind him. He scrambled out quickly as she came up, sputtering. He took his towel over and stretched it out beside hers and lay down. She made a face at him and swam by herself for a time, varying her stroke with each length of the pool. He lay with his cheek on the towel, watching her, enjoying the way she looked, the slim, tanned arms reaching up out of the dancing, green water, flashing droplets in the sun. The sun was drying him, hot on his shoulders.

At last she climbed out of the pool and came over and sat on one of the shabby rubberized pads and dried her hair vigorously with her big, yellow towel. She offered him one of her cigarettes and he took it, leaning forward for the light.

"You're pretty white, Brock. This sun will cook you."

"I tan easy."

"Do you work inside or something?"

"I'm not working. I'm loafing. I . . . got out of school a while back."

"You graduated? You don't look old enough to———"

"Sophomore year. Where are you in school?"

"Southern Cal. I was in my freshman year. But I dropped out in February."

"Going to go back?"

She seemed uneasy. "Nothing's very definite right now, Brock."

"I think I'll try a different school in the fall. What have you been doing since February?"

"Traveling, mostly. Daddy died four years ago. We were in Mexico for a while." Her uneasiness was quite pronounced. She was pouring lotion into the palm of her right hand, unselfconsciously greasing her long legs.

"Hope you'll be around awhile."

"I hope so too. Mother gets restless. Here, you better use some of this goo."

He took the bottle. "Thanks." The sun had warmed the bottle. The lotion had a sleek texture. He greased his arms and legs and chest and shoulders and began trying to spread it on his back.

She held her hand out for the bottle. "Roll over. Let me."

He lay on his stomach, cheek on his forearm. She poured lotion on his back, spread it, and rubbed it in vigorously. Her hand felt capable and good. It made him sleepy. He heard the small sound as she recapped the bottle. He sighed. He felt as if he were drifting. There was sun glare off the pool water, bright against his closed eyelids. He moved his hand so that it shaded his eyes.

When Betty Yost awakened him, he didn't know where he was for a few moments and then realized that he was peering stupidly at her, dazed by sun and sleep.

"That," she said firmly, "is quite enough sun for you for one day, Brock. A quick swim and then you go get dressed."

"I must have been exciting company. Why didn't you roll me into the pool?"

"A kind heart. The others wanted to. Clyde especially. I wouldn't let him."

"You're not sore at me?"

"Why should I be? I guess it was . . . sort of restful."

He still felt sheepish. After they took a quick swim and climbed out of the pool, he said, "Have you got a date or anything tonight?"

She looked at him speculatively. "Mother may have something planned. I don't know. What sort of thing did you want to do?"

"I don't know. Outdoor movie. Ride around. Eat something at a drive-in. I'm not too money-heavy." She had kept her hair out of the water on this last swim. He liked the reddish glint of it in the sun.

"Could we make it Dutch?"

"We don't have to do that. I asked you."

"I'd rather. Come over to the cottage after you change and I'll ask Mother. We're in the second one."

"I was going to go home like this. The clothes I wore

are all damp, and I haven't fixed up a locker yet this year."

"Okay, why don't you walk on over with me right now."

They walked to the cottage. There was a deck chair in the late afternoon sun. Mrs. Yost took off her sunglasses and smiled in a formal way. She was a long, thin, brown woman with a simian face and black hair cut unbecomingly short. There was only a vague resemblance between mother and daughter.

"Mother, this is Brock Delevan and he's asked me to go out with him." Brock was astonished. Her words had come out in a confused rush. She acted ill at ease and years younger. All her quiet poise was gone.

"How nice, dear," Mrs. Yost said. Her voice was practically a baritone. "I've met your sister, Brock. Lovely child. It's so comforting for Betty to meet some nice young people." There was a subtle accent on the "young."

"Mother, I just wondered if——"

"Don't just stand there dithering, child. Run in the cottage and bring out more chairs."

"No, thanks, Mrs. Yost. I want to go back to the house and change. Is it okay if I take Betty out?"

"If you don't, she is certainly going to have a dull evening. I'm going out to a dinner party. Can't you see she's happy as a clam that you asked her?"

"Mother, please!"

"Have I said something wrong again, dear? I want you to have a nice date, dear. A nice gay young uncomplicated date with this nice boy."

Betty was looking down at her toes. "Please," she said in a barely audible tone. The tension between them was almost frightening. There were undercurrents of things he did not understand. It made him feel awkward.

He used a voice that was too loud and too cheery. "Well, suppose I stop back in about an hour, Betty. Will that be okay?"

"That will be fine," she said, glancing at him, her eyes suddenly warm and grateful.

"Nice to meet you, Mrs. Yost."

"Delighted to meet *you*, young man. More than I can say."

He left them there. The anticipation of the date with Betty was partly spoiled by the odd scene. He couldn't understand what had happened. There was something between them that was not right. And it was tied up, somehow, with Betty's uneasy manner when he had been asking her about school. He wondered if Ellen would know anything about it.

Chapter Seven

It was three o'clock on Thursday afternoon when Benjamin Delevan sent word that he wanted to see Mr. Quinn Delevan in his office immediately. Ben knew once word was sent that he would have to follow through with it. It was something he did not want to do. Yet there was information he would have to have. Important decisions must be made only when all relevant and obtainable information is in hand. An old rule and a good one.

Irritably, impatiently, he got up from his chair and stood at the window, looking down into the yard. He could see an edge of the loading platform where finished bolts were being hand-trucked into a red express-truck trailer. He remembered mechanically that it would be the rush order for Rochester, going out on time.

"You wanted to see me, Ben?" The voice was hesitant.

"Shut the door and sit down, Quinn." His voice was heavier than he had intended it to be. When he turned around, he saw a look of nervous alarm fade quickly from his half-brother's face. He wondered what Quinn had been up to, then decided that it was probably just the urgency of the summons.

"What's on your mind, Ben?"

Ben sat behind the desk. "I want to talk honestly to you, Quinn. Maybe I never have before. Something totally unexpected has come up."

"Yes?" The voice and question were guarded.

"This is under your hat. Don't tell anybody. Bess or anybody. I'll do any telling that has to be done. One of the big firms in the industry wants this mill. A merger arrangement. A stock exchange, share for share."

Ben saw the flicker of relief and wondered at it. Quinn rubbed his chin, his eyes puzzled. "I realize that you have to think of all the angles of a thing like this, Ben. I mean it might be advantageous or something, but after all, this place has been in the family for three generations, and we are making a profit. I'd say we were prettty healthy right now. What are the details?"

Ben waited a moment. Then he said softly, "I don't want to hurt your feelings, Quinn. If I do, it isn't without reason. I see no reason for giving you any details. You wouldn't understand them. I don't need any help in coming to a decision. I'll make the decision myself. I didn't call you in here for advice."

"I resent that, Ben! I resent being told that——"

Ben went on remorselessly. "I'll give you some more things to resent, Quinn. If you want to resent them. I've never talked this way to you before. I should have, I guess. A long time ago. You've been in the place for sixteen ... nearly seventeen years, now. You still don't know what the hell it's all about. There's no responsible job I can trust you in. Oh, you know all the technical words and you can use them the way a parrot would use them. You have routine duties that should take you not more than an hour a day. You make them last all day. About once a month you come to me with what you call an idea. Most of those ideas of yours give away the fact that you don't know the first thing about our operations. I don't know what you would have been suited for. It certainly wasn't this business. This business seems to bore you. You're lazy. Family firms always seem to have one or two around like you. You put on the big-executive act. Outside the gates you're a big wheel. Maybe you even believe it yourself. I doubt that you do, somehow. Yes, we're making some money. Because I've been carrying this place on my back. You are dead weight. If you'd been able to share the load, we might be making more. You are one of the luxuries the firm supports. Your salary comes right off the top of the net. But useless as you are, you are a factor I have to consider because you are my brother. Without me carrying you, what will become of you? That's what I have to know."

Ben paused, realizing that tension had made him go too far, had made him state the truth with a finality that was too ruthless. Quinn was one of the weak ones. There were a lot of them. They were like those little men in parades who carry big banners. Until the banner with its brave paint becomes confused with the man himself. And because the banner is top-heavy, it is very easy to knock it out of unsteady hands.

Quinn stood up and wavered and caught his balance. "You can't ... say things like ..." His face was moist chalk.

"Please sit down," Ben said gently.

Quinn sat down. His color was a little better. "You always had to run everything. I know that. Nobody else could do anything right."

"You may be right, Quinn. It might be my fault. But that doesn't change anything. If I let the mill go, we'll both be out."

"You too? But——"

"I'm not a team man. They'll bring in nice, orderly team men, with big books about policy and methods, and when there's any doubt, they look it up in the book. They won't run this place the way I would. I want to know about you, Quinn. You'll have a house and two cars and no savings and a hundred and something thousand worth of stock. You're thirty-six. If it wasn't for the responsibility of David, maybe you and Bess could pull your horns in far enough to get by. But I doubt that. You have a well-developed taste for luxury, Quinn."

Quinn leaned forward. "I don't see why you even think of giving it up."

Ben felt the return of anger. "You don't! You don't! My God, just because it's gone along so far, you think it goes on forever or something. Three fair-sized bad guesses in any fiscal year and this thing comes down out of the sky like a bucket of boiled rice. Because you can't kick the buildings down with your bare foot, you think it's here for eternity. Does the big sign on top of the plant comfort you or something? Damn it, man! You think I wanted to come in here in the first place? I had to, because there wasn't anybody else. Wilma and I had other plans for my life. I've spent a lot of nights lying awake, sweating about this place. I've got jangled nerves and bad digestion— Oh, the hell with it!"

Quinn was looking down at his clasped hands. "Maybe, Ben, you ... underestimate my contribution. I mean, I think the contact work I do helps us quite a bit. The trips ..."

"Do you know why you haven't been down to New York lately? Because Delahay risked his job to write me a personal letter begging me to keep you away from there. He said he had to spend too much time patching up the damage. He said you treated his big accounts as if Stockton Knit was doing them a favor dealing with them. Stop kidding yourself, Quinn. Go play golf all you want, but at least have the honesty to stop implying that you're being a big help to me out there on the fairway. I didn't mean this to turn into a squabble like this, but you act so damn blind."

"Why are you doing this, then? Why are you doing this?"

"Because you've got to make some kind of a plan for yourself and tell me what it is. Because I don't like the idea of being retired for five years and then suddenly finding out I have to support the three of you. Because it's a factor in my decision."

"So ... I'm some sort of a joke around here. A big joke."

"Don't go off on that tangent. All that phony tragedy, Quinn. Let's not get melodramatic."

"The most constructive thing I could do would be drop dead."

"What kind of a remark is that?" Ben said, feeling very weary.

"There's the insurance, isn't there? The business insurance."

Ben leaned forward and banged his fist lightly on the desk top. "Will you please, please stop looking so noble and blighted and get off this self-pity angle. I'm trying to wake you up."

"Thanks. Thanks a lot, Ben."

"I give up. Probably things will go on the way they always have."

Quinn stood up. "That's where you're wrong, Ben. They can't ever go on the way they always have, no matter what you decide."

"Will you do me the favor of getting out of this office right now before I lose my mind completely?"

Quinn left without looking back, leaving the door standing open. Ben sat and felt bitterly ashamed of himself. Regardless of Quinn's ineffectuality, one human being had no God-given right to do that to another human being. He had, in effect, helped Quinn create his own myth. If he had torn it down in the beginning, when the myth was weak. . . . But long ago he had realized that Quinn Delevan had a limited intelligence, a complete lack of any competitive drive. He was mild and decorative and a bit of a bore. Born into a different social stratum, Quinn would probably have been one of those men who, bolstered by a working wife, drift through many jobs— floorwalker, salesclerk, doorman, usher, hearse driver— reasonably contented, mild, half-alive.

Ben knew that out of his own selfish fear had come the hope that he could wire a verbal explosive to the seat of Quinn's pants and shock him into awareness, into independence. It had been done, and he would have given a great deal to undo it. For a little time he had hoped he could force apart the jaws of this special trap. The hope had come from Griffin. But the springs of the trap were too strong. He thought of Griffin and of how contemptuous Griffin would be were he to know this special aspect of family responsibility.

He knew he had handled it very poorly. Had administered a shocking wound. Yet, he thought, perhaps you cannot inflict a deep and lasting wound when the injured party lacks depth. The meaningless people of this world seem to have a peculiar knack of self-delusion. Perhaps that is the measure of their meaninglessness. Already the ugly interview would be suffering a subtle distortion in Quinn's mind. All the protective circuits and devices would be operating. By evening Quinn would remember words that were not said, and would have forgotten words that had been said. Delehay's reaction would be construed as being the result of jealousy. Big brother Ben had been off on one of his usual tangents, trying to frighten the hired help. It would all be twisted and altered and changed, so that after a few days the rents in the toga would have mended themselves, and Quinn would pull it carefully around himself once more and stand proudly and smugly, made warm and safe by the fiction he constantly wrote for himself, the stories wherein he was always hero.

You could not smash the foolish ones, because the sledge bounced off their rubbery texture. It is awareness and sensitivity that fragment so easily. And he began, without warning, to think of his son. And as the sickness began, he turned his thoughts away. He had not yet been able to think it through. It hurt too badly. It involved too many losses, of hope and dreams and pride. Love was still there, stubborn and indestructible, but the good reasons for it were gone. And he could not yet permit himself to think of it.

Back in his own office, Quinn sat at his desk. The glossy trade journal was still open in front of him, open to the page he had been looking at when Ben had summoned him so abruptly. He looked sightlessly down at the color cut of the huge loom, a thing of Martian strangeness and endless complication, a device with an electronic brain which received its instructions from a plastic tape, a

chirping, chuckling monster that sat and fed itself and
excreted intricate patterns, full of stainless dreams of a
day when the last man would leave the last mill and close
the door.

Quinn sat alone and tried to remember when and how
it had happened. It hadn't happened in Ben's office. It had
happened a long time ago. He remembered the first day,
the strangeness of it. A Ben who was sixteen years younger
taking him around that day. *This is my brother. He's
coming in with us. This is my brother. He's coming in
with us.* Busy faces and quick grins and the handshakings.

Start at the bottom. Strange smells and strange methods
and confusion and new words to learn. He had wanted to
learn. They weren't natural with you—not the way they
were with each other. You were a Delevan. And somehow
it wasn't like a job. It was more like playing a part. And
Ben kept shifting him around so much. It was confusing.
There were a lot of things you never did get to understand
the way you should. You were supposed to pick it all up
quickly because you were a Delevan. You made mistakes
and they said it was okay.

There must be one specific moment when it happened.
One day back there when the decision was made. So that
from then on you drifted along with it, stayed out of
trouble, gave up any sincere idea of contributing anything.
And you learned to nod in the right way when they talked
over your head. And you learned all the defensive devices. *Yes, you may be right. We'll give that some consideration. I'll check with my brother on that. It could
stand looking into. It would have to be a policy decision,
of course.*

And once those defensive devices were perfected there
was little point in trying to learn more. Stockton Knitting
had been going on a long time. The technical people had
been trained for their jobs. Supervisory personnel made
the minor decisions. My God, it wouldn't collapse if you
didn't happen to know every little facet of the business.
Ben kept things under control. He even *liked* it. The thing
was to look wise in every job Ben gave you and wait

patiently for the office of your own and the desk of your own.

But something had changed him into precisely what Ben had called him. Maybe it was a change so gradual he hadn't noticed it.

Or maybe it had happened on a day long ago, a day during the time he had been assigned to bookkeeping. Sitting, drowsing over the intricacies of the accounts receivable, computing the discounts on the old manual machine with its worn keys, matching the discounts against the amounts taken by the customer firms. There had been a delay in getting some kind of new form from the printer. It was supposed to be ready, but for some forgotten reason, the printer couldn't deliver. Burney, long years dead now, had asked him to go pick up the forms. He had left the office on a clear, cool October day and driven over into the heart of the city, parked on a back street. The yellow Ford, wasn't it? The job press was a noisy place, presses thumping and clanking, paper whispering off into neat piles. The old man in the green eyeshade had shouted over the noise, "It's half run off, son. You need them in a hurry, you take a stack back with you. That'll hold you and we can deliver the balance tomorrow."

And he had stood there thinking of the clear beauty of the day, of the dusty drowsiness of the bookkeeping section, of the wind that was touching the skirts of the sidewalk girls.

"They told me to get the whole order. How long before it will be done?"

"An hour I'd say."

Quinn had looked at his watch. Three thirty. He'd still have time to get back to the mill before five. And it was too noisy, of course, to even think of using the phone in the job press. "I'll be back in an hour," he said.

The old man shrugged and turned away. Quinn had walked out into the sunshine. It felt good to walk. He stopped in at a quiet bar where the wood was old and dark and the ale had a taste that was like the smell of burning leaves, tart and smoky on that October day. And he sat at the bar where he could watch the sunny side-walk. He had forgotten to call Burney. And time went too fast. It was quarter to five when he got back to the job press.

The old man leaned close and yelled, "Fella come and took most of the order back with him. Got here a little after four. Little fella with glasses with gold rims."

Burney himself, and a needless affront when he could have sent someone else. "The rest of it's finished. You can take it along now, son."

The offices were nearly empty when he got back. He put the thin packet of forms in the storage cabinet. Burney glanced up at him and then returned to the work he was doing. Quinn turned and looked at Burney's thin shoulders. He was annoyed at Burney. What the hell difference did it make? Would the walls fall down because some forms were late? Damn elderly little accountant, taking himself and his job too seriously. He shrugged. There was no point in sitting down at his assigned desk and working just because Burney probably thought he should feel guilty. Maybe Burney was waiting for some kind of an excuse.

He turned toward the door. At the doorway he paused. "Good night, Burney," he said with great casualness.

"Good night, Mr. Delevan," Burney said, not looking around.

And before that it had always been Mr. Burney and Quinn.

Had it started then? Or the next day when Burney, without explanation, had given the accounts receivable job to the girl who had been doing it in the first place, and Quinn had spent most of the day wandering around the mill, carrying a meaningless sheaf of papers in his hand, thoroughly bored. . . .

He sat and tried to summon up righteous anger, anger at Ben. He tried to tell himself Ben had kept him ineffectual, Ben didn't want any competition. It didn't work. Ben was right—hideously, irrevocably right. He thought of what Delahay had written Ben, and he felt his face get hot. Probably everybody in the plant had seen through his masquerade. Everybody in the family. Everybody in the city.

A girl came in quietly with a sheaf of checks already signed by Ben and placed them on his desk, stood quietly waiting. Quinn closed the trade journal and placed it aside, pulled the checks over, and countersigned them automatically, paying no attention to amounts or payees. One of the routine tasks. One of those little jobs which, added up, made up the one hour a day. The girl waited, fiddling with the clasp on a bracelet. He wondered what would happen if he should demand of Ben a full explanation of one of the checks selected at random, before adding his own signature. That was absurd. Childish. And the explanation might be too complicated to understand, even if Ben were willing to give it. He handed the checks to the girl and she walked out. After she had gone, he realized that she had not said one word to him. She had put the checks in front of him as though running them through some sort of machine. Oh, he has to sign the checks because he owns stock or something. No, he never looks at them. He just signs.

His world had gone very cold and he searched through it for warmth. He thought of the one place where he would find it. He got up quickly and went out into the mill and went up to her, aware of her quick surprised look of alarm. He pretended to be watching what she was doing. "I've got to see you," he said. "I'll wait for you at your place."

She gave a barely perceptible negative shake of her head, lips compressed.

"I'll wait for you there," he repeated and walked away. He saw the other girls glancing at him. He knew he had given them a ripe basis for speculation. It did not matter.

He walked from the offices to the garage where he had left his car. It had been repaired. He drove it away. He parked in front of the old house on Fremont. He had never been there in daylight before. He walked across the shallow, defeated yard and around the corner of the house to the private entrance. He used his key and let himself in.

In the daylight it was unexpectedly dingy, with lumpy-looking upholstery, stained wallpaper, a rug so worn that the brown cording showed through the sparse pile. And there was a silent smell in there, as though no one had been in the apartment for a long time. Yet her morning cup was in the sink under a dripping faucet. Each drip made a varying musical note. He stepped into the tiny kitchen and wrenched at the faucet. The cadence of the drip slowed, but it did not stop. He moved the brimming cup and saucer. The drops made a fainter splatting sound against the stained enamel.

He went into the bathroom. There was a wiry brown hair in the lavatory. He picked it out with a piece of toilet tissue and dropped it in a metal wastebasket adorned with an incongruous picture in bright color of a cottage with a white gate and roses. He ran the water and cupped his hands and splashed his face. The water ran down the drain with a retching sound. The only towel was slightly damp. It held a smell of soap and flesh. He held his breath while he dried his face.

He had never been there alone. It gave him a feeling of secretiveness and curiosity. A tiptoe feeling. Like long ago, a Sunday afternoon when the family was out and he had gone into Alice's room, looking for something he could not define, knowing only that it was a part of the new mysteries that had taken her off into unknown places.

He found personal things in a bureau drawer. Legal papers, letters, photographs. The photographs were odd. She had talked of her family. He had seen them through her eyes. Idealized. But here were the pictures. Strange rough-dressed people looking uncomfortably into the camera. It made Bonny seem more a stranger to him.

He read parts of the letters:

. . . Well, there is nothing more to say, so I must close now, wishing you luck in your new job.

. . . Ruth is living in Schenectady where Paul is working for the G.E. and she says it is a good job but you know Paul and if it is good like she says you can bet he will not be keeping it long. Ha. Ha.

. . . Sis, you got to go back up there when you get a chance and get that sewing machine away from her. Sally thought you got it and like you said in your letter you thought Sally got it and the way it turns out neither one of us got it and you no dam well that if Mom was alive to no about it she would be sore as Hell. So dont let her give you any lip the way she will want to do and tell her we want it. It makes me so dam mad Sally renting one here when there is the one right in the family Mom bought and paying that dollar and a half a week on it for God knows how long and if you get it you send it express collect because Sally can sure use it. . . .

He put the letters back. He found a high-school friendship book:

Roses are red, Violets are pretty. Let's us get married and live in the city. Your true friend, Sidney.

No matter how old and wrinkled I get, you're one true friend I will never forget. Maria Teresa Rooney.

He dropped the book back in and banged the drawer shut. These things turned her into someone else. And he did not want that to happen. He opened her closet. He knew her clothes well. He knew the feel of them against his hands when she was warm inside them. They hung like empty promises. Brushed and neat and mended, and so few of them.

It was too silent in the room. He turned to the small radio she had accepted from him with such strange reluctance. *So that's the end of the Giant threat in the top half of the seventh, and the first man to bat for the Braves will be*—He clicked it off. The voice seemed to echo in the room, brassy, full of simulated enthusiasm, and then the memory of the voice went away and the room was quieter than ever.

There was no magic in the room. It was a girl's room. And the girl was trite and too young and meaningless. Here were all the grubby mechanics of a person living alone, a stranger. All the magic there had been in the young flesh now seemed a magic that had been self-induced. It was a circus ground by daylight. It was a magician seen from the wings, so that you knew how the trick hinges worked and where the pigeons came from.

He took off his jacket and shoes and loosened his tie and stretched out on the day bed face down. The tapestried cover smelled of dust. A transient room with nothing enduring about it. A room for the weak ones. Ben and Bess were strong ones, sure of their place. Walking the earth heavily, looking about calmly. Bovine and steadfast in their own sense of belonging. While the small ones scurry about and are eaten by giants.

When he heard the sound of her key, he rolled over onto his back. She hurried across the room to him, her eyes full of concern, and edged onto the day bed beside him, so that her round, warm hip fitted into the hollow of his waist and she rested her hand flat against his chest as she looked down at him. "Quinn, honey, what's wrong? What happened? You shouldn't come here like this. Your car out in front—talking to me like that in the mill."

He pulled his mouth tight, thinking he would cry. He reached for her and pulled her down and held her, but it was no good because all the mill smells were caught in her hair, and there was a sweatiness about her, and the taut skin over the hard cheekbones was faintly oily. It was no good, and there was no desire in holding her.

"I'll talk about it later," he said. "I just wanted to see you, Bonny."

She seemed to sense his restraint and she pulled away. "Let me clean up, then tell me, darlin'." She went over and took clothes from the closet and turned and gave him a bright nervous smile and went into the bathroom and closed the door. He heard the metal thunder of the old tub filling. He lay there and pictured her as carefully as he could, using the images of her in an attempt to awaken and quicken desire, needing desire for her the way, in crisis, strong drink is used to wipe the mind clean of other things.

The tub noise stopped. Soon he heard the soft wet

sounds as she bathed. He tried to imagine her soaping firm breasts. His mental pictures were without flavor or meaning. And the old fear was with him again. He got up quickly and walked soundless in stocking feet to the bathroom door and opened the door and walked in. The room was steamy, the mirror blurred. She had turned on the harsh overhead light.

She looked at him and gasped and held her arm across her breasts in the Venus gesture. There were blobs of suds on her shoulders, a soaked, blue sponge in her hand, and with her mouth open that way in surprise, the harsh light glinted on a metal filling. She tried then in a strained nervous way to smile at him, and he wondered if it was supposed to be a seductive smile. It was a thin grimace that did not touch her eyes. She held the sponge out shyly, tentatively. "Wanta scrub my back, hon?"

He turned and pulled the door shut behind him. He tied his shoes quickly, slid the knot of his tie up, shouldered into his jacket on the way to the door. He half ran to the car. The evening traffic was heavy. He half heard the scream of brakes behind him as he turned out into the traffic. He felt as if the world had gotten vague. His face felt as if something sticky had dried on it and the steering wheel felt too small in his hands, small and flimsy so that he could not hold it properly.

The evening traffic of Stockton crawled through the old streets, snarling and evil-tempered, honking at delays. Old men sat on high porches and watched the glittering evening river. The narrow old streets emptied themselves onto the wide velvet of main arteries leading out of town. The traffic sighed and the speedometers climbed and temperatures dropped and gear ratios thudded softly into the highest of highs. They swept out of the city toward mortgaged greenness, toward window walls and storage walls and corner enclosures for stereo speakers—toward PTA and the bowling league and the asbestos mittens that came with an apron embroidered JOLLY HOST—toward the new issue of *Holiday* and toward the twi-night double-header on TV and the bills that came in the mail and the book that came from the book club because somebody

forgot to send in the slip saying you didn't want it—
toward blacktop driveways that were parking areas for
small red bicycles and small yellow space ships on wheels
—toward a tossed green salad and one small lamb chop
and skim milk and no dessert because this was the year
you lost twenty-five pounds—toward matchstick draperies
and the incredible chomping din of the disposal and the
mutter of the deepfreeze.

Metal river racing from stone of city to grass of
suburbia, and in one car was Quinn Delevan driving with
quiet face and chewing the inside of his left cheek and
thinking of his dead loins.

Chapter Eight

The tennis, the swimming and the long shower had
made Ellen Delevan feel delicious and absolutely
ravenous. She glowed. This was going to be an absolutely
perfect summer. One of the last little nagging worries had
faded away when Brock had decided to come out to the
club. He'd been so funny ever since that trouble at school.
Nobody would talk about it. She knew he'd done something
that made Dad act as if he despised Brock. Like he
had committed a crime or something. And Brock acted
different. Even today. Sort of . . . well, timid with people.
Not like he used to be, always kidding around. More
serious. As if something had happened to him that made
him older all of a sudden.

She had brought a blue, imitation-leather hatbox with a
zipper that ran almost all the way around it. She had
toweled herself dry. She took out her fresh underthings
and put them on absently, thinking about Brock. It would
be nice if he and that Betty got along. She was nice. Sort
of odd and different. Funny-colored eyes. A perfectly

marvelous tennis player. She'd beaten Brock even, and Brock could take Clyde and Bobby Rawls. That Betty Yost certainly had a mind of her own. Funny how she seemed to take to Brock. They'd been talking at the club about how she was a man-hater. A lot of the older boys had tried to date her and had been called out on strikes. Brock had been sleeping as if he was awfully tired. And when Clyde had tiptoed up to roll Brock into the pool, that Yost girl had whispered, "Leave him alone!" and her eyes had looked like the flame on those Bunsen burners in high-school lab. She grinned, remembering the way Clyde had stopped and stared at her and then instinctively backed away as though he thought she was going to bite him on the leg. Betty Yost had been real fierce about it. It made her proud of Brock in an odd way to have the Yost girl take to him like that. She was very pretty, actually. And she had that sort of quiet grown-up manner that Brock had ever since coming home before school was out.

She put on her new pale-green cashmere cardigan, her light-tan skirt, the dark-green sandals. She pushed the cardigan sleeves up above her elbows. Her hair was still damp but drying fast. She pulled it back and put the little silver clamp on it, wishing it would grow faster, and wondering if she should have it cut short again. It was such a darn no-color. Not blond and not brown and not anything. Scared mouse. That's what Clyde called it.

She went out to the other room. Norma Franchard was sitting at one of the little tables, fixing her face. Ellen sat next to her and dug her lipstick out of her purse. "I'm absolutely starving," she said.

"I'm having a job keeping from snapping at this lipstick," Norma said.

"What are the plans?"

"Gosh, I don't know. Nobody said anything. I wish we could think of something exciting to do. Bob and Clyde were saying something about bowling and something about that new roller rink. Not for little Norma. I'm worn to a nub. Anything I do from now on is a spectator sport. At least *almost* anything." And she turned to Ellen with an exaggerated leer.

Ellen felt obligated to laugh in a knowing way. Norma was so darn crude sometimes. Almost as if she felt she *had* to keep reminding you that she slept with Bobby. Everybody knew it. Ever since sophomore high school. It didn't really make her cheap, because they seemed practically like old married people. That was what Mother didn't understand. Things had changed. If you were going steady for just years and years, then it was all right. That didn't make you cheap nowadays. If you slept around, then you were cheap and everybody knew it. And nobody respected you. But you didn't lose any respect if you were going steady. You had to know what to do to keep from getting caught, because if you got caught, it was a disgrace that somehow made you cheap like the ones that slept around. Ellen guessed that the kids probably thought she and Clyde did it. Clyde acted sometimes like he couldn't understand why she wouldn't. It made her feel funny to think what the other kids must be thinking about the two of them. A sort of uneasy feeling and yet kind of smug, too. Let them think what they wanted to think. It wasn't exactly that she was scared, even though she was scared, a little. She guessed it was sort of not being sure of Clyde. He seemed so kind of crude sometimes. And he liked to show off his muscles, like standing so long on the diving board before diving. Things like that.

Anyway, she wished Norma had more ... reserve or something. She was cute and a lot of fun.

Another reason was going to a different school in September, so far from Clyde. If she was going to go to Cornell, like Bobby and Norma and Clyde, maybe it would be different.

They went on out together. The boys were waiting. Ellen had her blue hatbox and Norma had a canvas zipperbag, like a basketball player. Ellen looked over toward the pool and saw that Brock was awake and swimming again with that Yost girl.

"Before either of you say a darn thing," Norma announced, "be it known that Ellen and I could eat the tires right off that jeep."

"It's a conspiracy," Bob said. "What are we for? Exercise 'em, drive 'em around, feed 'em, and start all over again. I'd rather have a cocker spaniel."

"Has anybody ever heard of a joint called Brannigan's?" Clyde asked in a dreamy voice, his eyes closed.

"Fat burgers with the works," Ellen said reverently.

"Canadian ale with dew on the bottle," Bob sighed.

"One of those big baskets of crisp, crunchy French fries," Norma said.

They piled into the jeep and took off with Clyde spinning the wheels on the gravel of the parking lot. It was too hot to eat out in the jeep, so they went in and sat in a booth. Norma went over to the juke and turned and said, "Hey! Frank Sinatra!" Both boys groaned. But she put in coins, pushed buttons, and came back happily. They had two burgers apiece except Clyde, who had three, along with two bottles of ale. Bob forcibly restrained Norma from going back and replaying Sinatra. They sat in contentment and Clyde said, "What now, people? The bowling? The skating?"

"Out!" Norma said. "Definutely."

"No exercise," Ellen said.

"There isn't a good movie within fifty miles," Clyde said.

"I can think of one thing," Bob said. He gave Ellen a quick speculative look. "Hell, I don't know."

"Give, man," Clyde said.

Bob leaned forward, became conspiratorial. "Dad gets his vacation the first two weeks in July. We've got the place on Lake Sheridan. You've been up there, Clyde."

"Sure. It's nice."

"He's been beating on me for the last week to go up there and get the dock in the water and get the water pump started and shovel out the joint. Usually we get mice in the winter. He was up there a couple of weeks back, took some friends up and they went after lake trout. But he couldn't do all that. No, it's got to be Bobby. So what I was thinking of was two birds with one stone. We could all go up there and stay overnight and you could help me with that stuff he wants done, Clyde, and we could take some food along. It's only twenty-five miles.

It'll be cooler up there, but there's a good woodpile. I should know."

"All of us?" Ellen said. "They wouldn't let me do that!"

"Call your mother and tell her you're staying with Norma. And Norma, you call your folks and say you're staying with Ellen. It ought to work."

"What if they check?" Norma asked thoughtfully.

"The odds are they won't. Even if they do, we can think of something afterward," Bob said.

Norma was looking at Bob. She took his hand, lacing her fingers in his. "I'm game, darling."

"I'll tell my people I'm going up there with you," Clyde said. "To help."

"And my folks will be glad I'm getting energetic," Bob said.

They all looked at Ellen. She felt their excitement. "I don't think I want to do that," she said primly.

"Don't *you* go chicken," Norma said sharply.

Ellen looked down and she knew she was blushing. It made her feel young and stupid. "But I just don't want to."

"Good God, you'll be chaperoned," Norma said. "Robert and Norma, professional chaperones. Protect your loved ones. Come on, kid. Don't be like that. It's a wonderful idea."

"Don't go chicken on us, Ellen," Bob said.

Ellen fiddled with her watch strap. She knew they were all looking at her. She didn't want to look back at them. Her knees felt weak. She let out a long sigh. "Well ... okay, then."

Clyde patted her back and said, "Good gal." Norma reached across the table and shook hands ceremoniously with her.

Bob grinned and got up. "I'll phone first," he said. He was gone about three minutes and came back and made a circle of thumb and middle finger, beaming. Clyde left and came back in about the same length of time, making the same gesture. Norma did the same, but her call took

longer. They all looked at Ellen, and Clyde got out so that
she could get out from her position against the wall.

"Well, here goes so much nothing," she said. She smiled
but it felt stiff. She went back and dug a dime out of her
purse and used the wall phone. "Mother. This is Ellen.
Mother, can I stay overnight please with Norma Franchard? Yes. Norma. On Poplar Crescent. No, I don't
have to because I've got nearly everything I need with me
and I can borrow pajamas from Norma. What do you
mean, Mother? I certainly wasn't aware that I was sounding funny, I assure you. Of course not, Mother. No,
Mother. All right. Thanks. Yes, I will. What? Oh, no, I've
eaten already. I was hungry. Yes, I will. All right. Good-
bye, Mother." She hung up. It would have been so easy if
her mother had said no. That would have ended it right
there. And it was certainly almost inevitable that her
mother would think of some other instructions or advice
or something and call the Franchards and then things
would really be messy. She went slowly back to the table.
If her mother had said no, then it wouldn't be her fault.
And then nothing could be done about it.

She was at the booth and Clyde, standing there, waiting
to let her in, said, "Well?"

"Gee, I'm awful sorry but she said I couldn't."

"I thought I heard you thanking her," Clyde said
suspiciously. "What were you thanking her for."

"That was sort of sarcasm, I guess."

They were all looking at her oddly as she slid in to sit
by the wall. "What was the reason you can't?" Norma
asked.

"She just said I couldn't. You know how they are. You
don't have to look at me like that. I tried, didn't I?"

Bob Rawls sighed. "Okay, my lamb. You tried.
Anyway, it was a thought. Where does that leave us?"

Norma's expression was unpleasant as she looked across
at Ellen. "It leaves us minus one gal. Who else do you
know, Clyde?"

"If Ellen can't go, then it's out," Clyde said.

"I think that was kind of stinking," Ellen said to
Norma.

All the good feeling of the day was gone. The excitement and daring of the idea had quickened them, and it had all gone flat, and Norma was being bitchy. Ellen felt as if the gulf between her and the three of them had widened. She was going away to school in the fall. Clyde, Bobby, and Norma had had one year away at school. She felt that Clyde, too, was annoyed with her, even though he had voiced his loyalty.

Ellen looked at her wristwatch. "There's one thing we could do," she said, lowering her voice.

"A fast hot game of scrabble?" Norma asked icily.

"It's early. And it's only twenty-five miles. We could all drive up and then Clyde could bring me back and then we could drive out in the morning. And . . . well, leave you and Bobby there, Norma."

Bobby looked a bit uncomfortable but Norma's expression changed. She leaned over and patted Ellen's hand. "Dahling, you make delightful sense. And then you'll be at your house to cover for me in case she who brung me up should phone."

"If she phones before I get home, you're on your own, gal," Ellen said.

"A calculated risk."

"I don't much like it," Bobby said. "Suppose the four of us got caught. Okay, we could bluff. You know. Just having a happy young time. But if it's just you and me up there, Norma, and we get caught, all kinds of hell are going to break loose."

"And you'll have to marry me, won't you?" The ice was back in Norma's voice. "Does that distress you, dear? Or are you reminded of that old yuk about catching a streetcar."

"I didn't mean anything like that," Bobby said defensively.

"Then show a little more enthusiasm, dear. You're not exactly flattering."

"Knock it off, you two," Clyde said.

Ellen, conscious of the tension, was glad to be able to change the mood. She saw two high-school boys come in the door of the place. "Dig those cool threads," she said, in a parody of a local disc jockey who had a massive teen-age following. The boys were about sixteen, slight, sallow, dark-haired boys. They were dressed in their best. Pants cuffs so narrow they were fitted with zippers, pale jackets with lapels that rolled all the way down to the first button below the natural waistline, jackets that were tailored snugly across lean hips, shirts with tremendous collars dwarfing the black string ties. Their hair was long above the ears, brushed back. They went to the counter, moving with ultimate casualness, slow sophistication, and, before sitting on the stools, looked around the place with slow, complete disdain. Norma half stood up to see them over the back of the booth and then sat back down with an immediate attack of giggles. Ellen caught the infection. Bobby and Clyde started laughing. Ellen saw one of the boys look around at them, his face reddening. She tried not to look at them. She hoped they would think they were laughing at something else.

And Ellen was aware, even as she laughed, that had Clyde and Bobby been younger, were they still in high school, it was entirely possible that they would dress in a way that, though not as extreme, would show the influence of this latest fad, this rebirth of the prehistoric zoot suit, this sartorial derivative of what they now all seemed to call healthy music. But Clyde and Bobby were lost and gone into the Cornell costume, moccasins and white socks and flannels and padless shoulders, a uniform that seemed derived in equal parts from Dartmouth and Princeton. She recognized one of the boys and knew she had seen the other one around. The one she knew was Jack Sheddler, and she remembered that his father worked at the mill, had some sort of job in the office.

There was a derisive unpleasant note in Clyde's braying laughter, and Ellen put her hand on his arm to silence him. The young boys looked very uncomfortable, and Ellen was no longer amused.

"Please," Ellen said to Clyde.

He pulled his arm away and leaned across the table and said to Bobby, "A rolling stone gathers no moss."

"A penny saved is a penny earned," Bobby said.

"A stitch in time saves nine," Norma added. The two boys got up from the booth, Clyde carrying a half glass of coke.

"What were you saying?" Ellen asked Norma.

"Oh, it's a kind of a code. Coining phrases. Just watch. This will kill you."

As they walked behind the two boys on the stools, Bobby pretended to trip Clyde. Clyde stumbled awkwardly and the half glass of coke jetted onto the back of the brightest of the two jackets, the salmon-colored one the Sheddler boy wore.

Clyde turned around and roared at Bobby, "What the hell you tripping me for?"

"I didn't trip you. You fell over your own big feet."

Clyde turned to the two boys. They had turned around. The Sheddler boy looked as if he were close to tears. Clyde said, "All right, you wise guys. Which one of you tripped me?"

Ellen got quickly out of the booth and walked to the door and went out. She turned instinctively toward the jeep and then turned away from it and began walking down the shoulder of the highway, remembering after she had gone fifty yards that her racket and case were still in the jeep, but not wanting to go back after it. She kept thinking of the way the Sheddler boy had looked. It was funny the way they had come in and looked around, but maybe they had had that sneery look because they were maybe shy about the new clothes. Like the time her mother had taken those stitches in the front of her formal and she had gone into the girl's room and cut the stitches and pulled the thread out and then gone back out onto the floor, walking more boldly because she felt shy. This day had certainly dropped dead. This day was a mess. The Sheddler boy would have recognized her. Big deal. That Delevan girl with her college friends. Big older guys who threw coke on your new threads just for kicks. She felt ashamed. And she felt as if, all of a sudden, she didn't like Clyde anymore. Or Norma or Bobby. Or anybody she could think of.

She heard the feet, the sound of running coming behind

her, and she walked on, not looking around, neither
quickening nor slowing her pace. Clyde took her arm
roughly and pulled her around. His face looked heavier
and thicker, the way it always did when he got angry.

"Where do you think you're going?"

"As soon as you let go of my arm, I'm going home."

"What's the matter with you anyway?"

"You know what the matter is."

"That gag? You've got no sense of humor. You should
have heard Norma laugh."

"Norma likes a lot of things I don't like."

"What do those punk kids mean to you? Are they your
high-school boyfriends or something?"

"I just don't think it was funny."

He began to look uncertain. "Okay, so maybe it wasn't
exactly a riot. So what?"

"So it was cruel."

"Cruel! My God, I was doing the human race a favor.
Those punks, they're . . . unnatural." The jeep swung off
the road onto the shoulder close to them, Bobby at the
wheel.

"How you doing?" he asked.

"She didn't like the gag," Clyde said.

"Get in, honey," Norma said.

"I'm going home," Ellen said.

Clyde sighed heavily. He said, "I give up, Ellen. You
win. It wasn't a good thing to do and I'm sorry about it."

She looked at him searchingly. "Do you mean that?"

"Of course I mean it. I wouldn't say it if I didn't mean
it. I shouldn't have done it. We shouldn't have done it.
Right, Bobby?"

"Right!"

"Well . . . okay," Ellen said dubiously. Bobby and
Norma stood up and got over into the back. Clyde got
behind the wheel. Ellen went around and got in beside
him. Clyde found a hole in traffic and wrenched the jeep
out onto the highway again.

"We've got to make a grocery stop, old pal, old
buddy," Bobby said.

"Are you going to stay up there?" Ellen asked.

"She talked me into it," Bobby said. "She plain old ordinary talked me into it. I've got no sales resistance at all."

After they picked up the bag of food, Ellen found that she was in a better mood again. They sang on the way up to the camp. Dusk was on the way. The hills were blue. Clyde had a good, steady baritone.

When Brock was on his way back to the cottage to pick up Betty, he found himself hoping that Mrs. Yost would not be there, and that Betty would be the Betty of tennis court and pool. He had rechecked with Bess on the use of the car, told his mother he would be out for the evening, changed to good slacks and jacket. The sun had burned him just enough so that he was conscious of the scratch of his clothes against his body. There was a good soreness in his muscles, and the skin of his face felt tight.

The sun was nearly gone when he walked across the grass to the cottage. He could see a foursome holing out on the eighteenth, standing in the long-shadowed, grass-odored quiet, standing in an almost devotional patience for the cramped and measured click, the long, white run of the ball toward the hole while putter swayed in anguished guidance and far out on the rolling fairway the next group waited and swung the impatient flashing clubs at the inevitable dandelions. On the club terrace the clinked and chittered cocktail throng made insect sounds while waiters moved among them. And a woman's laugh was like something silvery and wild that flashed quickly through the long tree shadows.

She was sitting where her mother had been and she got up as he came toward her. She wore a white, fleecy skirt and a black sweater and green beads. In tennis clothes and in her swim suit there had been a suggestion of ranginess about her body, an illusively rawboned look. But dressed she looked softer, more feminine. She looked older and more poised. She looked very special.

"Mother left a few minutes ago," she said, as though she had been able to read his mind.

He felt awkward with her. "Got any suggestions?"

"This is your town."

"Well, it used to be. I've been away."

"Do you want a coke or a beer or something while we decide?"

"A beer would go fine," he said too heartily. "Can I help?"

"No thanks. You sit down. I'll bring them right out." Another chair had been brought out. He sat and waited, heard the chunk of the refrigerator door. She came out with a tall glass in each hand and he stood up and took one and lighted her cigarette and his own and they sat down and sipped, and smiled at each other.

"I like this time of day," he said.

"I don't know. Mornings I guess I like best."

"I'm a grouch in the morning. I don't seem to get up on my hind legs and operate until noon."

"I guess most people are that way."

There was a silence. He said, "Like Italian food?"

"Love it."

"There's a pretty good place down in Stockton. Then we could go to the drive-in movie on the way back."

"That sounds fine."

And that's the way the evening was. Too many silences. When they talked, they didn't say anything. He could think of no way in which he could make them say anything, nor did he know what it was he wanted to say. He felt inadequate with her. Too young for her. And he had the feeling that had he not met her mother, had there not been that incomprehensible scene, had they been able to go directly on from the poolside mood, it would have been fine. As it was, he felt as though both of them were discharging some unavoidable obligation in going out together, and were thus pledged to this quiet formality, this frigid sociability.

They ate and the food was good, candles in Chianti bottles, pepper seeds, meat sauce, spaghetti al dente, tart red wine, and hot sauce. They drove through the summery night and parked in the amphitheater of the shining cars, hooking the brassy speaker on the lowered window, sitting apart and watching the vast screen, digging into the buttery cooling popcorn in the box between them, careful to take alternate turns so that their hands did not meet. The big figures in impossible colors shifted and spoke and fought, and when it was ended, he turned on the parking lights and nosed out with the others in the obedient line which the traffic light released in thirty-car segments.

He drove her back and the cottage was dark and he did not know if her mother was still out or had returned and was in there asleep, her face in lined, simian repose, and did not wish to ask. He got out with her in the darkness and, with something near despair, reached and found her shoulders and pulled her toward him, kissing cool, unmoving lips and feeling the tension in her body, the restraint, almost to the point of her running away.

"I'm sorry," he said.

"It's all right. It's all right, Brock."

"It didn't seem to be," he said.

"I know . . . but I didn't mind."

"Now you can tell me you had a good time."

"You're mad at me now, aren't you?" she said, and he could not see her face in the darkness. "I had a good time, Brock. I did. In a way I can't tell you. Don't be mad."

"Okay. I'm sorry. I seem to keep saying that."

"Don't say it anymore. I'm sorry. For a lot of things." And she thrust herself quite quickly at his lips in a briefest of kisses, a sister-kiss, but with lips warm this time, and turning, she was gone, hand a whiteness waved, and nothing of her, just the white skirt and the white hands and faint suggestion of hair, disembodied. Until the cottage was lighted inside and he drove away, looking back to see her move across the lighted window, walking slowly.

He drove slowly back. Thoughtful. Curious. The evening had left an odd taste. It was the sort of evening that should keep you from ever wanting to come back for more. So you tell yourself, defiantly, a dim type. A damp lassie. A wilted wench. But knowing more than that. Seeing something behind it. So that it was all a barrier to be broken. So the thing could be seen clearly. And once seen, the very seeing would make a princess-change. The kiss in the brambly courtyard, and all the frozen things coming to life. And, driving there with a fifty-ish sedateness, he returned to knowledge of himself, and remembered that this was, indeed, no gleaming knight to awaken the virgin princess. Not with these lips besmirched. There were, of course, the prior adolescent investigations, those back seat, beach picnic, church cellar, hallway episodes, the darkened fluttering strainings —small spots on the armor, readily removed with E-Z-Way and steel wool. But this final corrosion was beyond the resources of any body and fender works. So you can't bitch, boy, if you get a dim evening from someone like her.

But for the first time he had forgotten for a little while. And that felt good.

And he wanted to go out with her again. Would go over to the club in the morning. Act like the last few minutes of the evening had not happened.

He put Bess's car in their garage. It was quarter to twelve. Their house was dark. He walked across the lawn to his house. The kitchen lights were on. He went in. There was no one in the kitchen. The rest of the house was dark. He guessed they had been left on for him. He started to turn them off.

His father's voice startled him. It came from the dark living room. "What did you say?"

"Leave the lights on, please." There was a funny note in his father's voice.

He went to the doorway, peering into the darkness. "Is something wrong? Where's Mom?"

"Sit down."

He felt his voice go thin and childish and the fear come up in his throat. "Has something . . . happened to Mom?"

"No. It's your sister. Don't interrupt. She isn't hurt or anything. I was late getting home. Your mother told me that Ellen was staying overnight with a friend of hers named Norma Franchard. You know her?"

"Yes. I saw her today. With Bobby Rawls, and Clyde and Ellen at the club."

"As your mother was cleaning up after dinner, she got a

phone call from Mrs. Franchard. She was calling to tell Norma something. Norma had asked permission to stay overnight here with Ellen."

"But——"

"We were frantic. I talked to Mr. Franchard. He said he would phone the Rawls' house and call me back. He did. Their son had phoned and said Clyde was taking him up in the jeep to their camp to stay overnight and get the camp open for the summer. Put the dock in the water and so on. No phone up there. Franchard told me that he and Mr. Rawls were leaving immediately to drive up there. We think the four of them are up there."

"Where did Mom go?"

"She drove over to stay with Mrs. Franchard until we get word."

They sat in the dark room. His father said sharply, bitterly, "I don't suppose you have a damn thing to say. I suppose this is just one of those things. A sign of the times or something."

Brock thought of how Ellen had looked, of Clyde sprinkling the grass on her, of how she had looked there, lazy-bodied and brown in the sun, physiologically a woman—labeled a child by the society into which he had been born. It made him feel a jealous illness.

"I don't believe it," he said with more firmness than he felt.

"Explain what you mean."

"There's a foul-up someplace. A misunderstanding."

"The kind of a misunderstanding I thought there was when that dean phoned me?"

"We're not talking about me. We're talking about Ellen. And if they did go up there——"

"If they went up there to stay all night, then what?"

But Brock had remembered the Norma-Bobby relationship. They had never made a secret of it with the other kids, not after that time way back when they had been sophomores in high school and Stella something-or-other's kid brother had caught them doing it in his tree house and they'd given the kid five dollars to keep his mouth shut but the kid had told Stella anyway, and she had told it all over the high school. So Brock didn't answer.

His father's voice was different when he spoke again from the darkness. Heavier. Sadder. "I'm talking about Ellen. And I'm talking about you too. And about Fred Harn's boy."

"Joey hung himself."

"That's what I mean. And the Selinger girl—they're trying to cure her drug addiction. And the Carroll boy killing those two old people with his father's car last year and trying to run. Harns, Selingers, Carrolls. They're good people. Good stock. They try to do what they think is right. Wilma and I have tried to do what we think is right." He sounded puzzled. "What the hell are people being punished for these days? What have we done?"

"I . . . don't know."

"There used to be a place for us. God, you have to work for something. Now it's like some force was trying to make us extinct. Eating our young. Breaking the bloodlines. Taking away pride. I read something a while back. Some fellow guessing as to what happened to the dinosaurs. He thought something pretty agile that liked to eat eggs developed. And they couldn't protect their eggs. So the egg eaters multiplied and then there were no more dinosaurs. There's something agile in the world that's eating our eggs. So what does it leave a man? Just work with no end result. No goal. I don't entirely go for this crap about leading your life for your children alone. A man has his own pleasures. But when things are rugged, children are one of the reasons why you keep plugging along. If that reason is gone, about all a man has left is just plain damn endurance."

The room was dark. It seemed a time of privacy. Of thinking out loud. Somehow, in spite of the worry about Ellen, it made for Brock a special moment. It brought his father, for the first time in his life, into perspective. So that he could truly see him. A stocky tired man whom he had shamed. And who was now being shamed again.

And encouraged by the darkness, warmed by this new vision, Brock said, "You can't talk to parents."

"Just what do you mean by that kind of a remark?"

"Don't get hard with me again or I can't say what I want to say."

"Go ahead. I'm interested in your opinions."

"I don't think you are, really. You want me to have your opinions. Not my own. You want me to think the way you think and believe in the things you believe. You can't make it so by wanting it to be so."

"You won't have to prove that statement, young man."

"There you go again. Okay, so maybe the kids are rough these days. I mean really rough. Not this kind of a jam. Or even the kind of a jam Ellen is in, if she is in one. I mean rough. Killing strangers to prove you're not chicken. I mean grabbing girls and ganging them. I mean busting up stuff all over just because you want to. I read what they say. They talk about broken homes and working mothers and overcrowded schools and low-paid teachers and television crime and comic books. Then why do the real rough ones come from all kinds of homes? I've thought about it. I mean, I've really thought about it."

"And you have the answer, I suppose."

Brock was emboldened by darkness. "You're damn well told I have the answer. It's because nothing can happen to anybody anymore. Nothing very good and nothing too bad. I'm not saying this right. You've got to try to understand. Nobody starves. The government takes care of that. And nobody makes a million. The government takes care of that too. So everybody is squashed right in the middle. Everybody gets to be alike. Take the things you can be. A doctor? So when I get to be one, I find out I'm working for the government. A businessman? Ulcers and taxes. A minister? Nothing in the churches but old ladies with hats and lots of politics. Government? Nuts. Anywhere you turn, you come out at the other end with a pension. So kids want to do crazy things. They get caught and some psychologist says they're just sick. I mean, Dad, suppose you had a big football game where they let you do anything but make a score. And let the other guy do anything except score on you. How hard is anybody going to play? You take my last year in high. We didn't even get marks, remember? You were either satisfactory or unsatisfactory. So with no marks, all you do is try to just get by. Look at George. He used to really try to build good houses. Now he's got some percentage designs and he just builds those. And take you. The harder you work the more money you make. The more you make, the more the government takes. So why not just look around for kicks?"

He sat back, flushed. After a long time his father said softly, "No penalties and no rewards. That's the way you look at it?"

"That's the way I look at it."

"And there's no . . . kicks in the old words. Decency, a sense of personal honor. Respect. Self-sacrifice."

"That's twisting it. I wasn't talking about me. I guess those words mean something to me. But they don't to most people. Most kids, I mean. And when you haven't got those words, there has to be something else to keep you in line. And what used to keep them in line is gone now."

"I'd like to think those words meant something to you and Ellen."

"I think maybe they mean more to Ellen than they do to me."

"Is that a car coming?"

They both got up. Brock heard the familiar sound coming up the hill.

"Jeep," he said. "Could be Clyde's."

It turned into their drive and the lights were turned off. They heard steps on the gravel and a heavy voice say something, and heard Ellen say in a waspish voice, "Don't bother. *Please* don't bother!"

There was a surly grunt and the jeep engine started again and the wheels skidded viciously on the gravel.

They went into the kitchen and Ellen came in. Her eyes looked puffy. She carried the blue case and her tennis racket. There was a long, fresh scratch on her chin and a bruised place under her eye and her hair was mussed.

"Exactly where have you been?"

She looked at her father, startled. "I've been out with that— Oh, gosh!"

"What's the matter?"

"I forgot to phone. I was . . . going to stay with Norma and then I decided not to."

Brock had moved off to one side. He could see his father's face. "You're lying, Ellen."

Ellen flushed. "Yes, I guess I am."

"Mrs. Franchard phoned here. You better tell the truth."

Ellen put the case and the racket on the kitchen table. She spoke quickly. "They had this idea—about the four of us going up and staying in Bobby's family's camp overnight. A dumb idea, I guess, and we were—the girls, that is—to make out like we were staying at each other's house. I was the last one to phone and Mom said I could and then . . . well, walking back to where they were, I thought it would not be the right thing to do and I guess to be perfectly honest I was scared and so I told them Mom said no instead of yes like she said, and then we drove up there just to leave Norma and Bobby up there and we were going to go pick them up in the morning, but as far as I'm concerned, Clyde can go pick them up by himself. As far as I'm concerned, Clyde can take himself a big running leap and drop dead."

"What happened to your face?"

"I fell."

"Call your mother, Brock, and tell her Ellen is home and she's okay."

"Where's Mom?"

"Over staying with Mrs. Franchard while Mr. Franchard and Mr. Rawls are making a trip up to that camp."

As Brock hurried to the phone he heard his sister say, in an awed voice, "Oh, brother!"

He got hold of Mrs. Franchard first and then his mother. He gave her the message. She started to ask questions he couldn't answer, and then said she'd be right home. As he had been talking he had heard the low voices of his father and Ellen in the kitchen. When he went back out he saw Ellen smiling and he knew that things were all right. She'd always been able to get around the old man. And never got away with anything with Mom. It worked just the other way with him. The books said it was supposed to be that way. But it seemed funny sometimes.

Ellen, still smiling, moved gingerly onto the offensive. "I guess I ought to be kind of mad about you thinking I'd do that, Dad, stay up there all night."

"And I could have a few things to say about you running around with a couple who will stay up there— would have stayed up there."

Ellen took the new advantage. "I'm through with them. They're sickening. So is Clyde." Her face began to break up. "Oh, why can't we all go away from here? I just hate it here. I hate it!" And she fled. They heard the door of her room bang. A few minutes later his mother drove in, came hurrying into the house, asked where Ellen was, and went off toward Ellen's room. His father asked him to please put the car away. When Brock got back into the kitchen, his father was pouring two glasses of milk.

He gave Brock a twisted smile. "Confusing evening. Milk?"

"Thanks." Brock took it and sat on the counter near the sink. His father leaned against the refrigerator.

"You were right about Ellen, Brock."

"She's okay. She's a little mixed up."

"What about that Clyde?"

"I don't much like him. I never have. He goes around bulging his muscles. I guess he's okay, though."

"But if Ellen had agreed to stay up there, he would have liked that?"

"Why not? I don't like him, but he isn't crazy."

His father frowned. "Is that the attitude you all have? About nice girls?"

"If they won't, they won't. If they will, they will."

"That's pretty damn cynical, son."

"Is it? I never thought about it. Look, Dad, suppose I look around for something to do this summer."

"I hoped you would. But I wasn't going to mention it."

"Then enlist in the fall. They're going to come after me sooner or later. I can get that over with and then be squared away to try to get in school someplace when I get out. What do you think?"

"I want you to finish college. I don't care when or how, but I want you to finish."

"I want to. I thought I knew what I wanted to do. Now I'm not so sure. So maybe with a break in the middle, I'll be smarter about what courses I want later on."

"Your mother isn't going to like it."

"I figured that."

"Let's sleep on it."

"Sure. Night now."

"Good night, Brock." And there was a tentative touch on his shoulder in parting, the first shy gesture of affection since Fiasco. Brock went to his room. He heard the muted feminine voices of sister and mother. The affectionate gesture had pleased him. But, as he prepared for bed, the pleasure faded. He realized that for a brief time in the dark living room he had talked directly and honestly, as himself. But in the bright kitchen he had slipped into a new role. The staunch penitent. The noble prodigal. Good God! A job that would louse up the summer completely. And then basic training to top it off. All that had been spur of the moment, like a toddler holding up a newly found green leaf in hopes of a pat on the head.

After his light was out, he lay in darkness and wondered if he were truly totally lacking in that something called sincerity. Play a moody part for a time and then slide from that into temporary honesty and then into a new part. Now he would have to be bluff and cheery and brave for a long time. What in hell was it that he really wanted? What were you supposed to want? Approval? He had placed a big mortgage on the future to obtain a tiny morsel of that. Maybe the best thing to want was no trouble. Smooth and easy. Food and a sack and some records to play and some thoughts to think and a girl to chase.

After the boy had gone to bed, Ben sat in the silent kitchen, the empty glass, milk-streaked, in front of him. He thought of his daughter. He had wanted to go with the other two men but had not quite dared. For fear of what they would find. Fear of himself and how he would react if they found it. For it was more than protection of the sweet young daughter. There was, and perhaps there had to be in these years of their father-daughter lives, a faint yet not unhealthy tinge of the incestuous. Both he and she becoming aware, almost simultaneously, of her as woman. And so in the rage which he feared, there would be the murderous intent of the betrayed, as well as the fever of the protective parent. He well knew that one day she would marry. And the wedding night would be, to him, a form of peculiar torture. A physical jealousy that could not be admitted.

And so he had not dared go up there. And had been reprieved.

But the true oddness of the evening was in the boy. The way Brock had talked had given Ben a strange nostalgia for his own youth, for those years when you thought often about the why of things, when philosophical discussions lasted until dawn. I think, therefore I am. What is God? All those old thoughts had slept uneasily in his mind.

Brock's words had brought them awake again, to stand on awkward legs, blinking at the light. What Brock had been saying was basically the old discussion of good and evil. It hid behind new words. Purpose and lack of purpose. Creation and destruction. Meaningfulness and lack of meaning. Once upon a time it had been the most important problem in all the world, in all of life.

But you grew up. And grew into acceptance, not of good and evil, but of a world in which they were so curiously intermixed, so mutually interdependent, that it became far easier to accept the inevitability of all compromise. Or was it because it just became so much more comfortable *not* to think.

You could not go into the men's bar at the club and start talking about the meaningfulness of existence. Not sober, at least. You would embarrass them and, perhaps, alarm them. An old friend would take you aside and suggest a physical checkup.

Or start the same discussion with your wife and she

would interpret it as a general dissatisfaction with life, and she would put it in her personal frame of reference and see an implied criticism of her.

There wasn't anybody to talk to anymore. Even when your own son opened the subject, you could not talk to him without attempting to instruct or command.

So the thoughts went to sleep. You kept them quiet. You made them sleep. If they started to stir in their sleep, they could be safely Miltowned or martinied. Or eclipsed by the excitement of the new flesh of a stranger.

These are the things that put the doubts to sleep, but there are other ways to weaken them if they stir into wakefulness. Repetition, endlessly, that life *has* to be good. Because the white walls are pristine, because the dishwasher kills germs as well as washes the dishes, because the lawns are free of crabgrass this year, because there was enough left after taxes to buy some more Hudson Fund, because the doctor stood—grave, smiling, bakelite of the stethoscope hanging against starchy white— saying you were healthy as a horse [why is it always a horse?], because the joke you were dubious about, the joke that kicked off the speech [the tightrope walker and the four-dollar beer] convulsed them all, because the newsletter reports that dealers' stocks are moving rapidly, that retail sales are up 2.7 percent over the same month last year, that rails and motors are leading a market resurgence, because the twenty-pay-life is at last paid up, yes, yes, because of all these things it is good and it has to be good, and nobody has it any better, and no generation in any time of history ever had it any better, it has to be good, and pray leave us have no juvenile, adolescent, sophomoric maunderings about truth and beauty, good and evil, and man's destiny. Merely be the little engine that could, that has, and is, and will continue to be.

And what has this got to do with that so cold and so functional Thomas Marin Griffin, he who walks his jungle paths alone with never the click of claws or gnawing sound of teeth, and who now in all fairness and honesty and remorseless logic is waiting to chew you up and spit out something that is no longer you—is instead a man in a bright shirt and beaked, straw cap and fat legs sunburned, fishing from a tidal bridge, and boring his neighboring catcher of sheepshead, and grunting stories of ancient glory, of ivoried splendor of work sheets which now mellow and yellow in the green file, of warrior methods of forgotten sales meetings, of bold jousting with obsolescence. Saying it just right. To convey shrewdness without self-glorification. To hint of this and that, dropping names that land solidly. And one of the names would be, of course, Thomas Marin Griffin.

He looked around the kitchen with the sudden impression, close to alarm, that he was in a strange place, in a room he did not know. And his heart hastened with an excitement he did not understand. Then he got up and rinsed the glass and set it on porcelain with a tiny click and turned out the lights, the mercury switches soundless, and went to bed, hearing wife and daughter still talking in low voices, wondering what they still found to say to each other, wondering if he would sleep well and hoping that he would because this had been a bad day, all in all, and Friday would not be any easier.

After her mother had gone, and after the lights were out, Ellen sat up and flounced her pillow and turned onto her side, palms flat together and under her cheek, knees hiked high, feeling the warmth of herself in bed and trying to think only of coziness and warmth and curled up and warm and soft and each slow breath like falling softly off something into deeper warmth and softness.

Then she grunted and rolled over onto her back, flapping one arm down in exasperation, lying spread and rigid and wondering. What would it have been like?

The boys had brought their trunks and took a swim in the dusk-cold lake, the frigid, spring-fed lake, while she and Norma had made the sandwiches, feeling very housewifey in the old camp kitchen, giggling at the barbarisms of the camp equipment, and then the boys had come howling and blue up into the camp, into the kitchen, jumping and flapping in an agony of coldness, and the sun-golden hair of arms and legs pasted flat, but springing and curling and standing out again when towel-rubbed. Clyde had built the big fire in the fireplace and then they had dressed and Bobby had poked around, muttering and slamming cupboard doors until at last with cry of triumph had held aloft the bottle, almost full, saying that now they could get warm on the inside too.

So the boys had drunk a lot of it and Norma almost as much and she just enough so she felt far away from herself, numb-lipped, making faraway laughter at everything and nothing. So that the sandwiches were things eaten in a half-remembered state. And somehow time got mixed up so that a second was a long, long time. Or an hour was nearly nothing. So that she was on the floor, curled, facing the fire, Clyde behind her, knees against the backs of her knees, arm around her, so that the fire coals were steady warmth against the front of her, and Clyde warming close the back of her, and she kept drifting off and coming back with a start when his hands would move on her and she would push them away, not wanting to be touched, but just held like this.

Then pushing his hands away became too much trouble and she let him touch her, and the touch made things seem to slowly shift and melt inside her, made her feel as if she were enormously heavy, a sweet-swollen, dreamy, helpless thing there, unprotesting when he turned her around so gently, and his lips were stone against the soft membrane of her own lips. And then it began to turn into a fumbling, into an awkwardness of fumbling that broke the mood, so that she frowned against his lips. Then heard, in the camp stillness, in the night-lake silence, an odd sound, an odd regular sound. It could not be translated and then, in a moment of shock and horror she realized that it was the dogged, insensate, blinded creak of springs of one of the old camp beds in the nearby bedroom, and she began to fight Clyde silently and with all her strength. He fought to take her. They grunted and gasped, rolling dangerously near the fire, and she wrested one arm free and hammered twice at his stone face with her fist, holding it as though she were stabbing with a knife. Then, wiggling free and pulling her leg out from under him and half rising to run as he caught her ankle, she fell but pulled free and rolled and jumped up and backed away.

She stood, breathing hard, her eyes watering from the sting of the bump of her cheekbone against the floor. With Clyde ten feet away, sitting on his heels, braced with one knuckled hand, arm straight, against the floor in front of him, the pose of a football lineman, though horridly different, and no light but the red coals so that half his face was red and the other half in blackness, and the creaking had stopped.

It was a frozen time and she felt the stony purpose of him there, waiting for him to come at her, thinking that when he moved, she would grab the chair near her right hand and hurl it at his legs and take that moment to run out into the night.

But it seemed to stop in him as suddenly as a motor stops. He stood up slowly, turning away from her, fixing his clothing.

"You better take me back now," she whispered.

"Damn you, Ellen. Damn you to hell." His voice was too loud.

"Just take me back," she said. "Don't talk to me. Just take me back home."

"Suppose I don't want to?"

"I'll go out to the highway and hitchhike."

"You would, wouldn't you?"

"Yes, I would."

"Just tell me one thing. What are you saving it for? What makes you think you're so damn invaluable? You ought to wake up. You better snap out of it, kid. I don't like a teaser. You don't know how close you came to taking a hell of a beating."

"You scare me, Clyde. See how I'm shaking? I'm terrified."

"Oh, shut up."

"I'll be out in the jeep," she said, and went out and off the porch and glanced up at the stars, beyond which, in childhood, had sat an old old man with beard and white robe and look of pity and mercy. She heard him yell to

Bobby that they were leaving. He came out and thumped into the jeep.

He drove silently, with a vicious recklessness. They did not speak. He passed wherever he came to a slower moving car, close to hill chests, close to curves. She knew he was waiting for her to object. She had often complained about his driving. She sat with her hands clasped in her lap, squeezing them together at the dangerous places until her knuckles hurt.

She sensed from his driving, as they neared Clayton, that his mood was changing. As they neared the Jolly Pig Stand he asked gruffly, "Barbecue?"

"No thank you."

He did not speak again until they were nearing her house. His voice was softer. "All I can say, Ellen, is I'm sorry as hell. I guess it was the bourbon. Or the fire or something. I got out of control. I'm really sorry, kid."

"I'm afraid that as far as I am concerned, that is an entirely meaningless statement. I couldn't possibly care less."

"Aw, Ellen. Snap out of it, kid. I said I'm sorry."

"And that ends it, I suppose. Now I'm supposed to get all flushed and rosy and grateful and let you kiss me. I'll put it in language you can understand: The hell with that noise, buster."

She took her things and got out of the jeep.

"I'll give you a ring tomorrow. We got to talk this over."

She was walking away. She turned and said, "Don't bother. *Please* don't bother!"

And that was it. The record of a truly dreadful day. Dreadful all the way around. And she remembered that he was there in the bedroom, in the darkness, grinning at her. She went over and fumbled for his picture and found it, and folded up the stand and lowered it soundlessly into the plastic wastebasket and hurried back to bed. There were things to send back. The Christmas bracelet. The little musical box. The three Brubeck records.

Once she had decided to wrap them up and get them mailed, she felt vastly better. And she began to wonder if she had ever really liked him. Lots of times he had been fun. He was the most fun in games—tennis and swimming and golf. Not so much fun when there was a party with dancing and so on. But it had always been nice to be his girl. Because he was big and everybody knew him, and a lot of the kids had been after him. But liking him, really and truly. Well, there was something about him that was so ... so darn beefy. Thick-like. And never shy or humble or anything. Almost but not quite a wise guy. It would happen someday, but not with him. With somebody different. Dark and shy and gentle and humble and loving. Sort of a Gregory Peck type. Ethereal, sort of. Not like Clyde who sort of made you think of a bull or something. You kind of instinctively knew that if it was Clyde the first time, it would hurt something awful. Because he was so impatient about everything.

And then she started to think of Norma and Bobby and how it was inevitable that they would be caught in bed together, and what a hideous scene it had probably been up there, with Norma crying and Mr. Franchard cursing and raving and Mr. Rawls all ashamed and bitter about it. It would be awful. Norma would make it easier on herself by blubbering. She could start crying anytime she wanted to, just like that. Well, the group was gone now, for good. Today had busted it all up. Today had ruined a lot of things but it had made things easier, too, in a funny way. I wish we could leave this darn place. All of us. Just go away and never come back because I am truly desperately sick of it.

She sat up and flounced the pillow again and tried the other side, hands under her cheek, knees high. All warm and soft and sleepy and like falling. . . .

Wilma Delevan was awake and thinking of what Ben had mumbled to her when she had come to bed. So odd, a question like that.

"Willy?"

"Yes, dear. I thought you were asleep."

"Willy, are you having a good time? I mean are things the way you want them?"

"What a funny question!"

"Well, I just wondered."

"I guess I just don't think about it. I . . . I wish you didn't have to work so hard. And I wish you and Brock would get along better. And I wish Ellen would make some different friends. She needs to make new friends. Those other children are too old for her. She's easily led, you know. Impressionable. I wonder if we ought to keep her another year before she goes away to school. She could take postgraduate at the high school and learn typing and things like that, and it would be good for her." She stopped and heard Ben's heavy sleep-breathing.

For a moment she felt annoyed, and then it changed to a feeling of being puzzled. It was an odd question for him to ask.

"I'm happy," she whispered into the sleeping night. And with a shade of defiance she whispered gain, "I'm a happy woman."

And then lay as though waiting for something or somebody to give her an argument.

Chapter Nine

A girl of twenty-five with tousled, pale hair awoke in a strange room knowing only that her sleep had been heavy and the room was strange and her name was Susan Walton. Sleep had been so heavy that curiosity stirred sluggishly, and it was not important to know more. She shifted a bit and her naked hip came in contact with warm flesh and in that microsecond of first contact she knew at once that she was Susan Delevan, in love, on her honeymoon, in a Washington hotel room on a sunny morning in June, now warmly and safely married, and in a little while Robbie would be awake and then they would make morning love on this sunny morning, and it was a good thing to think about, both before and after, because it was a thing that truly kept improving with them even after you had definitely decided that you stood on the highest peak of all.

She moved gingerly away from him, not wanting him awake yet, removing the contact which might bring him up out of sleep in his ready need.

It was a nice luxury not to have to get up and become the brushed and brisk Miss Walton, she of the quick neat heel-tapping sound down the governmental corridor, bright hair strained back and bunned so tightly it seemed to tilt her gray eyes, all trimly and sexlessly girdled under the neat office clothes, the efficient and decorative and discreet Miss Walton, unfrivolous and highly valued for her tact and accuracy and promptness.

Yet it was a luxury tinged a bit with sadness because she had enjoyed the role. She had been hired in Washington when she was nineteen. CAF-2. Clerk-typist. Assigned to the Pentagon, to a subcommittee of the National Security Resources Board. After all the sympathy notes had been answered and the flowers acknowledged, back there in Cleveland. She had sold the house in which she had been born, sold the house and everything in it except what could be placed in two heavy suitcases, and she had purchased her one-way bus ticket to Washington, checked the bags at the station, taken the bus to the cemetery for one last look at the plot, at the old grave of Dad, the older grave of Bud, the raw new grave of Mother. And stood there and said a silent prayer that her life would not be as theirs had been, that her home would not be a place of sullen strain, of concealed bickering, of raw-nerved continual warfare that deprived the children of a chance to love them.

And got a seat by the window of the bus, and got off at one in the morning in Washington and took a taxi to the Y.W.C.A., and the next day made arrangements to transfer the substantial bank balance to a local bank, and rented a pleasant room with surprising ease, and settled herself in, and went to the Commission the next day, was tested and hired, and began work right after lunch for a very young man with an air of international importance.

The tensions that had soured her home during childhood had made her alert, watchful, secretive—quick-moving, with closed face, immaculately clean in body and habit. And it had given her a taste for intrigue, an instinctive perception of mood, an almost chameleonlike knack of melting into background and emerging at precisely the right time. It was these attributes, acquired for self-preservation, which had made her so quickly successful in government work. She inspired trust and never betrayed it. She gave any office a look of efficiency and importance. Yet she never let herself forget that she wished to be married. She never let herself be deluded into thinking that the world of files and reports, corridors and buck slips was her predestined environment.

She soon found that Washington was a city of attractive young women who shared her own desire. They pursued their objective in many ways, ways that had only the common denominator of ruthlessness. Sometimes she despised herself for this carefully calculated future, sensing a coldness of purpose. Then, alone in her bed at night, touching her soft breasts, she would know it was not coldness but the need for warmth and love and safety. And in the morning she would search her face, looking at the skin around her eyes, the skin of her throat, looking for the hard tiny lines, the look of crepe that would be the first sign of the hardening into a rigid spinsterhood amid the organization charts, the babble of officialese, the terror of departmental budgets.

For a time out of loneliness and despair she drifted into a halfhearted affair with a lean and melancholy naval officer who sat slunched deep in chairs and fingered his hawk nose and said wry things that made her want to laugh and cry.

Finally there came a day when, after she had worked up through many ratings and had become an administrative assistant to an important man, that man offended someone he should have flattered. And she stood nearby, feeling sad, as the big wise bumbling man cleared out his

own desk, wishing to do that little task himself, already
speaking in his soft growling voice about being back in
industry where, by God, he belonged and should never
have left in the first place.

And looked up at her and slanted a hairy eyebrow and
said, "Suzy, how about coming with me?"

"I really appreciate that. But thanks . . . no, sir."

"What do you really want, Suzy? Everybody wants
something most."

And to her own horror she blurted, "I guess I want to
get married."

He had grinned at her. "Tough proposition right here,
Suzy. Let me see. Resignation or no, I can still do a little
something. You better not hear this phone conversation,
child. Wait in the other office."

After a time he came out and winked at her and said,
"All set, but you don't know anything about it."

Twenty days later she was in Rome with State, learning
the clerical intricacies of visas and quotas and permits.

Even the sound of the name of the city now made her
feel slightly ill. That year had been a fiasco. Not
professionally. Her work had been praised. She had
worked even after her heart had been torn and trampled,
worked harder than before. A complete emotional fiasco.
She should have known. She sensed the selfishness in him
in the very beginning. But he had that warmth. Mike, he
of warmth and good laughter and the sensuous strength
that pulled her down with him into that small spring-
blinded world, into an affair which, she had believed,
shook both of them and brought them together for forever. But she learned that she had been the only one who
had been shaken. That it was Mike who always knew all
the words and who could pretend to anything, and who,
when restlessness moved him again, got up from her bed
and mildly and apologetically, and even shyly, said
farewell and it has all been dandy. As directionless and
unguidable as a breeze in summer. Not cruel, even kind.
But utterly free, and that was the way he wanted to be
and the way he would forever be until he was an old man,
and even then there would always be people around him

because of that warmth and his innate courtesy and the way everyone always liked him.

When the transfer to Mexico City had come through, she had left Rome in much the same mood as she had left Cleveland nearly five years before—with an intensity of cold purpose and a refusal to look back. She went in with two other girls in an apartment in Chapultepec. Tile floors and deep narrow windows and always the smell of charcoal burning. Mexico City was high and clear and bright, and it was there that she first saw the hard little lines barely visible around her eyes. And in the bathroom with its too high ceiling, and the cranky *rapido* for hot water, which was anything but, she had locked the door and stripped and stood on the closed toilet lid, looking back over her shoulder, feeling more than a little ridiculous, but wanting to look at the backs of her thighs, suspecting even before she saw them the little puckered areas where the flesh had lost young firmness, a matching condition to the slight but noticeable sagging of her breasts where tissues had been weakened by the years of the taut constrictions deemed suitable for office wear.

She had wept later. Not from any idea that the chance had passed her by. She knew she would marry. But the gifts were less. They had been lessened by the morose naval officer and by Mike and by the years. And so the bargain she could make would be less good and someone as yet unknown had been cheated in a way in which she had not intended to cheat him.

Remembering the tears, with Robbie asleep there beside her on this sunny morning, she smiled in a rueful way at the Susan of those first weeks in Mexico City. Because not long after that she had met Robbie. To walk hand in hand with him down Juarez and into the park across from the Del Prado. To drive in that brisk little MG that belonged to his Chief of Mission out to the Plaza de Toros on Sunday afternoons at four for the drinking of manzanilla, the whistles when the torero danced fearfully away. To have dinner at Jena, or El Parador, or Las Casuelas with its raucous music on the absurdly tiny balcony over the tables. To eat, with a sense of danger and daring, the freshly opened oysters from Vera Cruz at the little restaurant in the public market. To walk and talk about everything under the sun. And they rode the hills in the little car and picnicked at high places and smelled the wood smoke made by the charcoal men and were in love. She could not tire of looking at him. The good brow and the good jaw and the darkness. His apartment was next to that of his Chief of Mission so they could not go there. And they could not use her apartment. And a Mike-born caution made her squelch so firmly his first tentative suggestion about a weekend at the Hotel Victoria in Taxco that he made no such suggestion again. Yet she felt that even had she accepted, they would still have been married. But it was a point that she was glad that she had not tested, even if it did seem to give marriage the flavor of an asking price.

They exchanged confidences. She knew he was not such a fool as to think her a virginal twenty-five. He told her of a silly-sounding affair in New York, and a rather grotesque-sounding intrigue of long ago. She suspected more but rested content with that. And told him of Mike, making it longer ago as it had been too recent, changing his name, leaving his character relatively intact, and killing him off in a satisfactorily heroic way in the war. Even watered down, it turned him pale with physical jealousy.

He told her of his family. She told him of hers, and told him the entire truth of it, so that he wept at the vision of the quick, pale, light-stepping girl in that Cleveland house of acid things, because more than she meant to tell of it had gotten into her voice, more than she had ever told anyone.

Now warmly, safely, and excitedly married. More than the bald word. Married to Robbie—which gave a different impact to the word. Made it more than that goal so long sought. More than what had either been bargained for or, perhaps, deserved.

Tomorrow she would meet the family and that would be a serious and important thing.

She turned in a stealthy way so that she could watch

him asleep. It gave her a vague feeling of guilt to watch him sleeping, and gave her pleasure.

Yes, this was the giving up of the crisp and brisk Miss Walton. And she was realist enough to know that many aspects of that life would be missed. Yet, as she had begun to understand Robbie, begun to see what he was, the sort of person he was, she detected that taint of weakness in him. It did not make her love him less. Rather love him more because she knew that only through his weakness could there be for her an outlet for her own executive and administrative talents, her efficiency, her subtlety, her knack of gentle guidance. Were he a strong and determined and self-sufficient man, marriage would be less satisfying. To be so objective as to be almost cruel to Robbie, she could characterize him as a large and amiable and decorative man who had been reasonably successful in his chosen field merely because of his impeccable background, knack of light conversation, willingness to take orders, and lack of any dangerously observable ambition. He was a good aide.

Perhaps, as she had been looking for him, he had been looking for her. Looking in foreign places. And now, having found her, wished to carry her back proudly to the place from whence he had come. It would, she knew, be a good life for them. He was confident that his older brother, his half-brother, would take him into the family firm. There would be a house to build, his career to guide, a social stature to attain, children to have. A good warm safe life, and in this home there would be laughter and there would be love and the ready evidence of love. It would be the home she had made believe about those times when they used to lock her in her room.

His weakness was not in any way offensive, because he was not aware of it. He believed in his own strength of purpose because he had nothing to measure it against. Ruthless people and ruthless actions puzzled and annoyed him. He was sure of his place in the world and thus was not easy to hurt or disconcert. She knew that she would maintain his own illusions for him so long as they both should live. She seemed to amuse him when she seemed

slightly vague. And he obviously liked to have her ask
him questions. Very well. The role she accepted was the
role he wanted.

She lay watching him and marveled at the length of his
eyelashes. His night-grown beard bristled in delightful
maleness. There was a little scar at the corner of his
mouth. She had never noticed it before. She would ask
him what caused it. There was a nostril hair which
fluttered at each exhalation. A pockmark over his right
brow. Several enlarged pores at the base of his nose. All
the mysteries of maleness here sleeping beside her while
she watched and thought of many things. And smiled at
him. And now stopped thinking of things with that alert
and ready mind and began to think with the tissues and
fibers of her body. Began the thoughts of his hands and
of the breadth of his smooth back and of the strength of
his long thighs, and felt then the good tingling of herself,
the tiny glowings, the muted throat-tightening inner
shiftings. And leaned over and pressed her lips against his
sleeping ones, her eyes open so that she saw his eyes flash
wide open and then his lips came alive under hers, and his
eyes narrowed from their surprise, crinkling a bit, and she
whispered good morning against his mouth as his hands
found her and were good against her.

Chapter Ten

When George Furmon awoke on Friday morning, he
was immediately aware that something important had
happened the night before, and before he remembered
what it had been, he knew that it had been important and
troublesome and not flattering.

He remembered then and rolled over heavily in his bed
and saw that she was not yet up, was in fact sleeping. She

faced him, her mouth grave and still and her eyes shadowed in sleep, looking younger than she had any right to look, and looking like a stranger, which he felt was obscurely unfair. Her arm was bare, elbow bent, the hand made into a loose fist, which rested near her chin.

The clock was on the night table between their beds. It faced her. He reached out and turned it around and saw that the alarm would go off in another ten minutes. He reached out cautiously a second time and turned the alarm off. And frowned at her.

It had been a damn funny evening. She had acted a bit strange when he had come home. He kept catching her staring at him. Fourteen years of marriage had generated considerable caution and he made a brief survey of his conscience and began to feel a bit indignant because his conscience was quite clear. After Mrs. Bailey had been taken down to the village and after Sandy was asleep, Alice began to make frequent trips to the kitchen, coming back each time with an alarmingly potent-looking highball. That was totally unlike her. By nine o'clock she had definitely started to come apart. Her face had fallen into a new pattern, a looseness.

He threw his magazine aside and said, "What the hell are you trying to do to yourself?"

"Courage. That's what. Courage out of a bottle, dear."

"Courage for what?"

"Con . . . confession."

Sharp alarm pierced him and faded quickly as he quieted his own unreasonable fear and managed a smile. "What have you been up to, girl?"

She laughed and it was a laugh that was not like her. "It's what I haven't been up to. Isn't that funny. A sin of omiss . . . omission."

"Okay," he said patiently. "What haven't you done?"

"Don't look at me. Look other way, dear. Then let me talk and talk."

She rambled on for a long time. Her voice was blurred, and sometimes the sentences didn't end at all. He looked rigidly at the wall. Though her words were blurred, there was no mistaking her meaning. Frigidity. Pretense. All

these years. And the feeling that he had gone away from
her somehow. Not sharing any significant part of his life
with her. Restlessness. Walks. And today something
confused about seeing a young farmer and his wife. He
couldn't quite get that part of it. But whatever it was she
saw, or hadn't seen, had given her a new look at herself,
or something like that, and now maybe for the first time
she was ready to be a part of the physical side of
marriage, but she couldn't be if she didn't have his help
and his patience, and please help her, and please let her
share more of his life. Rambling and rambling into a lot
of incoherence that ended in tears. It wasn't a damn bit
like Alice. My God, she even looked sort of messy. And it
was an awful blow to a man's pride to find out that all
these years, all these fourteen lousy years she had just
been enduring him and pretending to like it just to make
him feel okay about doing it. A hell of a blow to your
pride. Like being told you were impotent or something.

And so he had taken her up to bed, and it had been the
damnedest situation imaginable. Such a long drawn-out
business. And her crying again and saying it was no use,
she couldn't, she couldn't and it was a mistake to tell him
and all. But him persisting, almost out of some sort of dull
and obstinate anger, fraying his own nerves, exhausting
himself, but being gentle and patient and not letting her
quit until finally, to his enormous relief, all the rising
shuddering tension went out of her unmistakably, and she
made a strange cry that he had never heard from her
before. And thanked him and thanked him in a dull,
blurred voice making him feel embarrassed and strange,
and then cried softly for a short time, crying her way into
sleep.

The damnedest night he'd ever spent. A man didn't
know where the hell he was. Stranger still when you
thought that after fourteen years of marriage this was the
first actual sexual experience she had had. Ridiculous.
And he wished he didn't feel like such a damned fool
about it.

Now there was this other stuff, about shutting her out
of his life. He wondered why he should have the crazy

feeling that he'd shut both of them out of his life. Man couldn't shut himself out of his own life, could he?

He got up with bearlike stealth and lumbered into the bathroom. He patted his belly disapprovingly. Got to get some of this lard off. Three months over forty. Too young for all this slob. Tough on the heart. Shortens your life. And can't be so damn appetizing for her to have to look at all this fat gut. That was an entirely new thought and it shocked him a little. My God, George, instead of just talking about it to yourself every morning, why don't you *do* something about it. Get along without all those calories that come in a bottle for a while. Why spend your evenings in a fat stupor? That can't be much fun for her either. God knows she was no prize after the sixth drink last night. You any different? Any better?

It was hard to realize that it was Alice in there still sleeping. You adjust to one woman and then find out you have a different one to deal with. Had her all sized up. Good-looking girl you could take anywhere. [Don't take her out much, though.] Not a hell of a lot of sparkle to her but nice manners. A little on the cool-acting side. Never thought of her as frigid. Just not too eager for a romp. Sure she disapproved of a lot of things, but you were doing all right by her and the kids. Where's the complaint?

You know damn well where it is, George.

Funny that it should seem like it was the first time, last night, that either of them had really talked for years and years.

And that wasn't right. It wasn't fair. To either of them. They used to talk. Good talk. Lots of it. Fun, too.

After his shower, when he went back into the bedroom, she was in her robe and sitting at her dressing table, brushing her hair. She gave him a quick guilty glance and her face turned pink and she got up quickly and came to him and hid her face against his chest.

"Oh, George, I'm so ashamed."

"No need to be."

"I got awful messy, I know. But ... I had to or I couldn't say what I had to say."

"I'm glad you said it. You should have said it a long time ago."

"I've cheated both of us, George. I . . . love you."

"I love you too, Alice."

"I'm saying the word a different way. I really love you."

"Fourteen years married and we start the morning like this?"

She looked up at him, her face still red. "One day married, George. If you want to help me pretend."

"I want to. It's a hell of a lot of time wasted, though."

"Not wasted, really. Maybe it couldn't have happened before. But . . ." She hid her face against him again. ". . . easier next time. I feel . . . well, like Christmas morning and looking under the tree."

"For gosh sakes!"

"Don't you *dare* laugh at me, George. Don't you *dare!*"

"I won't."

"You should, though. I'm a silly woman."

"Look, girl. How about this. Let's take a trip. The two of us. Talk Bailey into staying here with Sandy."

"Let's!" she cried and looked up at him eagerly.

He looked at her, puzzled. "You know, you are a damn good-looking female."

"Pish and tush."

An hour later he drove up to the job on Hillside Heights where he was building four houses on speculation. He hummed to himself as he parked the car and walked across the raw dirt of an excavation. He stooped and looked around him. It did not look the way it had looked yesterday. He had the feeling that he was not looking at it with the same eyes he had used yesterday.

Janitz, the foreman in charge of the job, came out of the house. He was a bitter, spidery-looking man with continually angry eyes.

"George, damn it, I don't mind cull lumber. I don't mind using scrap. But look at this stuff we got to use for studding. It's green. It leaks sap. It's going to warp so bad it'll pull the nails the hell out."

George beamed at him and said, "Gooood morning, Herman."

Herman Janitz stared at him. "What's with you?"

"It is a fine, fat, lovely morning, Herman."

"The big saw is broke again."

"Smell that air, Herman."

"McCarthy didn't show again. I think he's on another binge, George."

"There's nothing so rare as a day in June, Herman."

"What's with you? At this point you're supposed to be jumping up and down, George. You're supposed to be cussing so loud they can hear you in town."

"What's with me? Herman, I do believe I'm in love."

"Act your age, George."

"I am acting my age. I was eighteen yesterday. Let's see the lumber, Herman. Get somebody to load the big saw in the back end of my car. If you see McCarthy, tell him he picked a lovely time of year to get drunk."

"You baffle me, George."

They looked at the lumber. George clucked. "Have you used any?"

"Just that much."

"Rip it out and restack it and I'll have Federal pick it up when they bring some decent stuff."

"Are you sure you're all right, George? You're supposed to tell me to go ahead and use it. You're supposed to lean into my face and roar. You're supposed to tell me we're in this business to make money."

"Get the saw loaded, Herman."

George walked slowly around the raw skeletal house. It was like looking at the face of Alice. Like seeing it for the first time. But it had been pleasant to look at her sleeping face. It was not pleasant to look at this house. It was not a happy thing to look at something you were building with greed and spit, just barely squeaking by the building code, setting up a white elephant for some slob to spend the next twenty years carrying on his back. The slob would just love his home when it was spanking new, when the paint and the interior trim covered the hasty, rough carpentry. In a year there would be a dozen things sticking and warping and crumbling. In three years the roof would leak. The fine paint job might last a full year. Wavery flaws in the picture windows, scrap plywood under the kitchen-floor tiles. Cheap labor that left owl eyes around all the nailheads. Cheap glossy plumbing, with a chrome coat so thin it would start to flake before he'd made his third mortgage payment. A nice margin in a deal like this. You didn't twist the slob's arm. He wanted the house. He looked at it and liked the smell of it and the newness and he wanted it, and his wife just adored the gay colors of the kitchen.

The other builders knew what you were doing. So did your own crew. But you were smart, all right. That George Furmon, by God, he's making it while he can. No experimentation. Slap 'em up and sell 'em and get out from under. They all knew it, and it didn't bother you a damn bit. You could go home every night and forget it. Take on a nice comforting little load and forget it.

Herman came up and said, "The saw's loaded."

George gestured toward a pile of cinder block. "Have a seat, Herman. I'd hate to see you fall down."

Herman sat down warily, staring at George. George sat beside him and gave him a cigar. They lit up. "Herman, what do you think about putting up some good houses? I mean good. Make 'em just as good as we have to when we have an architect who's on the ball riding our tail. Good inside and out."

Herman studied the wet end of his cigar. "I would say maybe you are getting smart, George, and I would say I don't know whether it's too late or not."

"What do you mean, Herman?"

Herman studied the cigar for long seconds and then hurled it away. It hit and bounced. He turned and stared at George and his small eyes were angry. "I was on my own. You know that. I had pride. I did a house. It meant something. The name meant something. Go look at my houses. Twenty years ago I built them. Like rocks they are. I made a little money on every one. A little, George. Not as much again as it cost me to build. Okay, I'm a foreman. Does that mean no pride, George? My pride is in my hands. Look, George. These hands. Putting up cheap shacks for people to live in. A hundred times a day I want to puke. I say I can get used to it. I say I don't have to live in them. Is that any good? Never, George. I'm never used to it. I won't be. I have to try to do just as good as I can with the crummy materials and the punk labor you give me. I have to keep trying to get better stuff, and you lean in my face and yell about not being in business for love.

"Maybe I am in business for love, George. Maybe that's what it's all about. But you better not be kidding me, George. You better mean this. Like I said, maybe it's too late. You don't think I know? Stockton Savings won't take the paper on your houses anymore. That gets around, George. The little people talk. A guy comes to buy. He knows something about building. He looks around. He looks where other people don't look. And then he looks at me, George. It makes me ashamed. It makes me so my food doesn't sit good on my stomach, George. A Furmon house. It meant something. Now what? Does any architect tell the customer to get you to build? Not anymore, and you know it. Those jobs come only when the customer knows you personal. So don't give me any cigar and make jokes and then start roaring and leaning in my face, because this time I quit for good."

George sat for a long time. He scuffed sand with the side of his shoe.

"I'm ashamed, Herman."

"That's good, George. You should be."

"Why didn't you tell me this before, Herman?"

"Tell you! Tell you? Have you ever listened? For three years I've been telling you. Janitz. What does he know? A foreman? Yell in his face. You know what I do? I go home. I build cabinets. Fine wood. Things that are nice to touch. Things for a hundred years. Two hundred. Then I'm happy."

"What can we do about these four, Herman?"

"Burn down the bastards."

"I can't do that. Can't afford it. We'll have to use the materials we can't return. Let's us take a look at the bill of materials and the specifications and see what we can do."

"How about labor? Punks and drunks?"

"Can you get some of the old ones back?"

"I think so. I can try."

"I was going to try to move these at seventeen five, Herman."

"So?"

"They'll move better at fifteen."

"Good. That takes away some shame." Both men were standing. Herman stuck out his hand. George took it. Herman said, "It isn't a mistake, George. Believe me. You know the cream is off the market. They got to be good to move. And they got to be better to live in. Good materials. These houses, George, they are dull. Little rooms like boxes. We can make them like that one we did on Treydon Road."

"The Wilcox house? Stop dreaming, Herman. That was an eighty-five thousand dollar job."

Herman frowned. "Here is what I mean. That house had air, light, a good place to live. So does the wood have to be redwood? Does the glass have to be Duo-therm? Does there have to be rubber tile, not asphalt? Does the stone have to come from some bottom of a lake out in Michigan, for God's sake. And can't there be two bedrooms, not five? The materials, they can be honest. These houses, George, twenty years ago I was building the same design only better."

"See what you can dream up. With cost estimate, Herman."

Later, when George left, Herman stood with his hands on his hips watching him go. "What did you say happened to you, George?"

"I told you, Herman. I fell in love."

"That's bad stuff for a married man, George. Especially with kids."

"I fell in love with my wife, Herman."

"George, you better wear a hat out in the sun like this. Even if you are crazy, it is a good thing. Second thought, George—skip the hat. Get lots of sun."

From the Hillside Heights project George drove into the hills south of Stockton, to a fashionable residential district where a crew foremanned by Dug Lister was putting up, on a bid basis, a house for some friends named Duffy. The house had been designed by a clever young architect named Raymond Riker. The bid had been fifty-four thousand, six hundred, and George knew he had been on the invitation list only through the insistence of Duffy. He had put in the low bid, banking on Dug Lister to take full advantage of the relative inexperience of Raymond Riker. But it wasn't working out too well. Riker seemed to have a knack of arriving on the job at the critical moments. George had begun to worry about breaking even.

He parked by the house, went in. Dug Lister was a burly man with a very small head. An old throat injury had reduced his voice, long ago, to a husky whisper. And Lister had seemingly acquired all the conspiratorial mannerisms to go with his confidential voice. He was a man with a habit of looking back over his shoulder with quick nervous movements of his head. He was not one to inspire confidence. Yet on this sort of a project he was invaluable.

Lister nodded at George and came over and they went outside together.

"I was hoping you'd show, George." He squatted on the ground and unrolled a set of the prints and put stones on it to hold it open. "That damn kid hasn't showed yet, George. I'm stalling a little. I want him to come and look around and go. Then we can do this," he whispered. George, hunkering down beside him, listened while Dug explained. It was a clever evasion of the specifications, done in such a way that the evidence could be concealed quickly and thoroughly. George estimated that it would save somewhere around five hundred dollars.

"The kid'll have to ask us to rip it out again, here and here, before he can check it. And I don't think he'll do that, George. He'd look too damn simple if it turned out he was wrong. He won't take that chance. What do you think?"

"I don't know."

"Hell, the house will be just as good. These kids overspecify everything. They think they're designing the Taj Mahal or something."

"Lister, I think we better stick to the prints. All the way."

Lister stared at him. "Is there something I don't know, George?"

"Yes, I think I can say there's something you don't know."

"Are you sore about something?"

"No."

"Oh, I get it. You got another job lined up through the kid. And you don't want to take the chance. I thought for a minute there you were sore about something."

"No short cuts, Dug. None."

"I get it. Sure, boss. Just like the prints from here on in." He nudged George with his elbow. "But we've saved a little, haven't we?"

"Not enough, Dug. We'll be over."

"I'll keep it down as much as I can."

"But stay with the specs."

"I got you."

They stood up. A small maroon convertible turned into the slanting driveway. Raymond Riker got out. He had a set of the prints with him. He spoke politely enough, but he didn't smile. "Good morning, Mr. Furmon. Hello, Lister." He went on into the house.

"You better go on in, Dug."

George waited in his car. Riker was in the house for a full half hour. When he came out, George strolled over to the convertible. Riker got inside and started the motor. George leaned on the door. "Do you like the way it's going?"

"It seems all right, Mr. Furmon. I check it frequently."

"I know."

Riker gunned the car motor impatiently. George said, "I want to say something to you, Ray. Is that what people call you?"

Riker turned off the motor. "I might as well tell you right now, Mr. Furmon, that I have no intention of making any kind of a deal whatsoever. I know very well you're going over the bid. I can't help that. I protect my client."

"You think I'd try to pay you to goof off?"

Riker shrugged. "I might as well be frank. I don't like the work you've done in the past. When you got the bid, I knew I was going to have to do a lot of checking. I've kept the job tight. You won't make the bid. You'll lose money on the job. I expected that. So what *could* you want to talk about?"

"Open up your prints, Ray. I want to show you something."

Riker shrugged. "Sure." He unrolled the prints, held them flat against the steering wheel. George had him turn to the third sheet. He explained quickly what Lister had suggested.

"What would you have done, Ray?"

Ray frowned. "Frankly, that hadn't occurred to me. It would have worked. Why are you showing me?"

"Now back to page two, Ray." He showed him two short cuts they had gotten away with on page two, and another on page four.

Riker looked at him evenly. "Is that all?"

"That's all we could manage. You've stuck pretty close. What are you going to do about them?"

"You better tell me why you've told me this, Mr. Furmon."

"Just say I've gotten religion, Ray. I gave Dug Lister explicit orders today. No more short cuts. We take our loss."

"I don't get it. I'd never have found these things. Now you're going to take more of a loss. I'll have to have them fixed to conform with the plans, Mr. Furmon."

"Now we come close to what you said before. A deal."

"What kind of a deal? What do you mean?"

"You know what we did. Figure what we saved on those three items. I'll accept your figures. Deduct it from the bid. That's cheaper for me than what it would cost to rip them out and replace. It's up to you."

Riker said slowly, "You didn't have to tell me. Actually, they aren't serious." He looked up from the plans, looked hard at George. "Is there an angle here I don't understand? What are you after?"

"You design a nice house. Maybe I'd like to build another one someday."

"This is a damn funny way of going about it."

"Is it?"

Riker smiled. "You baffle me, George. I was warned that you're sharp. You're out of character."

"One favor. Don't tell Lister. Don't let him know you know. And tell Duffy you changed the specs. Then you can do as you damn please about future bids, about your future clients."

"Anything else?"

"I'll give you as full access to my office records on any job we do together as though they were cost-plus contracts."

"Now I'm supposed to be overcome. We turn out to be great pals. Is business slipping, Mr. Furmon?"

George's smile slipped a little but he readjusted it. "I deserve that, Ray. We'll talk again, maybe. After this one is done."

Ray looked at him bleakly for a few moments, then nodded and started the car again and drove off. George wondered if he had been too much of a damn fool. It was a funny feeling to go around feeling as though you had to make gestures of appeasement.

He stopped and looked at the only other job in progress, a house he was building to order, and then drove back to town to his office, in the Palmer Building. He had a staff of two, Emily Garver and Tom Herrick. Emily did the secretarial work, the bookkeeping. Herrick chased materials, made some of the estimates, made himself generally useful. George's own office was half the room, divided from the other two desks by a temporary partition. He stopped and told Herrick about leaving the saw off to be repaired, and when he could pick it up and take it back out to Herman. He went into his own office and phoned Federal about the lumber they'd delivered, got their promise to replace it and pick it up for credit.

Emily brought him some checks to sign and told him

that Mrs. Benjamin Delevan had called and wanted him to call back. Emily was a fat, nervous girl who ended every sentence with a short meaningless laugh, no matter what she was talking about. He signed the checks and called Wilma.

"This is George, Wilma."

"George, are you going to hire that Schermer boy?"

"He starts July first. Why?"

"Well, George, I want to tell you what happened last night. It was really terrible. We were almost frantic with worry. It's about Ellen and that Schermer boy. It seems that . . ."

George put his feet on his desk. He closed his eyes. My God, how the woman could talk. On and on and on. Takes her forever to get to the point. She finished the whole story. "What do you think of *that,* George?"

"Quite a hassle. Good thing Ellen got out of there."

"That Schermer boy ought to be in jail. Attacking a young girl."

"The point is, I guess, you don't want me to hire him."

"Well, you won't, will you?"

"Now, Wilma, you think this over. Do you want the boy hanging around, or do you want me to give him a summer like he's never had before. He'll be so pooped by quitting time every day, he won't think of anything but going to bed."

"Well . . ." she said hesitantly.

"His old man asked me to give him the job. And I said okay."

"Will it be . . . hard work?"

"As hard as I can make it."

"Maybe you're right, George."

"Don't worry about it, Wilma. Seen Alice today?"

"Why no. Why do you ask, George? Do you want me to give her a message or something?"

"No. No thanks."

He sat with his hand on the phone for a time, then lifted it and dialed his home. "Hello, punkin. Go get your mother. Run. Tell her it's an emergency, punkin."

He heard Sandy yelling in the house. Alice came on the

line. "George? George, what's the matter?" She sounded
breathless.

"I thought you ought to know it's a lovely day, baby."

"What? George, you fool!"

"Don't you agree?"

There was a silence. She laughed softly. "A fine day,
George. Yes."

It reminded him of those telephone conversations in the
teen age of long ago. The silences, the meaningless, meaningful things.

"I thought you ought to know."

"M-m-m."

"Be good, girl."

"Good-bye, George."

He hung up, grinning at nothing. Then he sobered,
pulled paper toward him, began to list his assets. Home,
cash, investments, equipment. It made a comforting total,
but not comforting enough. There would be losses. This
whole change of pace might sink him without a trace.
Then everything would have to be thrown into the pot.
There was a way it could be done more safely, he
decided. He could change from a single proprietorship to
a corporation. That would mean in effect a double tax on
income, but it would safeguard the home, the investments.
They wouldn't go into the pot then if he went broke.

It would be a nice safety play, but he had the peculiar
feeling it would take some of the joy out of it. If you
believed in something, then you wanted the risk. You
wanted a battle, with something at stake. He felt as if he
had suddenly climbed onto a horse, with milady's colors
tied to the lance. Then he was forced to grin at that image
of himself. Hell, a man had to scare himself every once in
a while. This was the time. Forget why he was doing it.
For the love of it, Herman had said. Right now that
would do as good as any other reason. After dinner tonight
he would fool around with some sketches, based on
Herman's idea. Alice might have some ideas too. No more
than two drinks before dinner then, or he'd be designing
houses for Martians. Rough sketches, then go over them
with Herman, and then take them to an architect. Use

honest short cuts in construction to save money, and then pass that saving along. Maybe Riker could help. The kid has good ideas.

Chapter Eleven

After two sets of tennis Brock's blister began to bother him so he told Betty and they agreed to delay the play-off set until the next time. They swam and got some sun. She was like she had been the day before. He had brought clothes this time, rented a locker for the summer. She went back to the cottage to change and then met him down in front of the club and they walked down the highway to the bean wagon for lunch. They sat at the counter and had two hamburgers and a milkshake apiece, and he told her about Ellen.

Betty nodded. "I like her. And the Rawls boy is sort of sweet and nice. But I don't go that Franchard item. Not one bit. Catty little beast. And the Schermer boy is just a nothing. A storm-trooper type."

"Get definite ideas, don't you?"

"I'm a definite-type person. Or hadn't you noticed?"

"Just that you're a definite type."

"Lines I get yet. Now what do we do?"

He looked at his watch. "One o'clock. How about a walk? Back of the course. Pine woods. Nature-study deal."

"Good."

"I'm going to find out if you're as tireless as you act, Miss Yost."

"Or as tiresome?"

"That too. Let's go."

He cut across the course, setting a long-legged pace. And she kept up easily. Beyond the twelfth fairway he

located the path that led up into the hills. It was quite
steep. They went down into the valley between the hills,
crossed the creek on the steppingstones, and went up the
far bank and up the second hill.

"Does this superhighway go anyplace in particular?"
Betty asked.

"Ready to give up?"

"Not until I drop, and may I add that it won't be long
now before I do."

"Just a little bit further, Miss Yost, please."

There was a level spot on the crest of the second hill.
Somebody with hatchets, rope and energy, possibly a
scout troop, had made a rustic picnic table with benches
and some rustic armchairs, badly weathered. At the edge
of the level spot there was a steep drop. Betty crossed her
eyes and pretended to snap sweat off her forehead, and
then she saw the view. She walked over to the edge and
put her fists on her hips and looked out across the wide
valley, seeing the distant highway, tiny cars glinting in the
sun, patchwork farms on the gentler slopes beyond the
highway.

"Hey, now," she said softly. "Almost worth the trip."

"Not many people know about this place."

"Not many people would want to know about it, after
the first trip up here. But I like it, Delevan. I like it
much." She came to where he sat on the rustic table,
swinging his legs, and took a cigarette and went over to
the nearest chair and sat down, long legs crossed at the
ankles, sitting on the end of her spine.

"On that tree there, Betty, just below that sort of scar,
you will see a deathless inscription. See?"

"Where . . . Oh, I see it. A sort of bulgy-looking heart
with a crooked arrow through it. And initials. BD. That
would be you. Who was MB?"

"A deathless love named Marian Brastlehauer."

"Nobody has a name like that. You made it up."

"No, really. I used to think it was the prettiest name in
the world. Brastlehauer. Brastlehauer. Her father was a
freight agent for the railroad. She had one crooked front
tooth. That intrigued me. A flaw in my beloved. A lovely
flaw."

"Did she ever see that touching inscription?"

"See it! I got arm-weary when I was half through and she finished it for me. We used to come up here and kiss breathlessly. She never had much to say. I guess I did all the talking. We came up here in winter once. The trail was icy. She slipped and bumped her mouth on her own knee and that crooked tooth cut the inside of her lip. Such red red blood."

"Tell me more."

"We used to bring salami sandwiches. And bottles of chocolate milk. We were both fourteen. My first love."

She looked at him soberly. "That's always a good love. That first love. And you know, you're kind of grown up to be able to talk about it in just that way, Brock. I mean you're not building it up or tearing it down. You just tell it, and it's kind of sweet that way. What happened?"

"I do not cut a handsome figure in the end of this tale, Betty. She came to school with tears in her eyes and told me the railroad was moving her father down to Buffalo. And that, of course, was equivalent to Southern Rhodesia when you are fourteen. We kept saying our final good-byes for a full month. We made the mistake of saying the final good-bye in her front hallway. I guess it was pretty emotional at the point her father walked in. He chased me all the way down to the corner, with Marian screaming like somebody was tearing her wings off. That was the last time I saw her. We wrote every day for about ten days. Then not so often. Then not at all. You know, funny thing. I don't think I'd know her if I met her on the street."

She ground her cigarette out against the ground, leaning over to do it. And straightened up, looking too sober.

"Brock, I didn't think you'd come back after last night."

"Why not?"

"I felt all night as though I was behind glass."

"That's a good description. That's what it was like. But I didn't mind, really. I mean I knew it wouldn't always be that way. It was just last night. But, well, I want to say something if you won't misunderstand. I sort of want just

... a date. Somebody to go around with, without it getting all complicated or anything."

"There's somebody else?"

"No. Nobody else. Just that I ... I've just gotten over enough complications to last me for a long time, that's all."

And she gave a surprisingly sharp flat mirthless bark of laughter.

"I thought you'd misunderstand. I didn't say it right."

"You said it right. I just happen to be in a position to understand perfectly exactly what you mean, that's all. And it's funny. It's ridiculously funny, Brock. That's all."

"But——"

"And that's what I want, too. So let's make it a deal. We'll be each other's ... companion. Dreadful word, that."

"A deal." By leaning far over, and with her stretching, they were able to shake hands.

She smiled into his eyes. "I like you, Brock. You're a nice guy. I'll be better fun next time we go out. But it will be Dutch, like last night."

"I ought to object, but it means we'll be able to go out oftener if I don't. Practical. A Delevan trait."

She gave him an odd, questioning look. "You told me about your first love. Would you like me to tell you about my last love?"

"If you want to."

"I think I better tell somebody. Maybe it is the story of my life. That sounds impressive, doesn't it? The story of Elizabeth Fletcher Yost. Third person? Easier, maybe. Betty was the only child of Mr. and Mrs. Fletcher Herron Yost of San Francisco, Paris, and Bermuda. As Mr. and Mrs. Yost were pleasure-loving people and enjoyed the delights of travel and had friends all over the world, and had *mucho dinero*, young Betty was frequently left at their main base of operations in San Francisco. At first with nurse, maid, and handyman. Later, of course, with governess, maid, and handyman. At the age of nine she was sent off to a very highly rated school in Switzerland and later she went to a convent in Paris. Four years ago her father died rather suddenly. While attempting to water-ski behind a float plane. All his friends said he was very young for his age. I remember him as a large tan grin full of white teeth, and too much money in the mail. Her mother described the estate taxes as being vulgar. It is one of her mother's favorite words. Since then . . ."

She looked at him then, a clear, bright, almost startled expression, and got up quickly and went to the edge of the drop and stood with her back to him. He did not know how to react, what to say.

"Betty?" His voice was uncertain, tentative.

"It's all right," she said, her tone flat. "That was a mistake. I thought I could be bright and sassy. But it's too close. And it isn't something I can just sit and smile and talk about. Even though I feel as if I ought to."

"Then maybe you better not try."

She walked back slowly, scuffing her heels. The high sun made bright spots through the trees, touching the brown, soft bed of needles, the split and peeling bark of the rustic furniture. She sighed as she sat down again and gave him a slightly wan smile.

"Anyway, with Daddy gone, she's been living my life instead of her own. They shoved me out. I learned my defenses. I got behind my wall. Now I'm supposed to act as though nothing had ever happened. She needs me and I know she needs me, but I can't feel warmth. She's a neurotic sort of woman, Brock. And possessive. And kind of overpowering. Maybe I was trying to escape from her. I don't know what it was. But I got into . . . a bad mess at school. I don't want to talk about that. Mother said it was vulgar and impossible. Maybe it was. He was older. So she took me off to Mexico. I told her and told myself that nothing would ever change the way I felt. Now he's gone sort of vague in my mind. You know? The outlines aren't clear anymore. And I can't tell her that . . . her plan is working because that's too much of a defeat to take right at this point. So here I am. She keeps riding me about it. When I'm twenty-one, I get the money Daddy left. It isn't very much. But enough to be free on. In the meantime I do as she says. I wouldn't really have to. I know I could work. I know I could get along. But ... it would do something to her that I don't want to do. I wish I could be ruthless, but I can't. And if I tell her now that she was right, it means that there will be just that much less of me."

"I know what you mean. Mine wasn't that way. The mess I got in. Because I was wrong and they all know I was wrong and I know I was wrong, and what do you do then?"

"How do you mean?"

"There was a girl. I guess I went a little crazy. I let everything go to hell and then I got kicked out."

"Because of your marks?"

He looked at her. All he had to do was nod. It wouldn't even take words, this lie. But there had to be a starting place. "I got kicked out because she needed money and so I stole it from a fellow I knew."

Her eyes went wide with concern. "Oh, Brock, how awful for you!"

"Awful for my people, I guess. It seems to me as if it really didn't happen. But I know it did. And so that makes me not what they thought I was. You know a funny thing? They want you to be something. They want it so bad that sometimes you have to kick it all apart, like kicking over furniture. Just to be something that is entirely yourself, good or bad. Last night I felt sorry for the old man. I mean that business about Ellen rocked him. He feels things. They get at him. He doesn't show it much. Not usually. So I went into an act. And got myself all sewed up. Job this summer and enlist in the fall. You know, noble and sorry and trying to make it up and so on and so on. I like to talk to you. You know what I'm talking about. You said awful for me. I liked that."

He realized that he had spoken too intently and he felt his face get hot as he looked away from her. She said, "You have just heard our weekly broadcast of the confession hour, friends. Be with us this coming week at the same time and once again we will ... now I'm stuck."

"We will hand out towels to the studio audience."

"I'll buy that."

They talked for a time of other things, and the sun patterns moved and then they stood ready to go back down, and she traced with her finger the ridged, gray scar tissue of the old tree carving, as he stood beside her. "Marian Brastlehauer," she said softly, "with one crooked tooth. Does she think about this place?"

"I don't know. Like I said, I never could tell what she was thinking. That was part of her charm. She never said anything."

"And you kissed her here."

"With my heart trying to jump right out my chest."

She turned to him. "I need a young kiss. A child kiss. The kind you had with Marian Brastlehauer."

He kissed her. She felt tall in his arms. It was a light kiss, without hungers, and then they held away and grinned at each other and started down the path.

She went first. He watched her and saw how she was quick and good in the steep places, where you had to grab the small trees for support. He watched the way she handled her body. They went up the first hill, she above him, and in looking at her, the look of her changed for him. He had watched Marian long ago in this same way, but not in this same way. There had been the old imaginings then, of soft and hidden delights which could only be devised from pictures, from passages in forbidden books, from washroom whisperings. Because they were not yet known. And now these things were known to him, so that he saw clearly as she climbed the reach and flex of flank and hip, and watching her he felt a deepening heaviness of loins, a specific want that was, not as in the times of Marian, direct and known and channeled. She turned suddenly and unexpectedly to say something to him and it was inconsequential. He heard her voice change in the middle of the short phrase and knew she had seen too much on his unguarded face.

When they moved down from the second crest toward the valley and toward the tiny erratic figures of the golfers, she did not move with the same easiness, but with a narrowed look of shoulders, a look of conscious compression about her hips and her carriage.

He knew that in that interchange of knowingness, something had been lost for them. There could never be another mild and Brastlehauer kiss on a high place. It made him feel stained and coarse, as though he walked thickly on hooves, hair matted in a jungly way. He knew she would think she had told him too much, and there was no good way to keep her from thinking that. He wanted back what had been lost, and yet at the same time he felt the excitement of this so sudden change in the relationship. Though he wanted it to be boy-and-girl, it was clearly man-and-woman, with all the racial awareness of full ability to breed true, with that deep instinctive knowledge, unaltered in ten thousand years, that these were the months of mating—yet it had all gone too complicated now in this time and place for the young.

She walked beside him toward the distant clubhouse. "Faraway, Brock?"

"Uh-huh. What are you planning to do?"

"I have to go into the city with Mother. Some shopping and then dinner and a movie afterward. Are you coming around tomorrow?"

"My youngest uncle is coming to show off his bride. He just got married. It'll be a big wingding around the place. I guess I'll have to stay around. Maybe Sunday, if I can work it. Monday I'll have to hunt for a job for the summer."

"What sort of job do you want?"

"Something on the rugged side, I think. Labor."

Where she turned off to go to the cottage they stopped and she thrust her hand out with an awkward gesture. They shook hands and felt slightly ridiculous about it. He went out on the highway. He tried unsuccessfully for a ride and when the Clayton bus came, he got on and rode to the foot of the hill and walked slowly up through the four o'clock sunshine.

As he neared his house he saw Quinn standing out by the shoulder of the road. Just standing there. He had never felt close to Quinn. Yet it was not because Quinn seemed to have too much adult reserve. His reserve seemed of another breed. The distant politeness of a bored

child. They made conversation, and it was usually meaningless. But something that had to be done.

There seemed to be an indefinable oddness about the
way Quinn was standing there. An odd place to stand,
and nothing in particular to look at. It gave Brock the
feeling that Quinn had lost something and had been
hunting for it along the shoulder and had now given up
the search and stood trying to think of some other place to
look.

He turned as Brock came up to him. "Hi, Quinn. What
are you— Hey! You shaved off your mustache!"

Quinn seemed oddly startled for a moment. And he ran
his knuckle across his upper lip. His upper lip was pale
against the golfing tan of his lean quite face. "Yes, I
shaved it off," he said, using the words carefully, as
though trying to achieve precision and understanding.
Almost as though he spoke a foreign language, having
learned it out of a guidebook.

Brock could see why Quinn had worn the mustache
ever since he could remember. The upper lip was too
long, and it was faintly convex from the root of the nose
down to the thin lip, so that it gave him a mildly rabbity
look, putting something thin and blinking and nervous
into his face that had been hidden before by the bold,
heather harshness of the carefully unkempt mustache.
Brock stood, wanting to go on, not knowing quite how to
break away.

"Back early from work," Brock said.

"I didn't go today."

"Oh, are you sick?" And Brock was aware of the
awkwardness of never having known precisely what to
call Quinn. When he was little, he had called him Uncle.
But that had seemed to become unsuitable when he was
about eight years old. And as that had been too early to
start calling him Quinn, he had slid into the perpetual
awkwardness of calling him nothing at all.

"No. I just didn't go to work today."

"I see," said Brock, feeling as though he had been
tricked into the position of inquisitor, wanting to get out
of it and not knowing how.

"How . . . uh . . . does Aunt Bess like the way you look without the mustache?" And Brock smiled, and felt as though his lips were stiff.

Quinn knuckled his naked lip again. "I . . . I guess I haven't seen her yet. She went off with David. His shot, you know. Glutamic acid. They're experimenting."

"Yes. I know. Well . . . I'll see you around."

"Yes," Quinn said.

Brock walked on. He turned and looked back. Quinn still stood there. Brock stopped and for a moment had the feeling that he should go back. Quinn stood in a way that suggested nothing. Not thought, nor patience, nor dejection. He was the figure of a man who stood quite still on a June afternoon. Brock half shrugged and went on toward the house. There was a small truck in the drive. There was a man on the kitchen floor, tinkering with the innards of the dishwasher. The front panel was off. Brock made himself a thick peanut-butter sandwich and poured a glass of milk. He sat on the counter top and ate and watched the man and listened with quiet amusement to the man's complete and utter condemnation of the manufacturer who had created this piece of junk, the plumber who had installed it, the electrician who had wired it, and the civilization which had spawned all of them.

Chapter Twelve

Bess walked back to the car from the doctor's office with David. It had simplified matters a great deal when Dr. Endermann had moved his office out to Clayton, closer to his home. Dr. Endermann was always so good with David. The way Mr. Shelter was good. But there was always that feeling that, good as they were, they didn't *like* him. No matter how gently they spoke to him, understanding how to achieve his always reluctant cooperation, Bess had the feeling that they did it because it was profitable and because it was their job, and if anything happened that changed the arrangements, they would not want to see him again.

There had always been so many shots. So many deficiencies to make up. It was Mr. Shelter who had suggested that he be taken to the doctor's office. At first it had been awkward because, unlike the shots taken at home, having them in a strange place had made David wet his pants. And so she had to bring changes each time. It was odd how David, so easily frightened and embarrassed by many things, did not seem dreadfully upset when he made a mess like that. He stood in horselike patience and waited to be handed the clean clothes, and went into the next room with animal docility. But he had not done that for a long time.

She was aware of her son walking tall beside her, and it was pleasant to think of just that, of walking by a tall son while the children in the park made the light quick sounds of play. Better to just think that and not glance up into his face, with the beard hairs beginning to fringe the pimpled mouth, the funny constricted way he walked.

She felt exhausted. It had been a strange unnerving session with Dr. Endermann after he had taken her into the other office, leaving David with the nurse. Dr. Enderman had seemed uneasy about it.

"Mrs. Delevan, I've been talking with Ralph Shelter about David. Understand I wouldn't talk like this if I didn't have some . . . professional basis for my opinion."

"I don't think I understand."

"As you know, Mrs. Delevan, we have never been able to find any evidence of actual damage to the brain or central nervous system. Physically he is what we call a constitutional inadequate. And his slowness and inability to cope have given him a serious emotional situation. So serious, you understand, that we have never been able to do any serious testing of his intelligence. Shelter tells me that at times there will be a flash of . . . well, call it a form of brilliance. Adolescence has been very difficult for him. Relatively speaking, he is worse now than when he was twelve."

"But he is ever so much better than . . ."

"Relatively speaking, Mrs. Delevan. Please understand me. He is more integrated than when he was twelve. Easier to handle. But the gap between him and the norm has widened. Now he is approaching sexual maturity. In spite of his poor coordination, he is very strong. I guess you know that. With his emotional difficulties it is entirely possible—now, understand that I am saying possible, not probable—that he might take it into his head to approach some female person."

She had stared at him. "That's idiotic, Doctor. He's much too shy. Why, it's——"

"If we could communicate with him more successfully, Mrs. Delevan, it might set my mind at rest. But it is difficult to know what he is thinking about. Shelter reports an increase in sexual curiosity. We can expect that. We cannot predict how he will attempt to satisfy that curiosity."

"You're talking about him as though he was a criminal or something! Why are you talking like this?"

"It might be time to reconsider what we have talked about many times."

"Send him away? Absolutely not! He's making fine progress. Mr. Shelter is very pleased with his progress. You should see the——"

"Mrs. Delevan, I thought you would react this way. But I felt obliged to suggest it again. You don't hope any more than I do that we'll see a change for the better soon."

Her indignation faded slowly. "What can change him, Doctor? What can change him now?"

He shrugged thick shoulders. "It's hard to say. The shock treatments two years ago were a failure. We might try again."

"No. They were dreadful."

"You have to think of him as being in a sort of prison, Mrs. Delevan. A captive. Maybe he will be released some day, quite suddenly. Maybe, instead, there will be a slow increase in the learning curve. And maybe he will never change. We are dealing with something without a specific name. A severe emotional shock might jiggle the mechanism just enough so that the wheels would begin to mesh. Or it might break the mechanism beyond even its limited ability to function."

"You see," she said, leaning toward him a bit, her face frowning and soft and earnest, "his father and I, we were very healthy people and it just doesn't seem right that——"

"Genetics is a tricky thing, Mrs. Delevan. Mitosis is something we half understand, and cannot explain. The whole area of birth and growth is so enormously complicated that I sometimes wonder that so many functioning human beings are born, that the percentage of chromatid error is so small. I'm sorry I've upset you, but I felt that I had to say this to you."

And she had stood up, picking up her purse, thanking him, walking out with David.

"There are a lot of children playing in the park today," she said with that bright and special voice she used for him.

"Playing in the park today," he said in his deep, rusting voice. And she knew that he was far away now, hidden and safe somewhere behind the things that fenced him off from the world, making no effort now to see over or between the interstices of the barrier, responding only by repeating mechanically the last few words of anything he heard. There was a differentness about him that was subtle. Strangers would glance at him and see only a gangling, awkward, ugly young man. And would glance again and sense the alien, the stranger among them. And look a third time and then at her and then glance away, aware of some unknown guilt.

He started to go by the car but she stopped him and he merely stood, not questioning why he was stopped, and then she said, "Get in the car, dear."

He looked at it and got in quietly and sat and looked straight ahead while she got behind the wheel and drove around the park and up Gilman Hill. This was not one of his good days. This was one of the days when he was remote, unreachable. Oddly enough it was on such days that he seemed most deft about the mechanics of living, of dressing and feeding and undressing, washing and combing and tying knots. On the days of more awareness he fumbled more and forgot things.

She parked the car and after she spoke to him, he got out and walked directly toward the studio, not looking back, a thing that had been wound up and placed on tracks and thus followed the tracks without curiosity, awareness or interest.

She went into the house. The light was odd in the living room, the late sun slanting from behind Quinn, where he sat in his usual chair. He was not reading and the television set was dark. He sat there and looked toward her as she came in.

"Do you feel better, dear?" she asked.

"I'm not sick. I told you that."

She went to him preparing to hold the back of her hand against his forehead and stopped and stared at him, the hand partially raised.

"What happened! Where's your mustache?"

"I cut it off."

"But why? It always looked so nice, dear. And Robbie is coming tomorrow and . . . *really*, Quinn. You look so dreadfully naked. Why on earth did you have to do that now?"

He frowned a little and touched his lip. "I don't know. I just thought about it, so I cut it off."

"It will grow back, dear."

"Yes, I guess it will."

"Look, is something wrong? Is there anything wrong you ought to tell me, Quinn? You really are acting odd, you know. You're acting as strange as can be."

"I'm all right."

She held the back of her hand against his forehead. "You don't seem to have any fever, dear. But you don't look or act right to me. I think you're coming down with something. Why don't you take a nice hot bath now, and put on your pajamas and robe, and then go to bed right after dinner. It will make you feel better. Weren't you listening to me, dear?"

"I heard you," he said.

"Well?"

"I'm going. I'm going in a minute. Any minute now."

"You don't have to positively snarl at me! Anyway, I want to tell you what the doctor said today about David."

She stood over him and told him in great detail. He sat there and did not change expression.

"Well?" she said.

"I'll go take my bath now," he said, getting up.

"Haven't you got anything to say about what Dr. Endermann said?"

"Is there anything to say? You settled it, didn't you?"

"I don't know if there's anything wrong with you or not, but you're certainly in a terrible mood. And that's always the first sign when you're coming down with something. You always get grouchy. Take an antihistamine. They're on the second shelf in the linen closet. The big blue ones the color of robin eggs."

He was through the doorway and he did not answer. She sighed and went to the kitchen. She opened the deepfreeze and looked in. If he was coming down with something, he'd like something bland. There was a package of frozen shrimp. She decided she could cream them and have them on toast. There were still two of the huge steaks left. She would use those when they had Robbie and Susan to dinner. They would have to have them to dinner. And if David was having a good day, it might be possible to have him eat with them. Then it would have to be at the table. David could never manage a buffet dinner. She hoped Susan wouldn't be one of those critical ones. Things seem to get in a mess so fast. David's curtains aren't done. The house could stand a thorough cleaning.

She hitched impatiently at her skirt and tugged at her bra straps. Get things started and then change to something comfortable.

Why in hell had he shaved off his mustache just now?

She began to organize the evening meal, clomping around with cheerful heaviness, banging pans, her mood improving enough so that finally she began to sing in her true, husky untrained voice, singing something old about darkness on the delta and saying dum-de-dum at the parts where the words were gone.

Ellen, curled in the big chair, saw Brock come in slowly. "Hey!" she said softly and he turned sharply, startled.

"Didn't see you. What are you doing home?"

"Nursing a fat eye."

He came over to her. "Let's see," he said, putting his fingers under her chin, tilting her face up to the light. "Hmmm. Not bad. Sort of a smudge, like. Like dirt."

"Were you at the club?"

"Yes. Tennis and a swim with the Yost girl."

"She's nice. Was . . . Clyde there?"

"Didn't see him if he was. What's the word?"

"Norma called me. She was real bitter sounding. I guess it was a hell of a hassle last night when their fathers got there. She was alone in the house, so she could talk. Seems first off, her father and Bobby's father were sort of united front about it. Then Mr. Rawls said something about a little tramp—something like that anyway—and Mr. Franchard hit him and then they grabbed each other and rolled around on the floor grunting. When that was over, Mr. Franchard tried to hit Bobby and they started it all over again. Well, they got in the car and nobody said much of anything all the way back and right at the end Mr. Rawls said he wasn't going to see his son spoiling his life with any little baggage like Norma and Mr. Franchard said that the furthest thing from his mind was letting Norma ever see his delinquent son again. Now Norma says it looks like they want to keep her in the house every evening all summer and send her to a real strict school in the fall. But she says that given all summer to work on them, she figures she can get them to ease up, but it's going to take a lot of crying. And Bobby is already gone."

"Gone where?"

"His people put him on the train this noon. Out to some

place in South Dakota where there's an uncle who has a
farm implement business, and Norma said he didn't phone
or anything before he left. She says he's been getting tired
of her. She suspected it and now she's sure of it and it just
gave him a chance to sneak out."

"She sound sad?"

"Like I said, bitter. I told her I was through with
Clyde. She said we better find ourselves a couple of
boyfriends quick. I said I'd call her up sometime, for
lunch or something."

"Will you?"

She looked up at her brother and felt the unexpected
sting of tears in her eyes. "Darn it, Brock, I don't want to
see her. I don't want to see anybody. They're going to
make me take a p.g. year at the high school. I didn't do
anything. It's a mess. I just wish I was dead or something."

"Down, girl. Easy," he said softly.

"What about you? Is what they said true? I mean
enlisting."

"I opened my mouth at the wrong time."

"I wish I could. I just wish I could do something like
that. You like the idea, don't you?"

She saw his reflective, self-questioning look. "Maybe I
do. It seems corny. Tom Swift and his Brown Suit. But
maybe I like it."

"I just wish I knew what I was going to do with myself
this summer. It started out so good and now— Sshh!"

She listened, heard the familiar jeep sound, the popping
of gravel under the tires, the plaintive peep of the horn.
She stood up uncertainly and said, "Brock, please. Go tell
him to go away."

"If I tell him, he'll be back. You tell him. Only you
better get him on his way before Dad gets here. He's
due."

She took a deep breath and squared her shoulders and
patted her hair and went on out. Clyde stood on the far
side of the jeep, face moody, thick arms crossed and
resting on the top of the windshield.

"Get in, Ellen. We got to have a talk."

She stopped a neat distance away and felt neat and

prim and cold and contained. And she looked at him in a new way, seeing that he looked sulky and petulant and difficult, and not caring.

She looked at him across the hood of the jeep and said, "There isn't anything to say, Clyde."

"I don't blame you for being sore."

"But I'm not sore. I'm not the least bit angry with you."

She saw his look of surprise. "What?"

"I'm not anything. All of a sudden I'm not anything. I think maybe I've outgrown you, Clyde. If I feel anything at all, it's sort of pity. Like being sad at looking at old pictures. Now get in your jeep and go away and find yourself some girl who thinks muscles are lovely."

"Outgrown me?" His face turned red and then the color faded. "You're just a high-school——"

"Good-bye, Clyde. Have a nice summer."

For a moment he looked like a child watching the other children go to the party down the street. And she was touched a bit. Then his face hardened and he got behind the wheel and drove away, and she felt an enormous and wonderful relief, knowing that he wouldn't be back. Brock stood in the doorway watching her approach. She dusted her hands together as she walked, grinning, up to him.

Ben saw his children standing there together as he turned into his driveway at ten of six. This day had been bad. It had not been a day of recurrent crises, of threat of catastrophe. Those days were, somehow, easier to bear than a day such as this one. Because crisis seemed to generate a sharpening of mind and instinct, a quick-footed caution, so that in crisis there was something of the stalk and the hunt and the kill, and the exhaustion afterward was healthier. But this day had been like driving uphill over cobblestones in an ancient, gasping, springless car, with the cumulative effects of the tiny joltings sandpapering his nerves. In descending order of importance there was the Griffin offer, there was the scene with Quinn and his unexplained absence, there was the absence of the vacationing Miss Meyer, there was an expensive cancellation, a lost shipment, two minor accidents in the mill that would bring around both the insurance investigators and the state people, a troublesome breakdown of equipment, a wrangle about discount. Nothing in itself that had the smell of crisis. Just a day full of things pressing on him, and a trip home that, instead of releasing pressure, merely shifted a new load—the load of Robbie, of Brock, of Ellen—and the overlapping burden of Quinn. Quinn was not going to be permitted to be a petulant child punishing the world because his feelings had been hurt.

On the way home he had stopped at one light and had seen the parked cars, the long bar, the dim turbulence of the juke in the back of the place and had been half tempted to park and go in and soak the hard, white crinkling of brittle nerve ends into a welcome limpness, speaking to no one, ungregarious, taking the shots with the somber method of the diabetic measuring morning insulin.

But it was late, as it usually always was on Fridays, and he went on home. He got out of the car feeling thickened and coarsened and pulpy, wrinkled, sooty. An ancient sergeant who had made no brave charges this day but had manned the familiar walls, shooting without hope or fear at the half-seen figures on the murky plains.

"Hello, kids," he said, unsmiling, and stopped and looked at Ellen and noted in a corner of his mind how something young and careless had gone out of them in a single moment and how they stood with a certain wariness. "Was that the Schermer boy's jeep that was tearing down the hill?"

"Yes, it was——"

"He came up here a few minutes ago, Dad, and she chewed him out and chased him off."

"Where's your mother?"

"She said it was a committee meeting about the flower show. She said it might turn into a battle and she'd be late. I've done what she told me about dinner."

And he plodded into the house and poured bourbon on two ice cubes and carried the drink to the bedroom and set it aside to cool as he took off the uniform of the day: the dull gray armor—fifty percent wool, fifty percent da-

cron, the mailed boots—Nettleton, size 10 C, the breast-
plate—white broadcloth with button-down collar, the
battle colors—four-in-hand, maroon and gray diagonal
stripe, from Miss Meyer, Christmas two years ago.

He sat white and heavy in his underwear on the side of
the bed and looked at the wall and sighed and scratched
his hairy thigh and sighed again and took two long swal-
lows at the now cold drink. The warmth spread and ran
through hidden brittle passages and he was able to turn
his mind outward then, the sounds of the summer early
evening beginning to come to him as though a volume
control were slowly turned up. As though he had lived in
the silences inside him all day, hearing only what he
directed himself to hear, as though it were a special
deafness, an aid to concentration—coming out of that still
place now to be alive, yet still retaining a lingering
coldness, the memory of a day that was like a closed fist.

The world on that June evening rolled the band of dusk
shadow from east to west. The sun had heated the eastern
third of the United States for many days. The high
pressure area was moving north and east and below it,
coming up out of the southwest, was a mass of cooler air,
bringing line storms and turbulence and bright snakes of
lightning.

In Washington the headwaiter, smiling, holding his
stack of vast aqua menus, asked the couple if they would
like a table now and the young man, with a questioning
glance at the young woman, said they would have a drink
in the lounge first. Robbie followed his bride into the
lounge. Her shoulders were bare, her wrap over her
arm, and the tan of her was that perfection of Mexican
tan which, instead of being a harshness on the surface,
seems to glow up from a deeper layer. And as she swung
her arm and walked tall, he saw the movement of the
small muscles of her shoulder and he thought of her and
how she was, so that it made him feel dazed in that place,
dizzy with the knowledge of his luck, so much in love
with Susan that he wished for great deeds and a sad dying
in proof of it all.

Miss Meyer sat alone on the wide porch of an ornate old frame hotel overlooking Lake Wannolana. As the light faded she glanced up from her book several times and at last closed it, storing the page number in her memory with a tiny click. She looked out across the deepening color of the water, knowing that in a few moments the dinner gong would make its long sound, full of overtones, decaying slowly, and she would then go in to her table. After dinner—tonight it would be the New England boiled dinner—she would talk in the lounge with some of the others who always came back here, or read more of the book, or watch television. Knowing that this was one more day that could now be counted off before she could go back. Back to that grave, warm, and wise man she loved with all her heart. Back to that good sense of being a team, understanding his exasperations, his little irritations, making each day for him as smooth and safe and easy as she could make it, because once you had given up the hope of anything more than that, given it up long ago in awareness of the empty places in the road ahead, you took what was there, grasping it firmly, making it do in lieu of all the rest.

After Sam ate his evening meal, he took out the letter from his son and read it again. It was the same old story. Give up the place and come live with us. It's warm here the year round. You can fish. You shouldn't work so hard. You don't have to. Sell the place. And he knew he would give the same answer as before. The Crestholms had been on this land for three generations. Not much left now. The old place and four acres. Barn falling down. No stock. The Delevan land used to be the south pasture. Three hundred acres they'd had. But you work the land. You marry and have the kids and work and they grow up and they go away and she dies. How do you tell the boy? That even if you don't own it, even if you work for wages, there is something good about making things grow on that land. Not yet, boy. Later he went out and looked at the sky and smelled the change of weather coming. And went back into the old place which was forever creaking and settling and sighing and held within it all the known smells and flavors of boyhood, manhood, all the memories that were so strong that there always seemed to be somebody in the next room, so it was never what a man would call lonely. Not really.

And Quinn Delevan lay in bed, looking at the very last light of the day against the ceiling, smelling the soapiness of his body from the long hot bath, hearing the insect uncertainties of the sewing machine, feeling, in his belly, the thick, unmoving mass of the creamed shrimp she had insisted he eat. He made the surface of his mind a flat, silvery thing, taking care to see that it stretched evenly, covered all areas. And there was a thing in the middle of it that kept trying to bulge up and break through the flatness and silveriness, and each time it did so, he pressed it back firmly down and smoothed the surface and tucked the edges in just so, because that dark horror must not be permitted to hump its back and brace knotted legs and burst up through to where it could be seen.

And Bess guided the gay yellow material through the little metal mouth of the machine, making it take neat little needle bites, clucking her tongue when the stitches were not perfectly straight.

Bonny Doyle had washed her hair and done her nails and eaten her solitary dinner. Now she sat on the studio couch under the light in robe and slippers trying to think of things to put in a letter to her brother. It was hard to make a letter long enough lately, even when you wrote big. She bit the pencil in between the short sentences. From time to time she would listen intently, but there was no sound of his approach. He'd certainly acted funny. A lot of the time he was hard to understand. She sighed and considered the letter again and remembered something she could use.

Today a big woman named Christine I don't know her last name started to fool around when the foreman wasn't around and she made another girl named Blacky anyway they call her that sore and she tripped Christine into a rack of spindles and got her cut up so Christine is reporting she slipped on an oil place on the floor because if she squealed on Blacky who is pretty tough there would be people to give Christine a bad time maybe on her way home some night. Now don't worry about me because I say some of the girls are tough. It is *all right*. I don't make them mad at me for anything and I get along. You can stop telling me about the wonderful jobs you can help me get out there. I appreciate it and all but I *like* it here and it is good money and I am happy. My best love to you and Sally and the kids and write soon.

Your loving sister, Bonny.

She read it over and put it in the envelope. It wasn't much of a letter, but at least it was off her mind. She wished she could write about Quinn. But she could never put it in a letter so he would understand. She couldn't write it the way it was. And it would sound terrible to him, a married man and all, and it would be just like him to get off his job for a time and come roaring here and spoil everything because he wouldn't even try to understand. He wouldn't see how Quinn was so sort of funny and helpless, and not really able to understand what life was all about.

And with Sandy in bed and Alice out making a last check on the little guest annex where the newlyweds would stay, George Furmon sat hunched over the unrolled sheafs of house plans, jotting down cost estimates. The tide of pride and recklessness had crested during the day and he had made many decisions that could not now be changed. Now, without customary evening stimulant, and with the tide in full ebb, he sat and felt afraid. God, it could really go wrong. He didn't quite understand why he had taken so many irrevocable steps. Alice had jolted him, certainly, and made him take a good look at himself, not liking what he saw, but did that mean a man should try to change everything? Maybe if he had edged into it bit by bit.

Well, no sense in crying about it now. Get to work, boy. This is a new kind of corner cutting. Giving the client the most for the least money. Now the shower. Ceramic tile comes too high. Scored plaster with waterproof paint won't hold up. Plastic tile needs a pretty fair surface. Okay, so we try Marlite. Run it all the way up and then use molly screws for the curtain rod, and the rod better be chrome over brass. Terrazzo base, then run the vinyl floor up over the raised edge, and for a neat job, build the lavatory in and use the same vinyl on the counter-top effect. He tossed the pencil aside and bit his lip. And sighed and picked it up again as he began to wonder if you couldn't use a metal, prefab shower-stall and have some automobile place undercoat the sides that would be concealed, so that it wouldn't have that cheap, tinny sound when you hit your elbows on it or when the water drummed against it.

And Clyde Schermer stood and watched the girl who sat alone in a booth, watched her slide her eyes across him until he was absolutely sure, and then dropped his cigarette and turned his foot on it and started for the booth, taking in that moment the image of Ellen and forcing it back and down and out through a convenient trap door in the back of his mind, and giving the girl the hard practiced smile.

And Thomas Marin Griffin sat alone in his apartment. It was a hotel apartment uptown, just far enough off Madison so he could hear the more hurried sound of the uptown-downtown traffic. In the long day many things had come to his attention. As there had been no time to consider them, he had filed in his memory those factors he considered significant. Now he took them out. Assorted facts of many varieties. A court decision on a minority stockholders' suit. Discovery of a new natural gas field. A serious and expensive bug in a new transmission out of Detroit. A cut in the import duties on small motors.

He had learned long ago that creative thought is largely the discovery of relationships. In industry the most sensitive and accurate gauges are themselves gauged by metal blocks machined to an almost incredible accuracy of dimension. They are kept in a specific temperature and humidity range so that expansion and contraction will not prejudice their accuracy. So perfect are their mirrored surfaces that when two of them are pressed firmly together, the dry metal surfaces cling and they cannot be pulled apart but must instead be slid apart to break the molecular bond between them.

And in Thomas Marin Griffin's mind were those facts, the new ones of this day, and all of the known facts from all the rest of his days. And he sat in silence and sought relationships between these facts which were like the mirror surface blocks with which the gauges are tested. He turned them this way and that, pressing the surfaces together, seeking creative and profitable relationships. When two facts stuck together in the illumination of an inevitable relationship, he felt a warmth and satisfaction. When he could make three or more cohere, he felt a flush in his cheeks and a rippling flutter of excitement that seemed to start under his breastbone and spread both up and down. And when the inventiveness of his mind began to stale, he filed away the newly discovered relationships, setting himself a schedule of the action he would take on them. It was not greed that moved him, nor the need of power so much as the hard flutter of excitement, better than a woman, that came when surfaces matched, when corners were lined up, when two unrelated things became related and hence profitable by the strength of his disciplined mind.

He was forever setting up and arranging things that other men thought of just a bit later.

And in the studio David Delevan's thoughts crawled through his mind like small random animals which crawled under a dusty rug, making little places over their furry backs that moved with them. And when two of the moving places would converge and touch, there would be a moment of strain and motionlessness and they would diverge and move about again, in furry, dusty aimlessness.

Bobby Rawls rode the rattling coach, drinking from a bottle with a sailor while the night hurried by outside, the signal bells of the crossings bursting and fading into minor key, quickly lost in the rushing night. He wept inside for Norma while he and the sailor leaned red-faced at each other and talked boldness. And after a while the rye turned sour in him and when he threw up, holding his foot on the water pedal of the train toilet, the train lurched

and he bumped his head and spotted his knee. He went to
his berth and left the shade up and watched the wheeling
night. A train exploded by, going in the other direction,
shocking him, making his heart pound for a few moments.
Its diesel bray challenged all the still things, all the quiet
things, and Robert Rawls thought of all those who lay in
each others' arms and heard that beast sound in the
flatland night. And that way managed at last to make the
tears come. They did not sting. They were round and
bland and warm, feeling like oil on his face. The train
plunged west.

Chapter Thirteen

There is an old airport at Stockton, but the commer-
cial airlines do not use it anymore. It was started
back in the days of struts and wing-walking, of lumpy
grass and voices thin across the field from the temporary
stands the day of the jump from five thousand feet. A mile
up.

Later, in the late twenties, there was a time when all
civic organizations began to talk about the airport
improvements. New runways were laid out and paved.
Hangars went up. The air age was here. Lindberg had
flown to Paris. So on Sunday the cars would drive out and
park by the fence, and families would watch the takeoffs
and the landings. It was a magical time. A carnival time,
with men selling ice cream and whirring, little airplanes
tied to the ends of sticks.

But the hills nudged in too close, and the area was too
populated and the runways could not be extended. So now
it is a place where you can keep your aircoup or cub in a
dilapidated hangar for a small monthly charge, where the
wind rattles old signs, where students wait in overcasual

nervousness for their next lesson. Sometimes, at night, the hot-rodders get out onto the old cracked runways and drag race until the cops come. It is a sad place now, and the improvement bonds clutter the deposit boxes of the die-hards, the hopefuls.

The new airport is a tri-county project, far out on lonely land, actually closer to Clayton than to Stockton. There rises the building of blond stone, glass, and driftwood-gray trim, with restaurantlike operating rooms, bored chant of the tower, arrival-and-departure board, electric baggage trucks, magazine racks, red gas trucks, NO SMOKING BEYOND THIS POINT. It is a trackless railroad station, a wondrous and alarming thing turned now into dullness and routine, into a sort of bored civil-service efficiency. A man stands in the super-conny aisle, reading his newspaper while waiting to file toward the wheeled stairway with his eighty-seven fellow passengers. And in that gesture there is the end of all high glory. Subway in the air, it is. No more dope and struts and fabric and the exposed cylinder ends. No more the tiny figure on the high wing, and the great crowd's *aaaah* and the drop through sunlight until the chute blooms. It is now a matter of credit cards and confirmed reservations and, if you are sick, there is a special paper bag—if you don't get the Dramamine in time.

Flight 707 was scheduled for arrival at 2:08. Susan felt the plane letting down. Robbie, excitement on his face, was trying to see across her, and he pointed out things. She felt a pang of jealousy that here she saw for the first time an excitement in him that was not of her making. The signs about smoking and seat belts came on and the stewardess went up and down the aisle awakening those who slept. The earth tilted at an angle against the wing, with a toy group of buildings and toy runways below for a time then gone, and then they were down, Susan tensing for a jar of landing, waiting and waiting, then finding they were turning, taxiing, she unsnapped the belt.

"Nervous, honey?"

"Sort of, I guess," she said.

"They're harmless. They'll love you anyway. Hey, there

they are. See? Behind the fence there to the left of the gate. Wilma and George and Alice. I don't see anybody else."

Susan had seen pictures and she at last spotted them. At last they went down the long stairs, Robbie carrying her small travel case, hurrying, taking her arm and hurrying her along once they were down on the concrete. Again she felt that twinge of annoyance with him. Yet, after all, it was his family.

There was the confusion of introduction, with all the right words said, and a forthright kiss from Wilma, who seemed matronly and pleasant and proper, and a shy, cool kiss from Alice, and a walloping, let's-kiss-the-bride smack from hefty, club-joining George, who punched Robbie in the arm and told him he had gotten himself a nice dish, and then being left with the two women while Robbie and George went off to see about the bags. Yes, it was a very nice trip. No, not rough at all. Oh, I got this in Mexico. I'm glad you like it. I'm dying to meet all of Robbie's family. Yes, Washington was dreadfully hot, but we were lucky enough to get an air-conditioned room. Coming up we changed planes in San Antonio, and then had I think it was an hour and half to wait. Then the flight stopped in New Orleans, then Nashville, then Washington. [Trying all this time to find the right balance, enough warmth, enough shyness, enough brideness, and seeing in their faces that she was doing it correctly, seeing the general look of relief hidden by the politeness.]

They went to the car and George put the bags in the trunk compartment and with the three women in back and the two men in front they drove out of there, and Susan wished that Robbie had made more of an effort to sit beside her, because she needed to feel that he was close. He didn't understand that these were strangers. They were so familiar to him.

The guest annex on the Furmon house was new and pleasant. It had a connecting door into the main house and also a private entrance. There was a tiny kitchen alcove, with combination stove and refrigerator and a sink nearby. Alice Furmon said, "There's breakfast things in the refrigerator, and more towels in this cupboard. And, let me see, I guess that's all you have to know. We won't run everybody at you at once, Susan. Suppose you relax for a while and freshen up. The rest of the tribe will be over for drinks about five thirty, and then we're all going to the club for dinner. There'll be a lot of people to meet there, so maybe you ought to take a nap or something."

Then after Susan had protested about everything being so nice, about being so much trouble, she was at last able to close the door and lean her back against it and stick her underlip out and blow her hair off her forehead.

"That bad, honey?"

"Just sort of confusing. Hey, this is very nice, you know it? Private."

"Mr. and Mrs. Delevan at home."

"That still sounds crazy. How would you like it if all of a sudden you had to become Mr. Walton?"

"Do you like them?" he asked, suddenly earnest.

"They're nice, Robbie. They really are."

"Come here."

"Uh-uh. I've got to unpack so things will hang out. How will the women dress, Robbie?"

"I haven't the faintest idea. The club isn't what you'd call a very formal operation. A sort of a cocktail-dress deal, I'd say."

"Go ask Alice and borrow an iron, darling. Ask her what sort of thing she's wearing." He kissed her and went off. And while he was gone she sat on the bed and suddenly felt small, forlorn, and very much alone in a world of strangers.

When Ben Delevan got home at five thirty on Saturday evening he found Wilma waiting—all dressed, ready and indignant. "The children have gone over already. What *possessed* you, Ben, to be so late?"

"Couldn't be helped. Sorry. Something came up."

"Something always comes up. Now hurry just as fast as you can. I'm going on over."

"Plane on time?"

"Right on the minute."

"What's she like?"

"I'd say she's no fool, Ben. I think she knows what she's doing every minute. But they seem very much in love. I mean that's something you can sense. Now *do* hurry. I laid out everything for you."

He showered and dressed with just enough leisureliness to retain a sense of independence. And just enough haste to avoid too cold an eye from Wilma. He knotted his tie carefully and patted it into position and looked at himself with a proper measure of approval. As he walked across to George's place he could hear the chatter of the party. He stopped, out of sight, tasting the wind. There was a new flavor to it, a gusty humidity. The June leaves flapped over, exposing their pale undersides. And quick little winds flapped at his pants cuffs.

The party had a colorful look. His own children and Wilma, and the Quinn Delevans, and the George Furmons, and the Robbie Delevans. And Sandy, with a barometric awareness of weather change, running in silent, tireless, solemn circles on the wide, green lawn, curls bouncing, legs thin and brown and fleet.

They looked toward him as he approached, smiling, and he made a smiling half salute and went directly to the pale-haired bride, who looked up at him out of gray eyes, pupils made tiny by the terrace sunlight, late out of the west, and started to raise her hand toward his and then, as though on impulse, stood up and shook his hand.

"Nice to have you aboard," he said, wishing he could think of something better.

"Nice to be aboard, captain," she said, and something quick danced for a moment in her eyes, giving him the impression that she and he were for some inexplicable reason close, even in that first moment of meeting. Yet he had met many who had this knack and used it all the time with everyone and it meant nothing. So in caution he smiled and turned to Robbie and congratulated him and gratefully accepted bourbon from George, who knew enough to have something other than cocktails at a cocktail party. And, from the side, he watched Susan with the

others and felt pleased out of all proportion when he saw
that what he had seen in her was not something turned on
for the others too, but had been a quick and valid affinity
between them. He knew he would like this girl. He knew
her strength would be welcome.

Reassured, he turned his attention toward Quinn. He
felt guilty and uneasy at not having talked to Quinn since
the Thursday scene. And though Brock had warned him
about the loss of the mustache, he was still shocked at the
way the change enfeebled Quinn's face. At the way it
changed an ersatz strength to a look of uncertainty. What
had been bored appraisal was now shown to be a compressed shyness. He went over and sat next to Quinn and
said in a low voice, "Sick yesterday?"

Bess, overhearing, said rather shaply, "He was out of
sorts yesterday, Ben. This morning, too. I didn't think he
ought to come tonight, but he keeps saying he's fine. He
doesn't look fine. Would you say he looks fine?"

Bess's habit of talking about Quinn in his presence as
though he were a child or deaf always made Ben uneasy.
"You'll be okay by Monday, Quinn boy. Hope you will.
Things piling up a little. Got some stuff I want you to
handle." Saying it, Ben knew it was a feeble and awkward
attempt to make amends for the things he had said on
Thursday.

Quinn turned his head slowly and looked directly at Ben
for the first time. He frowned as though puzzled. "Monday? I'll be fine on Monday. I'm fine now."

"He keeps saying that, but he doesn't look it," Bess said.
"The cat's got his tongue. He just sits like that. And he
gets so cross with me."

Ben gave up. He looked over at Susan and saw that his
own children were monopolizing her. Brock, sitting on one
heel, talking with low-voiced enthusiasm; Ellen just sitting
and looking at Susan with warm love and admiration in
her eyes. If the kids were any indication, Susan was in.

George took his empty glass and said, "You need more,
bub. Back in a flash."

Ben watched George go over to the table where the
bottles were. Alice was there, putting hot things on a plate

of hors d'oeuvres, and Ben nearly gasped aloud when he saw George give her a quick caress that was furtive and direct and anything but subtle. He half expected Alice to bash him with the plate of hors d'oeuvres, and when she didn't, he thought that what he had seen had been imagined. Then he saw Alice's face and throat darken and saw her touch her cheek against George's shoulder for the barest fraction of a second.

Ben felt as though he had been peering under a drawn curtain. He marveled that he had been so wrong about them for so long. That he had so definitely decided that Alice, cool and withdrawn in all things, would insist on restraint and circumspection in all matters of love. Yet here was a sudden and unexpected key to a relationship that was apparently a good deal more earthy than anything he could have guessed. And was, amazingly, reciprocal rather than being merely endured by Alice. And was, even more astonishingly, progressing briskly after many years of marriage. He had to turn his head to keep from staring at Alice. He felt guilty, and at the same time he felt as though he had been cheated in some obscure way. He resented being proved wrong about people he thought he had known so well. And he began to look around at his other relatives with dim suspicion.

As the shadows began to grow longer it slowly became apparent to all of them that Quinn Delevan might very possibly ruin the evening. When the drinks had not come fast enough, he had gone and made his own. And now he had taken up his station near the bottles, looking through everyone. Drinking with metronomic efficiency. Conversation began to get too loud and too brittle, and everyone laughed too often, laughed in uncomfortable awareness of Quinn and not knowing how to stop him. Not with the bride present.

His face was masklike in the fading light, and his movements were wooden-toy, wind-up movements, almost audible the crinkling of coil spring, the brass biting of the little gears. And turned, saying nothing, empty glass falling on the grass at the edge of the stone, and walked away on stilt legs, back rigid, feet feeling for the grass and for the mechanical balance. In the silence of his leaving, his shadow moving long across the grass, Bess called out to him, called his name, trying to make her voice casual. But he did not turn and her voice, a flat cry, seemed to reecho among them, and then was covered with the conversation which dismissed him with its jauntiness, yet underlined his absence with the little edges that showed through.

Here was a new daughter brought from a far tribe, and they wanted to show her the solidities, the huts staunchly thatched, the crops tended, the good washing-stones by the river, the boldness of warriors, the fertility of women, the grace of their dancing, and the respect for taboos. But one of the greeters had violated taboo and shamed the tribe.

There was the one thin call and that was all.

They all heard the car sound, the high, hard roar of the motor, and though they could not see the car, they heard it leave the drive, shrill onto the pavement, take the long, fading plunge down through the dusk of the hill. Bess started to stand up and sank back, making no sound. Ben met Wilma's glance, saw that her lips were tightly compressed. Alice stood with the plate of hors d'oeuvres, poised, still, head tilted a bit to one side, her expression odd—the look of a person who has forgotten something and gets the first vague mental clue as to what it was that was forgotten. Then she bent and smiled and passed the platter to the bride, who took one, smiled her thanks upward, raised it to the fresh, red lips, white teeth biting firmly, delicately.

Ben met George's glance and nodded at him and they moved ponderously, too obviously, out of the group and met over on the lawn.

"Drunk as a hoot owl," George said softly.

"I know. Too damn drunk to drive like that. He'll kill somebody or himself. What a time to pick."

"What should we do about it?"

"I'll go in and use your phone, George. Ask to have him picked up. It'll be easier to hush it up if we ask, if they don't just grab him. I'll tell them to phone me at the club."

"I guess that's best. What got into him, Ben?"

"I rode him pretty hard the other day."

"That isn't enough reason. Is there something else? Is he in some kind of a jam?"

"I frankly don't know. I better phone."

"Go right ahead. Use the extension in the bedroom. So Bailey won't get an earful."

George whispered it to Alice. Ben came back and whispered it to Wilma. Ellen overheard her mother being told. She found a chance to tell Brock. Robbie asked Ben and Ben told him. And later, as they were going to the cars, after Mr. Shelter had arrived to be on hand in case David got upset, after Alice had kissed Sandy good night, Robbie whispered to his bride. So it was known by all of them. And there was a brittle covering of suspense over the life and movement and color of the evening.

Ben, in his nervousness, drank too much both before and after dinner. No word had come through. He tried to tell himself that drunks and fools have wry angels who protect them. He knew he had reached the point where, though in control of all physical faculties, he would talk too much and too often. He watched Brock dancing with Ellen, to the music of the four-piece orchestra that played at the country club every Saturday during the summer. Piano, drum, clarinet and muted trumpet. Balding, blank-eyed men who never referred to written music. Music that was for dancing, specifically, rigidly, uncompromisingly for dancing—*One* two three four. *One* two three four. *Oh, it's only a paper moon shining over a tea for two* . . .

He went through the side doors and across the terrace and down the four stone steps to the grass and heard the scrape of leather on stone behind him and turned to see his new sister-in-law slimly silhouetted against the light that escaped to the terrace.

"Mr. Delevan!"

"Ben. It's too confusing around here to call me anything else, Susan."

"I've been looking for a chance to talk to you."

"Come on then, I need some air. We'll walk and talk."

She walked beside him, silently for a time. They approached the first tee. He felt the bench and it was just a bit damp. Not too damp. "We can sit and talk."

"Sure," she said. He peeled the cellophane from a cigar, bit the end off, lit it carefully, turning it in the match flame. The music came across to them from the lighted club.

"Is something the matter?"

"Mr. . . . Ben, I mean. I don't know how to start. Well, because I don't want to sound disloyal to Robbie. I love him. That doesn't mean that love *has* to be blind. He's so . . . trusting about everything. And I don't want him to put you . . . or the rest of the family on a spot."

"How do you think he can do that?"

"He wants to work for the company. I mean he thinks that it's all right. Just to ask for a job and get it, and maybe he feels you sort of have to take him on because of the stock and so on. He's talked about the company a lot. It's not so much what he's said as what he hasn't said. And I've had business training, Ben. Even if I have been in government, I've worked for men who have been in industry. And, well, I've wondered about something. I mean there's hardly any dividends on the stock. Maybe you're modernizing or expanding or something and that's why. But he told me how old the company is. I guess I better be perfectly honest. He was going to resign. I made him take a leave of absence. I told him that maybe I wouldn't like it here. I gave that as the reason. I love it here. But I wouldn't want us to be . . . that kind of a family charity."

"Why not?"

"That's a funny question," she said with some heat. "I'm his wife. I want him to *be* somebody. And he *can* be somebody. I know that. He's intelligent. There just isn't enough push to him. I can provide that. I intend to— without being obvious about it. But I can't if he is in some job where he just goes and sits in an office and looks important and draws a salary for it. Why did you ask me that?"

"I wanted to make sure it was true. I wanted to make sure that there is another pair of shoulders in the family."

"Is . . . is it like that?"

"Just like that, Suzy. Maybe I've had just enough to drink so I can gripe. They all think everything is automatic. They all think their world has got . . . reinforced-concrete pillars that reach down to bedrock. They all think . . . the hell with it. I talk too much."

"No you don't. You don't."

"You know what I would give him? You know what I'll give him if he asks?"

"What, Ben?"

"Work clothes, Suzy. Sweat and sore muscles and pay to match. And they'll think I'm a bastard. He can take it or leave it. I can see how shocked he'll look. Me? Me! You can't mean it, old Ben. I make mistakes, Suzy. Bad ones. But never twice. Never, never the same bad one twice."

"You mean Quinn?"

He stared at her in the darkness. "By God, girl, you astonish me."

"It wasn't hard to guess. It couldn't be anyone else, could it?"

"No. I guess not. So there it is. So I'm glad you didn't let him resign. Because he wouldn't take it."

"He'll take it, Ben. I'll see that he takes it if you promise one thing. If you promise that you will do no single thing to make it softer or quicker or easier for him, and fire him if he needs it and promote him if he earns it."

"Yes, but——"

"We have some money saved. We'll gamble it. I couldn't risk letting the outside standard of living drop too far. But on that basis, I'll see that he takes it. And I think I know him well enough to know that he won't disappoint you." Her voice changed then, became deeper and more resonant. "You see, Ben, we're a good team, Robbie and I."

He waited long moments. "I moved too fast, Susan. There's something else. I mean something that may change the whole thing.

"What's that?"

"I haven't talked about it to anybody but Quinn. And it was a mistake to talk to him. I haven't talked to Wilma, anybody. And I'm not going to. It's a decision I have to make by myself. And soon. There are a lot of ... factors. A lot of things that don't have values you can write down and add up. I remember when I was little I saw a brown cow. She'd tried to jump a fence and got the front end of her over and hung up there, bawling and rolling her eyes. That's where I am. With no farmer coming to use cutters on the top strand. So keep him from asking anything until——"

She touched his arm lightly. "What's that? Listen."

The amplifier system they used for the music blurred the human voice, but they could hear it dimly and fill in enough of the blanks.

"Mr. Delevan. Mr. Benjamin Delevan. Telephone."

"Quinn!" he said softly and got up quickly and hurried toward the club and the telephone, with a feeling of something cold spreading through his belly.

Chapter Fourteen

Quinn walked over with Bess and met the bride and greeted Robbie. He held the bride's hand in his for a moment, and her hand was a bit clammy and he knew she was nervous, meeting them all. He was given a drink and the others came and he let the conversation become meaningless to him. If you listened just to the sounds of the words and not the meaning, listened mostly to the vowel sounds, then suddenly it would be as though they spoke a foreign language—and their words would come through in a hollow, meaningless way, like the voices of parents when you were a child and half-asleep in the back seat of the car.

The world had turned strange for him. It had happened on Thursday, driving home. An odd change in all things. A thin transparent membrane stretched slack across the road so that the front end of the car touched it and, speeding, began to pull it tighter and tighter so that at last the car thrust forward into a glistening pouch, and he could see through it but all colors were swarmy, like oil on water. And in a last moment of tension the membrane burst and the car drove through into this other world on the other side where nothing was quite the same. Where things were almost the same, but you had to be careful about them because they were different.

He had stayed home on Friday to better consider the differentness of things and test his steps in this world on the other side. The words of them were meaningless around him. He sat and considered the bride, sidelong and wary. And drank and thought of her. The mincing, simpering bride, securing poison candy inside her taffy hips. And black groom like a hammer. Like a blind club. Like a darkened machine for pounding soft things in factory silences. Two of them, sitting in their sated arrogance there, with their fleshy stink of evil, all tissue and fluids and the hidden pumps and churnings of the membranous bodies. So a God-thumb could come out of the sky and rub them both at once in a dark wet shining smear across the terrace stone. And cleanse itself on the grass, removing an unpleasant stickiness from the giant whorls and ridges.

Drank and watched sidelong her depraved legs, evil cup of lips. Drank and sensed the stickiness of all the others around him, the fatty rub of tissues together. Drank and stared obliquely at the giant breasts of his wife. All of them around him, heated in their flesh, veined and glandular, fat marbling the red meat of them, throats working wet, stomachs fisting shut and opening, fisting shut and opening, on the bits of food cut smaller than their hungers.

Got up before the scream began and walked away from

them and felt the scream subside before it was born, felt it
curl and nestle down, a soft rustling amid dryness of him.
Walked tall with a shadow long beside him scissoring its
dark legs. Sat in the car and turned the brass thing and
thumbed the chrome thing and trod on the rubber thing
and the motor roared back at all of them. Dived down the
hill, fingers like dried leaves on the wheel. Dived godlike
and straight, closing god eyes for a little time and opening
them slowly, casually, still aware of straightness, of precision like lines drawn.

When he was on the highway, after the shrieking,
wrenching turn around the square, after the truck that
filled his vision and fell away to one side, after the tree
that swung across in front of him, he took his foot from
the gas pedal. It took a long time for the car to slow down
almost to a stop. Then with delicacy he used his foot
which was now carved of finest wood, to touch the gas
pedal and bring the needle up to thirty-five. The needle
did not waver. Dry-leaf hands and wood-dried and carved
and polished. Clockwork heart and silver loins. Steel-dry
teeth and cordovan tongue. Jeweled eyes and paper lungs.
Function, balance, precision. Intersection of lines. Roll of
bearings. Predictable rotation of stone planet.

It was dark when he drove down Fremont Street. He
drove to the closed gas station. The night light was on. He
was surprised that it had taken so long. He parked the car
and turned off his lights and got out. He bounced the keys
in the palm of his hand. Ignition key and trunk
compartment for both cars. Front door, back door, studio
door. Office door. Locker at the club. Desk drawer.
Bonny's door. Eleven keys. They were on a chain. There
was a charm on the chain. A silver peso with a hole bored
through it. Worn smooth from years of carrying it.

He grinned ice-lipped at the night and wound up with
the exaggerated formality of the backyard years. He threw
the keys up and out and high, arching in the night,
hurting his shoulder, seeing a brassy flicker of them as
they passed the street lamp into blackness. For the
moment there was no traffic on Fremont. And he heard

them strike on a roof and bounce and slide, slide faster into a second of silence before landing on tin.

He walked across to Bonny's entrance, snapping his fingers as he walked, making the crisp dry sounds like things breaking, taking pleasure in the little sounds because it was something he had always been able to do well. Alice could whistle better.

Rattled his fingers dry on the door, seeing the light pattern from her window onto the grass, feeling with tongue tip a rough place on one filling as he waited, hearing her steps coming, grate of knob, clack of latch, tink of spring hinge, then light washing out at him, yellow-pale on his face, and her voice soft, "Quinn, I worried. Come in."

Went in and stood dry and godlike, watching her mouth move and seeing the expressions go and come across her face, and knew, without hearing the words, that it was about the mustache again and he wished that they would stop talking about it. Over here in this other place.

She came close to him, her face fattening against his eyes like a trick-movie shot, and she kissed him, taking a quick, shy, sly nibble at his underlip, and the face moved back again, moving into proportion. Then smaller than proportion as she grew tiny and the room slid in upon itself. These things you had to watch on the other side. Slyly, but showing nothing.

Stood smiling and watching her, watching the nervousness of her grow as he said nothing. Saw that she sensed that he now knew of the tricks. Go down three steps and open the door and a bell will ring and an old man will come out of the back, and there you can buy all the tricks there are. Itching-powder, lipstick, dribble glasses, breasts, worms to put in drinks, round thighs, disappearing coins, white bellies, rubber daggers, red lips. . . . He has everything there, and everything is for sale. And in the dusty stillness of the shop you can hear the old echoes of strained laughter. Like sobbings.

Looked at the trick body of her and the trick eyes and the growth of fright and laughed. Looked down at his own hand and saw that the knuckles under the skin were truly marble, ancient and avenging. Caught her as she turned in sudden wildness. Swung her back and timed the blow of the steel and leather arm and marble hand. Timed it into thick sound and redness. And held and struck and held and struck, and brought limpness up with mighty effort to strike once more and release and watch the red doll rolling, pleased to see the special precision. Arms just so. Legs just so. Red spreading out from under the still cheek. Not knowing it was precise and right until you saw it thus and thus and perfectly so.

He turned off the light and went out and closed the door quietly behind him. He went to his car and got in and sat for a long time. He looked through his pockets for his keys. He felt a strange rippling of uncertainty. He got out and walked down to Fremont and turned down Fremont.

Blur of places and light and sweat. Juke blast. Liquor bite. And a place with stools. Late. The god stuff gone. Felt furtive touch, looked down saw thigh-pressed the haired hand, looked into stranger face, with its stubble and grin of broken teeth and hit out at the face. Bump of head on wooden floor and then sirens, head hurting. Yanking, pulling at him—*whatsyourname*—*wheredyalive* —*whatsyourname*— Yank and slap. Leave me alone. Let me rest. Give me silence. . . .

Brock followed his father down the corridor to the room where a high counter stretched across half the room. Brock stood at his father's side, a half step back. There was an institutional smell. Green cakes of deodorant, dust, varnish, cleaning compound and ammonia salts.

"I'm Benjamin Delevan. You phoned me about my brother."

"We got him." Bored voice. Voice of Saturday night.

"Suppose you tell me the details and tell me how I can get him out of here, then." The hard authoritative cut of his father's voice surprised Brock. He looked at his father in surprise. He looked no different.

"Yes, sir. Ah . . . Car twelve made the arrest. He was in one of those queer joints on lower Fremont. Pretty drunk. Fighting. No keys or wallet or anything. We got his name off the label in his coat. About the same time his car was spotted. There was a pickup on it and it was in a gas station. It'll be towed in. He's been booked, so you want to take him along with you now, you got to post a hundred bucks bond."

"I brought the money. Do I give it to you?"

"Yes. I'll give you a receipt. Have him in here Monday morning at nine. Joe, go get me that D-and-D out of the tank. The tall one with the knee out of his pants. Name's Delevan."

Brock watched the money counted out on the counter top. The man behind the counter put carbon paper in a pad of forms and began to make out the receipt. His father turned and locked his hands behind him and began to stare at a bulletin board on the wall. Brock couldn't tell if his father was reading the dusty notices or just staring into space.

They brought Quinn in. He walked with a curious shambling limp and his eyes looked loose in his head. He tried to smile at them. They could not understand what he tried to say. He smelled of vomit.

"Here you are, sir. Nine o'clock Monday. Handle him okay?"

"We can handle him."

They each took an arm. He would have fallen on the steps outside had they not supported him. They got him into the back of the car. Ben got in with him, saying, "You drive."

"Sure."

It was a silent trip back. Quinn mumbled twice. Brock drove as close as he could to Quinn's back door. As they were getting him out of the back, Bess came out of the kitchen door. She had changed from her party dress to a robe.

"Is he all right? Is he hurt? Is he hurt, Ben?"

"He isn't hurt. He's drunk."

They walked him into the light, his head bobbing. Bess said, "Darling! Your trousers! Your best suit. Oh my darling! What did they do to you?"

She fluttered in front of them and they got him into the kitchen. Ben said, "Where do you want him?"

"I can take him from here," she said.

"Better let us. He's pretty heavy."

The fluttering stopped and she stood close and took Quinn's arm. "I said I can take him from here. Thank you very much. I can handle it very nicely by myself." She was proud and angry.

"Okay. We can stand by, Bess."

"I'd rather you'd go home, really. Ben, I don't mean to sound angry. I appreciate your doing this. But ... it's my problem. Good night, Ben, Brock. Come on now, darling. Go ahead. Lean on Bess. Lean hard, baby. Come on. That's the way, darling. That's the way, my poor darling."

"Come on," Ben said to Brock.

Once they were out in the night, Brock said, "Brother! That certainly took a half hitch in the evening."

"It could have been one hell of a lot worse."

"I know. I know it could."

"Tone it down for your mother, will you? And ... thanks for helping, son."

Brock felt a sudden surge of pride that nearly choked him. Pride in awareness of strength and maturity. In knowing that he had done a small thing, but done it quietly and well and without excitement or silliness, or assigning exaggerated values to what he saw or to his own participation. There had been a manual training teacher in grade school. Brock remembered his saying one day with unexpected heat, "If a man can drive *one* nail perfectly and that is part of something he is building, then it is a special thing for him to do." The class had thought the old joker was nuts. Some of the time he'd acted half-crazy. Taking botched work and slamming it on the floor and stamping it with his heavy carpenter's boots. It began to make strange sense, now, that business about one nail. Do one small thing well. And then the next small thing. And maybe they will be a part of something big and good. But if you try to do the whole big good thing at once ...

He drove the car back to their garage while his father walked across the lawn. He had to go out onto the main

road and into the next drive. As he turned in he saw the
light go out suddenly in the guest annex George had
added to the Furmon house. He saw it go out and thought
of his young uncle and the tanned, pale-headed bride and
his hands felt sweaty on the wheel. He had been astound-
ed at Robbie's luck. Even after seeing the picture of
her, he had expected the flaws he saw in all wives. Dumpy
ankles or a silly voice or a broad beam. This was Wife but
it was also Girl. And that made it confusing. Somehow
unfair that Robbie should have been able to acquire the
legal and unassailable right to take her to bed, this magical girl, with the full knowledge and consent of everyone.
That it was, in fact, expected of him. Her very desirability
seemed to indicate that possession of her was something to
be accomplished in stealth, in awareness of guilt.

Sitting there in the dark silent car in the dark garage for
a few moments, he thought of his father and his mother.
So there, too, there must have been a time when she was
both Wife and Girl. Magical and legal and wonderful. A
strange overlapping. It made him uncomfortable to think
about that. It was funny. You knew the words. You knew
the associations. But they were just words and sort of
hollow, unfilled-in facts, and then there would come a
moment of comprehension like this and you would fill it
all in and the words would have new meanings. Like the
trick where you ask somebody to pronounce first
MacDermott, then MacLaughlin—spelling them out each
time—and finally MacHinery. With the last word
expanding abruptly into a new dimension.

He got out of the car and stopped in the driveway and
looked in the direction of the dark windows, then plodded
toward the lighted kitchen of his home, thinking of the
stranger they had brought out, the mumbling man, all
stench and apology.

Robbie held her head against his shoulder and scowled
into the darkness. "Hell, I don't know why I should feel
apologetic. I mean it *is* my family and all that, but if
Quinn wants to be a damn fool——"

"You're not your brother's keeper."

"You think I could have———"

"Don't take that as criticism, darling. I meant you actually are not his keeper."

"Anyway, I found out this certainly isn't a thing that has been going on. He hasn't done this before. But you see, I feel as if I were convincing you of something. As if you had a right not to believe me."

"Robbie, Robbie. Oh, darling, you don't see how much there is here."

"What do you mean by that?"

"Things I didn't have. Ever. A sort of warmth and trust and love, and people taking care of each other. My father used to walk me down to the store. And we'd go in. And there'd be people there and he'd laugh in a funny way and say in a big loud voice, 'Suzy and me had to get out of the house before the old woman drove us both nuts.' It was one of his ways of taking revenge on her. Later I realized she had her own ways of doing the same thing. They, both of them, ran around to the whole world holding their hands out and saying love me and hate the other one. Don't apologize for your people, Robbie."

"Do you like them?"

"I like them all except Ben. You see, I love Ben. Not the way I love you. I like the rest of them. I didn't get a chance to really meet Quinn, of course. Or ... is it David?"

"He's the weird one. Brock told me there isn't much change. Damn sad thing. Gosh, this has been some day, wife."

"Say it again."

"Wife. Wife. Wife. Has a funny sound when you keep saying it. Ever do that when you were little?"

"Oh, yes. Say words over and over at night until they didn't mean anything at all. Until they got kind of creepy. There was one that was one of my favorites. Burner. Like on a stove. Try it."

"Burner, burner, burner, burner, burner, burner . . . hey, that does get sort of wild."

"What would somebody think of this conversation?"

They both began to giggle. And turned toward each

other. And her soft laughter began to change. And falter. And become something else entirely. There in the night on Gillman Hill. And thunder rolled toward them out of the southwest. Rolled and grumbled and then cracked loudly. Later the hard rain came. A thick-bodied rain that sounded like trains passing. When it stopped, toward morning, it left a thin layer of water in the rain-washed glass beside the terrace, the glass Quinn had dropped, the glass Mrs. Bailey had overlooked when she picked up after the others had left, when she had tidied up, wearing around her mouth that tight, sucked-in look of disapproval habitual with her when removing the evidences of drinking and smoking and carrying on.

Chapter Fifteen

Quinn awoke on Sunday morning at ten thirty. After he had looked at his watch and let his arm fall back, he knew that he was sore and sick. There were unaccountable aches and bruises all over his body. His forehead pulsed, his mouth tasted sick, his thirst was enormous. So immediate was his discomfort that it left no room in his mind for more than the contemplation of discomfort. He was but dimly aware that beyond this immediacy there crouched black things waiting, like patient animals. He got out of bed in gingerly stages, wincing at the brutal increase in head pain that resulted from each change of position. He made the four steps to the bathroom doorway and stood and held onto the doorframe, his eyes closed. His heart made a dry, hammering sound. He opened his eyes and saw the puffed and reddened knuckles of his right hand, flesh bloated so that the knuckles themselves seemed to be dimples rather than the customary bony knobs. But there was no room to think about that.

He held onto the edge of the lavatory and found the yellow plastic glass. He rinsed it out and drank the water eagerly. The first glassful had a faint and nauseating peppermint tinge of toothpaste. He drank five glasses, and the water bloated him. He adjusted the shower, peeled off his pajamas, damp with night sweat, and stepped under the water, leaning his shoulders against the cool wall of the shower, standing with face upturned, the rush of water stinging his face and chest. He stood there for a long time. When he went back, dried, naked, uncombed, into the bedroom, he felt uncomfortably tall, tottery, fragile. The head pulse had dulled. The long shower had puckered his fingertips. His long, white feet looked pulpy. Tan stopped at his throat and his biceps. The rest of him was the color of soap.

He put on nylon shorts, heavy, white wool socks. He went back into the bathroom and shaved himself with great care, though awkwardly because his right hand was stiff. His face was not marked. There was a bluish bruise under his heart, and his right knee was barked, freshly scabbed. He rubbed a lanolin tonic into his hair and combed it carefully. In the bedroom again he put on pale-tan slacks, loafers, a lightweight wool shirt, brown-and-white houndstooth check.

He went to the bureau for keys and wallet, cigarettes and lighter, pocket change. He could not find the keys. He stood with his hand poised in the automatic gesture of picking them up. And saw a brassy arc through the night, heard a slithering clatter. Something dry turned inside his throat, and a tremor as of excitement went through his chest. But excitement in which there was a flutter of terror. And no wallet. There was no memory to fit the loss of the wallet. No memory of going to bed.

He walked carefully to the kitchen. He wished he did not feel so grotesquely tall and fragile. As though he should duck for doorways. Yet they were high enough for him. All the colors of the house seemed richer, more clearly defined. The corners sharper.

Coffee stood over low blue flame. Note on the table:

There's lots of juice in the refrigerator. Coffee on the stove. Rolls in the oven. I've taken David to the drive-in church. Back by quarter of twelve. Hope you don't feel too bad. B.

He poured a cup of coffee and took it over to the booth, cup jingling in the saucer as he carried it, coffee slopping into the saucer as he set it down. He put his elbows on the table, straddling the cup, and pressed the heels of his hands hard against his eyes. Pressure made green and violet things shimmer against blackness. "God," he said aloud. It was a loud word in the stillness of the house, in the scrubbed and burnished place with its odd littered places where Bess had projects half-completed.

Memory was a child's kaleidoscope. You sipped the coffee. Then looked through the little hole and turned the tube. Sometimes the things would turn into a meaningful pattern. Most times they were just bits of colored junk. Hairy hand, cell door, keys in the air, Brock driving, siren, yellow, broken teeth.

The coffee did not taste right. He poured it into the sink. He opened the refrigerator and looked at the tall glass of juice. The orange of it seemed bright enough to hurt his eyes. He shut the door against the color of it.

So you got drunk. So it happens to everybody. So why do you feel you have come back from some far place. Welcome traveler. Why is your mind all blurred about the mustache? How many days have you been drunk, you great damn fool? You schoolboy.

And he suddenly remembered Robbie and his bride. And a great wave of crimson shame suffused his face, beading his forehead with sweat. He went outdoors. The world was washed and new. It smelled fine. His lips felt heavy and chapped.

Where the hell did you go? Who did you fight with?

He stood there, hands in the pockets of his slacks, looking down at the vivid green of the grass. He wondered if he had made a damn fool of himself with Bonny.

BONNY!

red doll rolling. red, dead, ragged, rolling.

Stood there in the terrible out-of-doors, in light of the frightful sun, stood small on the outer skin of the daylit world under the god eyes, figure at the wrong end of the lens, and the focus of that lens bubbled the gray brain fat under the bone sheath, under the animal pelt trimmed to fashion.

There are the troublesome mornings-after. When in the head are jumbled the unstitched pieces of long conversation, intermingled with corrupt bits of the night's dark dreams so that reality cannot be truly sieved from all the rest of it, and the day is spent in half remembering, half disbelieving, walking about full of a wary conjecture.

And he had reached down into the cooling pot and brought up this clear fragment, true and undeniable and horrid. He looked down at his right hand. It seemed far away from his eyes. The knuckles were puffed and sore. Right hand made sore by the girl-bones, by the girl-face, by the temple structure under that slightly coarsened skin across her cheeks. Girl who kept hurt things in boxes. Girl with a body-shyness, whose very fierceness had a timidity.

He turned and looked at the house behind him with faint surprise that it should be there, unchanged, that it had not become a Disney house for witches, dark windows for eyes and picket-fence teeth. He went in and the house was gay and bright and sharp and clear inside. It was a stage setting. They had been very clever about the lighting, using offstage floods that really looked like sunlight. And things were just enough worn, just far enough off the edge of shopwindow newness so you would swear it was a house where people had lived. But, of course, the play had not started. So he could walk through it inspecting it to make certain it would be satisfactory for the players. Stand here for this line, and then walk to there, and stop and turn and wait just long enough, and then say that dramatic thing, that line he could not remember but which was so suitable.

Didn't they usually wear their hats in the house? Identifiable typecasting. Or was it now polite young men who could be lawyers or insurance people or practically anything, asking permission to smoke and using the ashtrays properly.

Did you know a young woman named Bonita Doyle, an employee of the Stockton Knitting Company?

With the catch, of course, being the use of the past tense. *Yes, I knew her*, you might say.

We've lifted your prints from all over her apartment. Lifted? Why was it lifted? Don't they dust and photograph? *Sorry, you'll have to come with us, Mr. Delevan.* Or plain Delevan. Or nothing. *Just come with us.* For a silent, nervous ride.

Hurt your hand, I see.

Drunk, weren't you?

How long you been keeping her, mister?

EXECUTIVE INDICTED IN LOVE NEST SLAYING. Too long. They usually had ways of saying it in a shorter fashion.

BOSS SLAYS PLAYMATE.

The house sat still in the washed morning, the world hung out to dry, bright in morning sun. The house was still. He walked through the rooms and he was tall and made of glass. He went into his study and sat at the impressive and ornate desk. Gift from Bess. Split-calf accessories. Gifts from Bess. Brass student lamp. Gift from Bess. A leather file with nothing in it, and drawers full of junk. He opened one and looked in. Medicated, fancy-filtered cigarette holders he had used for a week or two and tossed in the drawer. Lighters that no longer lighted. A small stapler that no longer stapled. And the almost new impedimenta of some half dozen attempts to switch to a pipe. Some dark pennies and a corroded nickel. Packet of colored rubber bands.

When they went through his effects they found . . .

Effects. An effect is something that is produced, is it not? The result of something. So these drawers of junk were the produced results of his life, and thus they were his effects. Along with house, cars, land, some savings, some old pictures, a closet packed with clothes. Didn't they give away clothes? Salvation Army or something. And did the ones who put on the used clothes wonder for a moment or two about the man who had worn them? The gray flannel was new. Worn twice. Why would a guy give this away? Maybe he dropped dead, you dope.

And, as he had known he would, known it from the very moment of standing out there in the sun, he opened the bottom drawer. Took out the shallow, heavy box. Opened the cardboard lid. Colt Woodsman Automatic with target barrel. Long rifle. Joint gift from Bess and David last year. He and George had tied cans to strings and tied the strings to limbs and set the cans swinging and walked back from the edge of the woods and turned and took turns firing and found that it was dismayingly difficult.

He hefted the three gay little yellow-and-red boxes of the Western Super-X .22 caliber ammunition and found the one that was half empty. He felt far away from himself. His hands worked, busy and remote from him, on clumsy duty of their own assigning while he sat tall above his hands and waited for them to finish. They loaded a clip and pushed it up into the grip and it clicked into place. One held the grip and the other worked the slide and it was ready. He stood up with it and looked around the room and then, wary of his own fragility, of his brittle tallness, his farawayness, he walked to the couch and stretched out on it, knees bent high, feet braced on leather, wrists braced against his canted thighs, one thumb inside the trigger guard. He could see a little way down the barrel. The hole would look big and then little, big and then little, seeming to pulsate in the slow rhythm of his breathing, hypnotic, like standing on a high ledge over the beetle traffic on asphalt ribbon below.

He exerted a gentle pressure with his thumb, held the pressure and could not increase it.

It was too far away.

He got up and went over to the desk, feeling suddenly competent and rather official about it all. He took paper from the leather rack and wrote a quick note to Ben, giving her name and address and stating that he had

beaten her to death and nothing more. When he attempted
to lick the flap of the envelope, he was surprised to find
his mouth too dry. He nibbled at the tip of his tongue
until saliva flowed and licked the envelope and sealed it
and scrawled Ben on the outside.

And one to Bess. It was hard to compose. It had to
have a certain dignity. *Darling—Forgive me for what I
am about to do. Try to understand. It was the only course
open to me. It was a decision I had to make. With love
and regret. Quinn.* He read it over twice. It seemed all
right. Serious. Competent. Even efficient. And sealed it
and wrote her name on the outside of the envelope and
put the two of them side by side on the blotter and picked
up the gun again. It felt vastly lighter than it had before.

He put the muzzle in his mouth. It had an oily taste.
The metal touched his teeth. It gave him a crawling
feeling, the same feeling that certain sounds gave him,
such as a knife scraping along a chipped place on the edge
of a plate.

He felt irritated. Indignant. He stood up very quickly
and jammed the muzzle against the side of his head above
his ear and pulled the trigger. The sound of the shot
astonished him. In the open, shooting at cans, it had been
a snapping sound, a flat crack. Here in the room it was a
vast resounding *bam* that filled his right ear with a great,
dulled ringing. His head felt seared and he smelled burned
hair. He wondered why he was standing. He fingered his
head, turned and looked to his left and high and saw the
torn mark, a pale mark torn into the paneling close to the
ceiling where the slug had gone.

He heard the rumble and pop of the tires on the gravel
and the car stopping and the shutting of car doors and
Bess talking to David in that special voice she used for
him. The way nurses talk to you in the hospital.

He put the gun up quickly again and yanked on the
trigger again. The noise did not seem as loud. He guessed
that was because he was partially deafened from the first
shot. There was a silence outside. Bess called to him. The
burn had hurt his head again. He looked for the slug. It
had gone into the ceiling this time.

He heard Bess running into the house.

He went over quickly and sat on the couch. "You can't even do this," he told himself hopelessly. "Not even this."

And he thought of the way all inanimate things seemed to have always banded themselves together in conspiracy against him—nails bent, pliers slipped, knives wouldn't cut, cars wouldn't start. She was coming quickly, calling to him.

If the damn thing kept flinching up so that you kept missing, then find some way to steady it. He socketed the muzzle in his deafened ear, pushing it tightly against his ear, the front sight gouging him a bit, and he pulled the trigger carefully.

A great blinding sheet of purest white filled the whole world. He had a fraction of a fraction of a second in which to feel satisfaction that he had been able to do it, after all. The sort of satisfaction you feel when the starter on the car, after grinding dismally and too long, makes the motor catch and roar. And just as the feeling of satisfaction began, by micro seconds, to change into something else entirely, to change into a dreadful regret, he became nothing.

Chapter Sixteen

Ben turned into his drive, heavy and quiet with the feeling of Sunday, hunger turning slowly in his belly, sonorities of the morning sermon fading in his ears. As he got out of the car, he heard the screaming. He turned and looked at Wilma. Her lips were pulled back tightly against her teeth, flattened against them in the effort of listening and understanding.

"Bess!" she said.

And he went, running, wishing fleetness, conscious of

the thickened slowness of his running, aware that Brock was coming along behind him, gaining on him.

The screams were short and sharp and piercing, coming with each drawn breath, and all Ben could think of was that she was on fire and he remembered you had to roll them in something. A rug, a blanket.

He stopped in the kitchen, breathing hard, orienting the direction of the sound. "Study," he gasped and hurried on.

He went through the door and stopped and saw it then, saw in a half second exactly what it was. Quinn toppled on the couch, with the death-slack face, the gun between slack thighs, pointing at his crotch, a smell of powder and burning in the room. Bess stood with her back turned toward the body, eyes squeezed tightly shut, fists tightly shut, arms a bit out from her side as though she balanced on a wire, legs spread, feet planted, screaming with each breath. He reached her in two long steps and, in his nervousness, slapped her much harder than he intended, slapped her so strongly that she toppled back and would have fallen onto the body had he not snatched at her wrist, caught it, pulled her away. The screams stopped with the slap and her eyes were wide and dazed with shock. David stood silent and goggling, his face gray and his underlip falling loose away from his large, yellowish teeth.

"Get her out of here and phone Endermann," Ben said. He had directed the request at Brock, planning to get David out himself. But to his astonishment, David moved toward his mother and put a long awkward arm around her shoulders and said, "Come. Come ... on," guiding her toward the door and giving Ben a look in which there was defiance and even a certain pride. She went willingly with her son.

"You phone," he said to Brock. And Brock went to the desk and picked up the phone book as Ben, starting to turn toward Quinn, heard Wilma in the house, calling him. Heard Ellen's softer voice.

He went out into the hallway and they came toward him, eyes wide with identical concern so that they looked more alike than at any other time in his memory. "Don't come in," he said bluntly. "Quinn killed himself. Go take care of Bess, Wilma. You go tell George, Ellen."

"Oh, dear God," Wilma whispered. "Oh, dear God."

Ellen's face turned to chalk and she turned and ran.

"Dr. Endermann. Just a moment, sir."

He took the phone from Brock and saw Brock look toward the body and look away quickly. "Ralph? This is Ben. Trouble up here. Yes. No ... not an emergency. Quinn . . . shot himself. Dead. Yes. I don't know. Bess is pretty—Yes, of course. Thanks a lot. You'll phone them then."

He hung up, turned with reluctance toward the body, feeling the sick weight of guilt. "Dad," Brock said, "there's notes there. One to you."

Ben tore his note open with a hand that trembled. The incredible words blurred and then came clear. And he felt the lifting of that oppressive weight, but immediately felt shamed within himself that he could feel a lessening of sadness merely by learning that the cause of suicide had been other than what he had so grimly suspected. He folded the note quickly into his pocket, picked up the other one, saw that it was sealed, tapped it on the back of his hand for a moment, then opened it, avoiding Brock's eyes. The other note made no mention of the girl.

"Do you think she saw the notes, Dad?"

"I don't think so." He knew what his son was thinking and liked him for thinking it. "Cleaning the gun?" He went over to the body, forced himself to look at it, looking for the wound, saw the blackened pit of the ear. "I'm afraid that would be pretty difficult, son."

"Look, Dad. Up there. That hole."

"There's another one in the paneling. At least three shots. No, we can't make it work at all. I'll leave the note to her on the desk."

"What about the note to you?"

He looked at his son. "There wasn't any other note."

Brock looked startled and then nodded. "Okay."

They could hear, in the distances of the house, a woman crying. George came walking somberly into the room. He stood and looked at the body, his face unchanging. Ben handed him the note. He read it slowly, handed it back.

"Hell!" he said. It was a sound of protest, of indignation, and also of disgust.

"Anything I can do, Ben?"

"They won't want him touched. Let's ... get out of here." They went to the doorway. Ben was the last one out. He pulled the study door shut. "George, Endermann is coming. He'll give Bess a pill or a shot or something. He'll phone the sheriff's office and I guess they get hold of the coroner. There'll be an inquest, but it will be routine. I'll get hold of Durr and Commings. They can pick him ... it up after the officials are through."

George scuffed one foot, said meaningfully, "Any chance of——"

"Not a chance. He missed twice, at least. Then took it in the ear."

George's face darkened. "Isn't that just like him! Wouldn't he crumb it up so there's no chance at all. That son of a bitch never drew a single unselfish breath the longest day ... Hell, I'm sorry, Ben. I'm sorry I said that."

"It's okay. How about Alice?"

"Your girl was smart. She got me alone. I got to go back and tell her."

"It's going to hit her hard, George. Being a twin. Want me to come along? Or I could tell her myself."

George sighed. "Thanks. No. I'll do it. It has to be done. I'll do it. I'll stay with her. Tell Ralph to stop over after he gets through with Bess, will you?"

George walked away, head bent. Ben said to Brock, "I've got to make that call. Do you think you could go over and tell Robbie and Susan? I mean quietly, without a lot of——"

"Dad!"

"I'm sorry, boy." His smile was tired. "Go ahead now." Brock started away and Ben called him back. "As soon as the routine is over with, I have to go into town. I'm not going to tell your mother in advance. After I get away, you tell her I told you I had to check something at the plant, something plausible, connected with this . . . mess."

"I'll do that."

Brock walked down to the second house and tapped at the private entrance to the guest annex.

"Who is it?" Susan called, her voice cheerful.

"Me. Brock."

"Just a minute, huh?"

He waited and soon she opened the door. She wore a blue robe and her hair was tied back. She smiled at him. "Come on in, Brock. I had to get some lipstick on. Robbie's wallowing around in the shower. Making mooing sounds. He thinks he's an operatic baritone. Listen to him!"

Brock made himself smile. His mouth felt unused to smiling. "Sit down, Brock. The place is a mess. We've been dreadfully lazy this morning."

"I guess you were tired from the trip and all."

"What's wrong, Brock? What is it?"

"I . . . I better wait until I can tell Robbie too, Susan."

She gave him an intent look and then went to the bathroom door and knocked. "Robbie! Please hurry."

"Okay, okay," he called. In a few moments the sound of the water stopped.

"Brock is here," she called. "Come right out."

He came out quickly, belting his robe, dark hair damp, bare feet making marks on the rug, yellow towel over his shoulder. He looked curiously at their still faces. "Hi, Brock boy. What goes?"

Brock had the feeling his voice was going to break. He made it deeper and kept it firm. "It's Quinn. He . . . he shot himself this morning. He's dead. He . . . did it on purpose."

Susan made a small sound and put the back of her hand to her mouth.

Robbie looked as if he was trying to smile, as if he didn't quite get the joke. And then his face changed and he sat down. "Why in the wide world would he——"

"I don't know. I just don't know," Brock said.

"What a mess!" Robbie said. "What a damn stinking mess!"

"How is Bess?" Susan asked.

"She was in pretty bad shape. Mother and Ellen are with her. The doctor is coming."

"How is Alice?" she asked.

"I don't know. George is telling her, I guess."

Susan bit her lip and then walked swiftly to the connecting door and opened it. "I'll see what I can do for Alice," she said, and pulled the door shut behind her.

"I can't believe it," Robbie said.

"It's true all right. I saw him. I mean I didn't see him do it. I . . ." He swallowed hard.

It was nearly three o'clock before Ben was able to get away. Endermann had knocked out both Bess and Alice with heavy sedatives. The sheriff himself had come, a tall wide man named Harley with blunt eyes and a small, skeptical, puckered mouth. After the coroner was through, the slack thing that had been Quinn Delevan was wrapped in coarse cloth and strapped in a wire basket and carried out to the waiting vehicle by the employees of Durr and Commings.

Harley sat in Ben's kitchen, accepted a cigar. "Now, why'd he do it? The note doesn't say anything about why."

"I really don't know why, Sheriff."

"Health, money, or love. Those are the reasons. Take your choice."

"I really don't know."

"I'll tell you something, Mr. Delevan. You better know. Because the papers are going to be on your neck and you've got to have some kind of a statement to make, and it has got to satisfy them or they'll build it into some kind of big mystery, so as to help 'em sell their papers. If there's a reason they'll buy, they're usually pretty decent about a thing like this. But you tell them what you're telling me and you'll get yourself some page one stuff about mystery surrounding suicide of prominent businessman sort of thing."

Ben knew he was right. And he was highly conscious of the folded note in his pocket. Bess, in her life, had had enough of violence. Enough of shame.

He leaned toward Harley and made his voice confidential. "I'l have to pledge you to secrecy, Sheriff. In order to give you the facts."

"I can't promise anything. You know that."

"I'll tell you. I guess I have to. But if the news gets out it might make things financially embarrassing. You see, the firm hasn't been doing too well. Last Thursday we had an offer of a merger. It would be advantageous to the stockholders. But the executive staff would be out, of course. I talked it over with my brother. That was Thursday. I guess I indicated to him that I look favorably on the merger. I didn't realize it might hit him so hard. He hasn't any savings to speak of. And he's a comparatively ... he was a comparatively young man. And the family firm ... well, it meant a lot to him. Maybe more than it does to me. You know. Tradition. He acted strange and depressed ever since I told him. Everybody noticed it. He took off last night, right during a sort of family party. He got drunk and drove away. He got into trouble down in Stockton. The police picked him up. He was booked and I bailed him out and he was supposed to stand trial Monday. I'm not saying he'd kill himself over a little thing like that. But he never did that sort of thing before. But you can understand why ... for business reasons, I don't want this to get out. Why, he never came to work on Friday or Saturday morning. I think it was because we are ... to his way of thinking, losing the mill."

Ben leaned back and watched Harley's face intently. The big features slackened. "That would seem to fit. Depression. Toomey is hanging around out there. Good man. *Journal-Times.* I'll get him. You sit still. Let me do the talking."

Toomey was a little, slow-moving man. He looked to be on the verge of yawning. But his eyes had a terrier alertness.

"Sit down, Rog," Harley said. "You know Mr. Benjamin Delevan."

"Seen him around. What's the score?"

"Quinn Delevan, the fellow killed himself, did it on account of business worries. Financial reverses, you might say. Been depressed now since Thursday last. These people are having a hard enough time, Rog. Think you can keep the other boys off their neck?"

"Nothing worth holding an exclusive on here. Sure, Sheriff. I'll spread it around. Now if you can fill me in on the obit, Mr. Delevan."

Harley got up to go and Ben thanked him and then gave the bored little man with eyes that were no longer alert the information he wanted. As Toomey left he said, "I'll phone it around. Nobody'll bother you."

"Thanks," Ben said. And he had the sour knowledge that when the sheriff and the reporter learned what he had in his pocket, they would be merciless. He saw no chance of keeping it quiet. Maybe one chance in five thousand. But worth taking for Bess's sake. For the sake of the living.

He drove toward Stockton, full of apprehension and impatience. He found himself driving too fast, and then too slow. There was a Sunday afternoon sleepiness in the city. He cruised slowly down Fremont and spotted the number and parked. The old house looked quiet, dingy, drowsy. No official excitement. So either the excitement was over, or the body had not yet been found. He looked around warily, sensing that had the body been found, the vacant-minded curious would be standing and looking at the house, as though the sight of it would satisfy some strange craving, establish some twisted identification. Thus, were it as yet unfound, there might be some chance of removing any evidence of Quinn's visit. And without too much danger to himself, as the time of death once established would rule him out.

He heard the ringing of the doorbell, deep in the dusty house. A woman waddled heavily to the door, with a piece of the Sunday paper in her hand. "You want something?"

"I'm looking for a Miss Doyle."

"You go around that side a the house. The door on the

side. I don't know if she's in or not. I don't keep track a her. I got enough to do."

"Thank you. Thank you very much."

"Doan mention."

He walked around the house. He raised his hand and hesitated, then knocked on the door. He could not see through the curtained windows. He knocked again and waited. The city sounds were sleepy. Children whined at play. "It is not yours— It is so— It is not— It is so."

He took a deep breath and reached for the knob. Just as he touched it the door opened inward and stopped with a clink of the night chain. No one stood in the crack of the door. "What do you want? Who is it?" Girl voice, mumbled, distant.

"Are you Bonita Doyle?"

"Yes." His heart seemed to jump upward, land safely in a higher place in his chest. "Who are you?"

"Quinn's brother."

There was a long silence. "Just a minute."

The door closed and he heard the chain rattle. It swung wide. "Come in."

He went in, closed the door behind him. Her face was shocking. Her left eye was puffed shut, hard, shiny skin, eggplant color, shading off to the misshapen cheek. Fat broken lips protruding, too swollen to close across the teeth. Clumsy bandage along the line of the jaw. He could tell that she was young, that she might have been pretty. But nothing else. Facial tissue was too bloated to show expression. She moved oddly, as though her neck was stiff. She sat down with her hands in her lap and looked at him from the single expressionless eye.

"Yes?"

"Have you seen a doctor?"

"I thought I would go in the morning." It was difficult for her to articulate clearly. "Did he tell you why he did it?"

Ben sat warily. "No."

"He's sick, I think. I know he was drunk. But sick too. To do that. When I . . . came to, I phoned you. Nobody answered. I didn't want to phone his house. I thought his wife might answer. I think he's sick. I think he needs help."

"How did you two meet?"

"Meet? At the mill. I work there. Section nine."

"I'm sorry. I probably have seen you. But——"

"I know how I look. It's all right."

"What ... what do you plan to do about it, Miss Doyle?"

"I've ... been thinking about that. I don't know. Just try to make sure somebody helps him. But I don't ... I don't want to see him again. Hitting me like that ... it did something inside me. Nobody ever hit me like that. It isn't the hurting, or even being afraid. It's something else. I just don't want to see him anymore."

"Has he been giving you money?"

She sat quite still, but he saw her hands lock together. "It hasn't been like that, Mr. Delevan." The words came with great dignity from the ruined mouth.

"How long has it been going on?"

"Since spring."

"Did you think you loved him?"

"I think I did. But I don't. Not now. It broke something. Maybe that was what it broke. Holding me and hitting me——"

"I think you ought to see a doctor today. Maybe he'll want to take an X-ray. You might have a broken cheekbone or a cracked jaw."

"I don't think so. My front teeth are loose. But they tighten up, don't they? Sometimes, I mean."

"I think they do. Yes, I think they do."

"I want to give them a chance. I'm not going to bite on anything. They never match your teeth right."

"Miss Doyle, I ... the family feels responsible for this. I want to see that you get proper care. I'm going to insist on that and I want to give you something for ... this discomfort."

"I don't want anything."

"What do you feel about my brother now?"

"Not ... anything, I guess. Just empty, sort of."

"He thought he killed you, Miss Doyle."

"How awful! And you came here to ... He must be going half crazy. I've got a phone. Right over there. If you——"

"He left a note for me, Miss Doyle. He killed himself this morning with a gun. He shot himself in the head."

It seemed as though she hadn't understood him. She just sat and looked at him. Her hand lifted toward her face and she lowered it again. "He couldn't have. He didn't do that. There was no need."

She leaned back and closed the single eye. He watched her carefully. He realized that he liked her and was concerned about her. Once he had found that she was alive, he had planned to be completely ruthless with her, to bully her out of any idea of making additional trouble. But there was an obvious decency about this one.

"Miss Doyle, I think you're right in saying he was sick. Only a sick person could do that. And don't feel that you are in any way to blame for it. I think it would have happened anyway."

"It's ... a bad thing. For you and his wife and all of us."

The choice of words seemed strange. "All of us?" he asked gently.

She opened her eye. "I'm sorry. I guess I'm not a part of it. I meant all of us who sort of loved him."

"Will you let me do something for you?"

"I ... don't know."

"Is your family here in the city?"

"No. There's just a brother. In California. He keeps writing me to go out there. I think I'd like to go out there."

"I'll get you an airline ticket."

"No. I don't want to get there quick. I've never been out there. I mean seen the country or anything. And I think I'd like to go by bus. By the time I get there, I won't look so awful. And I'll see more."

He sensed how, already, she was turning her back on it, resolute, fatalistic. Strength in her. Not the same sort of strength as in Susan. This was a more primitive strength. Will of the organism to survive. She had been hurt deeply,

and now she would begin to mend herself. As perhaps
Bess might one day mend herself, though there was less
emotional resilience left in Bess than in this young girl.

"I'm not ashamed, you know," she said suddenly. "I
don't care what you think about me. I'm not ashamed at
all."

"I'll use your phone. I've got a friend who has X-ray
equipment in his office. I think he'll open his office up for
me. Then I'll drive you over and we can meet him there."

She touched her skirt. "I guess there's no need to
change my clothes. I guess I can't look very good no
matter what I wear. He'll know about teeth, won't he?"

"I think he'll know about teeth."

"Does ... his wife know about me? Did she see the
note you told me about?"

"No. Nobody knows now but you and me. And whoev-
er you or Quinn may have told."

"Neither of us told anybody. And don't worry. I won't
tell anybody. Nobody will hear it from me. It's funny, I
keep thinking I ought to cry. Ever since I woke up on the
floor with the blood all over my face, I've felt like I ought
to cry. But I can't seem to. He was ... so sort of lost,
your brother was."

"Lost. I guess that's right. Have you got a phone book?"

"Right in that drawer. I wish I had a hat with a veil. I'd
feel better going out if I had a hat with a veil."

He looked up the number. He heard the phone ringing
in the doctor's home. Sam would be annoyed. But he'd
cooperate. As the phone rang, he thought of what he
would do. Cash a check in the morning. A thousand
dollars. Advise her to change it to traveler's checks. He
had the uneasy feeling that it would be difficult to get her
to accept that much. But she would take it. He would
make her take it.